Book Three of The Siren Series

ACAPELLA

By

ALISA K. MICHAELS

ISBN: 978-1-959715-30-6

Library of Congress Control Number: **2023949471**
Published by **Belen Books, LLC**
St. Petersburg, FL | Winter Park, FL | Chicago, IL USA
Belenbookspublishing.com

Edited by Beverly R. Waalewyn & Paul Hight
Cover by Belen Media Group

10 9 8 7 6 5 4 3 2

Printed in the United States of America

For Laura & Alissa

"The small wisdom is like water in a glass: clear, transparent, pure. The great wisdom is like the water in the sea: dark, mysterious, impenetrable."

—Rabindranath Tagore

PREFACE

Fidgety and distracted, I sit on the terrace of our vacation villa overlooking the choppy waters of the Tyrrhenian Sea. Its undulating waves of cyan and aqua no longer tease of what is concealed below. I know exactly what it contains.

But today something is different.

Something ominous hovers. It hangs low in the atmosphere. It hangs like old, yellowed wallpaper peeling off tattered walls.

No longer am I lost in my overly zealous teen imagination or consumed with ancient shipwrecks and the buried treasures they protect. That ship has long sailed. Yet it is true. Lately, my mind rarely wonders if Davey Jones watches from fathoms below as unwary vessels glide along the surface enjoying the salt-kissed trade winds and the song of the sails as they fill.

Now, my conscious is filled with the realities of centuries ago when blood-thirsty gods and goddesses ruled the seas, their havens pregnant with gold and jewels obtained from temples of worshipping humans. As if I was there, I imagine their breasts heaving with pride as they ogle their offerings. All the while, their eyes twinkle with arrogance and they laugh at who they have corrupted, who they have deceived.

Then perhaps early one night as Selene's spring moon watches from high in the heavens, they hear it.

"Don't be afraid," the voice sings.

"We are not afraid, *Siren!*" they proclaim as if it were a curse, surprised at the sea nymph's gumption.

"Follow me… into the sea… in the ocean's waves we will play."

Recklessly, they venture out of their dwellings into the surrounding water. From the crystal-clear depths, a passing pod of sperm whales wakes them from their spell causing courage to transform to panic. Their Ids tell them to swim toward the safety of the caves, but their Egos take control urging them onward. Dread engulfs them, washes over them like crashing surf bashes against the shore and as the fear subsides, they are reminded that they are mighty. Then why are they compelled to venture toward the purple horizon in a self-defeating daze?

After all, Sirens are not as powerful as gods.

Or are they?

Acapella

Unfortunately, before anyone can address that question, the undertow grabs hold of their legs and begins to pull them out towards the open depths. Unable to fight against its wishes, they close their eyes allowing their bodies to surrender. A watery embrace devours them as their god-like strength fails and their lungs fill with salt water, yet they are not afraid. They are content for the first time in millennia.

Steadily, seductively, the liquid domain begins to fade as they drift into the emptiness, but in the distance, gliding toward them, are five shapes. As the shapes approach, they realize that there are four women and a boy. The first female, crowned with a golden-blonde cascade resembling early morning rays. The second is awe-invoking with long, curly, crimson locks, locks as fiery as the sun's first light accompanying a new day. The third and fourth are adorned with silk-like, onyx curls that spill downward like graceful tentacles. And the child; the child embodies everything angelic and pure.

To their dismay, the last things they see are their beautiful aquamarine eyes...

Acapella

Part One

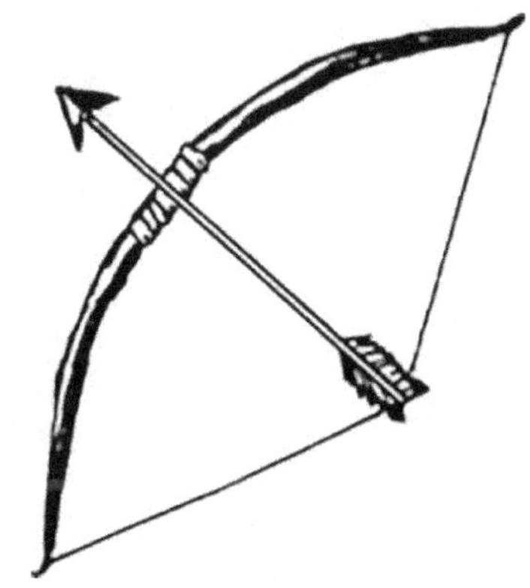

CHAPTER ONE

The pit in my stomach is growing exponentially while my heart threatens to explode from the sheer excitement of the moment. Instead of speaking, my mother and I tread water, holding our collective breaths. Waiting.

After a few more minutes, Mom insists: "Look down toward the floor of the cave."

Obediently, I do as I am told, but only see more darkness.

"I can't see anything," I whine, feeling inadequate.

"Adjust your eyes," she requests in her most supportive parental tone, and of course I try, but nothing happens, as usual.

"Will your eyes to see beyond," she encourages in our Siren language with a small smile.

Following her suggestion, I slowly glance around.

"Beyond?" I click and clack with growing impatience. "Beyond what?"

Displeased that I have given up so easily, Mom frowns.

"Beyond this world," she adds like some hippy-dippy shaman.

"You must have lost a lot of blood," I tease with a snicker, unable to control myself, earning a playful slap to the arm.

"Just try it," she huffs.

"Here goes nothing," I state, trying to impress her by doing something right, and just as I suspect, I still see only the brightness illuminating from Mom's irises.

"Don't worry," she soothes sweetly. "It will all fall into place one day. I promise."

"If you say so," I utter, giving her the benefit of the doubt, but not entirely believing it.

"Swim down," my mother commands motioning toward the bottom of the cave floor. "Follow me."

I do. I follow her, our hands clasped tightly, nervous at what we will encounter. Once again, I feel nauseous and as

Acapella

I continue to observe, Mom hunts the rocky wall nearest her searching for something. After several minutes, I hear her pull down on some type of device. The object sounds heavy and old. Then, without warning, she lets out a wail so loud, so blood-curdling, that I release her hand in order to cover my ears.

As the sound subsides, the water around us begins to glow and become warmer. The surrounding cave walls illuminate themselves as if thousands of tiny multicolored lightbulbs have suddenly been switched on. With the soft light, I realize that all over the rocky surfaces are drawings of sea creatures of all shapes and sizes along with shimmering diamonds, opalescent pearls, shiny shards of obsidian, an array of precious jewels, and polished metals that light our way farther down into the bowels of the sea like the lights lining the path of an airport runway.

Quickly, the brightness increases tenfold. Almost blinded, I squeeze my eyes shut, just in case I truly do lose my sight, but I hear my mother's voice pleading inside of my head.

'Open your eyes, Selena.'

Cautiously, I do.

The sight that greets me is overwhelming…

More incredible than anything…

Ever!

"Where are we?" I swallow the gigantic lump forming in my throat.

"We are home, my love." Mom's eyes glisten. "We are home."

"What is this place?" I mumble to myself, allowing my hands to glide over the bumpy wall as we continue along our path.

"This, my dear, is the Siren Grotto." Mom smiles with tear-filled eyes.

"Wait!" I exclaim halting my pace, dread increasing by leaps and bounds. "Won't the high concentrations of volcanic sediment poison me?"

Mom's happy expression suddenly fades.

"Possibly," she grumbles, still holding my hand.

"Well, that's comforting," I sarcastically jibe, feeling my blood pressure rising.

All the while, my mother concentrates. Her mind running through all that has happened and all that *might* happen. Physically, I can hear as every possible outcome is analyzed, scrutinized, weighed, and measured.

Then finally, she speaks.

"How long was I asleep?" Mom demands, ignoring my flippant attitude.

"A few hours," I reply, feeling my apprehension at its pinnacle. "Why?"

My mother releases a heavy sigh.

"You've been breathing in the sediment for the entire time," she grins.

"I have?" I grin back.

"Yes," her grin widens into a full smile. "How do you feel?"

Thoughtfully, I quickly do a self-check: breathing normal, stomach steady, vision perfect, mind clear and concise.

"I feel great!" I laugh. "Strong."

Mom nods in approval.

"Are you ready to continue?" she queries.

This time, it is my turn to nod.

"Let's go then!" she encourages, eager to introduce me to our sanctuary.

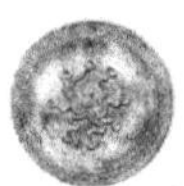

Our path through the Siren Grotto is magical. Actually, 'magical' does not do it justice. A better description is indescribable and overwhelming and as we navigate the long tunnel that leads from the cave into another chamber, my eyes adjust to the dim light. Up ahead, I see, *land?*

"Hurry!" Mom squeals her excitement. "We're almost there!"

Quickening my pace, I follow her toward the landmass, and in less than a minute, we break through the surface displacing the water like emerging submarines. However, the unexpected pressure in my ears warns that we have ascended too quickly. My mother must also feel the effect because she also touches her fingers to her ears, trying to subdue the slight pain.

"Are you okay?" she questions, still adjusting to the strange sensation.

"I'm fine," I admit with a nod, wishing I had a piece of gum as if I were on an airplane and needed to pop my ears.

"Don't worry, it will pass," Mom informs. "It always does."

"I thought that the Siren Grotto was the cave we were just in?" I probe, feeling a bit confused.

"No," Mom shakes her ebony-locked framed face and giggles. "Technically the Siren Grotto is the cave along with the tunnel that leads from the outer sea to where we are now.

"This land—" she announces waving her arms around like Vanna White before a wall of illuminated letters, "—is where Melpomene raised her offspring after giving birth."

"Oh!"

"Parthenope, Ligeia and Leukosia all grew up in this place," she continues. "Here they learned their craft. Here they learned what it meant to be a Siren."

I laugh, imagining three Siren toddlers running around causing havoc.

"Kinda like a Siren nursery," I snort, remembering the mangrove cluster back on Isla Flora where I was first taught my Sireny-skills.

"Exactly!" Mom snickers too.

"What do we call this place?" I query, glancing around.

"Yaya Parthenope once told me that your great-grandmother referred to it as a paradise, hence why it was dubbed, *Paradiso*." My mother beams.

"Paradiso," I mimic the word, enjoying the sound of it as it rolls off of my tongue. "I like the sound of it."

"I'm glad."

"Can we look around?" I question hopefully.

"Of course," Mom agrees. "I haven't been back here in almost twenty years."

"That's before I was born," I acknowledge Mom's confession.

"I know," she sighs, and I hear the sadness in her tone. "It's been too long. Much too long."

"C'mon, Mom," I urge, feeling her longing. "Give me the grand tour."

Then out of the blue, I recall Ariella, the tour guide on Anacapri, who I almost killed. Thick guilt chokes me as I attempt to brush it from my mind, but all the while, I know that if Mom, Dad and Ando were not there to stop me, I would have truly killed the young woman.

Next, the memory of the young man on the ship near the *Faraglioni* who resembles Andrew pops into my mind causing another tsunami of self-loathing to slam into me.

Will I ever purge these nightmares from my hippocampus?

"Selena?" My mother interrupts my mental anguish.

"Yes, Mom?" I gulp down the lump growing in my throat.

"Please, don't think about those events anymore," she states with understanding and compassion. "What's done is done. They are both fine."

"I can't help it," I reply sorrowfully then wince unexpectedly. "I almost killed two innocent people."

"I know," she whispers, diverting her gaze. "I was there. If it helps, you're not the only Siren to lose control."

That's a relief.

"How do I get rid of those thoughts?" I plead, hoping there is a magical potion or suppressive device I can use to keep in control.

"You don't," my mother replies, bursting my figurative bubble.

"Huh?"

"You do not get rid of them," she repeats. "Remember them always, so you never feel the urge to do it again."

Shaking my head, I vocalize my thoughts.

"I don't want to be a monster."

"Selena?"

"Yes, Mom?"

"Monsters do not feel pain or doubt or remorse, that's why they're monsters," Mom educates with a frown. "Sirens feel *everything*. More so than everyone else and being a young Siren surging with uncontrollable hormones, you must try even harder so that bad things won't happen to innocent people."

Comforted for the moment, I smile at her.

"Are you speaking from experience?" I jibe as a mental wall appears in my mother's mind, a wall that I cannot see past.

"Yes," she answers sincerely. "Yes, I am."

"Did you do awful things when you were my age?" I question, unable to picture my cool, confident mother out of her mind and out for blood.

"Unfortunately, I did many stupid things when I was younger," she pouts as I take her hand in mine, and we drift along with the current toward the shoreline of Paradiso. As the growing excitement overtakes me, I hear myself begin to hum.

Abruptly, I stop.

"What's the matter?" Mom asks, uncertain of why I have stopped so suddenly.

"Am I allowed to sing here?" I whisper as though I am in church.

Mom laughs and places a kiss on my forehead.

"On Paradiso," she beams. "We can do anything."

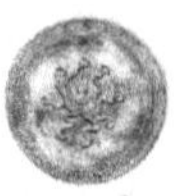

At a snail's pace, we allow the current to wash us up onto the powder-like, black sand shore. Curious of how it feels, I grab a handful. The texture is like talcum powder or corn starch or something equally fine and silky. If I rub too hard, it might dissipate.

"Why is the sand black?" I query, examining it.

"It is made from volcanic glass like what your pendent is made of," Mom explains as she gently touches the obsidian charm that hangs around my neck on a simple chain along with the black pearl that my stepfather gave me in Isla Flora.

"It's much softer than regular sand," I reveal, letting the grains fall through my fingers like sand in an hourglass. The minuscule granules tickle between my digits.

"The current down here is much stronger than the ones above and objects here are subjected to more stress," she informs and picks up a handful too. "Even the cliffs aren't that jagged.

"If your scales are up, you'll rarely get hurt here."

"Speaking from experience again?" I joke, earning me a finger poke to the side.

"Ready for the tour?" Mom inquiries with newly found cheerfulness.

Filled with anticipation, I nod, and grab another handful of the black powder to take with me.

Why? Why not?

When I glance back up, Mom is already halfway up the beach trudging toward the dense tree line surrounding the narrow stretch of shoreline. Somehow, it reminds me of the beach near our house on Isla Flora, except prettier, if that is even possible.

"Wait!" I shout, but she does not pause, so I run to catch-up. "Why are you in such a hurry?"

"I'm just excited to show you where our line began is all," she smiles brightly. "There are so many things to see, but not a lot of time to see them."

"How can it have sunlight here?" I question when I finally reach her, admiring the beautiful scenery encased by steep walls of stalagmite as I catch my breath.

"Remember the Blue Grotto?"

"Of course," I respond, recalling the amazing blue light that fills it.

"Look up," my mother petitions, pointing above our heads to the limestone cliffs stretching for approximately a quarter of a mile upward. "There are hundreds, maybe even thousands of small openings in the limestone stacks that allow sunshine, moonlight, wind and rain to enter."

"Limestone stacks," I repeat. "Like the Faraglioni?"

"Yes, just like those in the Marina Piccolo," she professes. "From the outside, the stacks appear like any other rock formation around these parts."

"What happens on rainy days or on cloudy nights?" I wonder aloud. "Are we in complete darkness?"

"No," Mom reassures. "I'll show you."

"Show me what?"

"One moment."

With that said, my mother releases my hand, and closes her eyes, concentrating on something unseen. The slight breeze filtering throughout the cave steadily increases until it reaches category-one hurricane strength. Almost immediately, the cavern surrounding the island starts to darken until there is not one ray of sunshine. In the darkness, I reach out trying to touch Mom, but cannot.

"Wa-what are you doing?" I ask, hating the dark.

"I'm moving the clouds, so they block the sunlight."

"Oh!" I exclaim, quite impressed by my mother's Siren talents.

Then it happens. The wind stops and Mom opens her eyes.

"What's going on?" I interrogate, my heart beating like a drum.

Unhurried, Mom raises one hand.

"Wait… one… moment," she requests, eyes toward the cavern ceiling.

At first, muted light similar to candlelight except softer spreads then expands with just a hint of brighter radiation so our eyes can adjust. It is like a hidden stagehand bringing up the houselights before a play starts. Or when God said, "*Let there be light,*" and then there it was brightening the wide expanse.

Next, all around us, everything from the ground covering and vegetation, to the brown-husked coconuts high in the palms, to the very limestone itself that hides Paradiso, even the black, volcanic sand beneath our bare feet begins to glow. Not harsh light. No. It reminds me of bioluminescent plankton and algae in my science book. The light is delicate and welcoming; soft and soothing.

"Wow!" is all I can say.

"Spectacular, isn't it?" Mom beams from ear to ear.

"It certainly is," I say in a hushed tone, grinning my approval. "Show me more."

With my mother leading the way, we enter the jungle. Carefully, we walk through prickly thickets of pineapple bushes, their slender leaves cutting at our legs. My mother does not seem to be bothered, but I, on the other hand, am being attacked.

"Ouch!" I cringe as a trickle of blood runs down my leg, alerting me to the gash in my skin.

"Call for your scales," Mom instructs pointing to her own.

It is then her scales appear, but only on her legs. Wanting to be protected too, I do the same, ecstatic to have the practical and necessary covering. Now, enhanced by the foliage, my scales look even more fish-like. Wondrously, they shimmer in varying shades of aquamarine, silver, gold, and emerald with just a hint of onyx. Finally seeing them as attributes, I deliberate on how I ever got along without them.

"We'll be out of this shortly," Mom knowingly informs as I follow obediently.

Taking another step, I hardly feel the sting as the knife-like blades of the fruits slash at me. Unlike the first time, the ridiculously resilient scales remain unharmed. They actually seem to adjust themselves in their hardness.

"There it is," Mom coos as she points to a pool of shimmering clear water being fed by several small waterfalls that break off from a much larger river. "Are you thirsty?"

"Most definitely," I pant, wiping the perspiration from my brow.

"Take a drink," she suggests, getting down on her knees to be closer to the water.

"Wait," I pause. "Isn't this salt water?"

"Trust me," she pleads.

So, I do.

Carefully, I kneel beside her, cupping my hands to form a bowl-like shape then gather some liquid and take a small sip.

Surprised at its delightful taste, I respond with a loud satisfied, *Ahh!*

"Good?" my mom giggles.

"Delicious," I respond as I cup my hands together again and take several much-needed gulps. "It's so sweet."

"Surprisingly so," Mom grins. "Hey!"

"What is it?"

"Are you hungry?"

"Always," I heartily profess, rolling my eyes.

Mom's face lights up as she motions toward a hilly area not too far ahead.

"Come with me!" she announces then takes off like a sprinter in a fifty-yard-dash.

Eagerly, I chase after her, willing my feet to move faster, but they do not and I am worried that I might trip and embarrass myself in front of my perfect mother.

"Where are we going, Mom?"

"You'll see!" she exclaims like a teenager at a concert trying to be heard over the din of screaming fans.

At the base of the towering mango grove, Mom suddenly stops and drops to her hands and knees. Immediately, she begins to dig near the roots of the tallest tree.

"Mom?"

"Huh?"

"What are you doing?"

"Retrieving something," she puffs, out of breath.

"Retrieving what?" I pant too.

"Something that I considered to be my pride and joy once upon a time," she giggles. "Before you, your dad and Ando, of course."

Her exuberance makes me giggle too.

"Of course," I smirk.

"Ah ha!" she yells after another few seconds.

"Did you find it?" I ask, excited to learn what *It* is.

"Yup!" she squeals, holding up something wrapped in weathered burlap.

With shaking hands, she unwraps the parcel. Inside is a beautifully crafted wooden bow, probably made from a strong, yet bendable wood, perhaps birch. A thick strand of horsehair is fastened to act as the bow's launching mechanism. It is rustic, but elegant in its simplicity. Carved in the wood are ocean creatures: starfish, a stingray, a couple of turtles, and other species that I do not recognize. Near the center of the efficiently made weapon is my mother's name neatly written, I assume with the tip of a talon. Along with it is a quiver of six razor-sharp, pink shell-tipped arrows.

Mom beams.

"You made this?" I gasp with another bout of admiration.

Blushing, she nods.

"Does is have a name?" I question, knowing that my mother loves to name her most favorite items. Back on Isla Flora, all of her prized orchids have names. Why does she name them? Who knows? She just likes doing it, I guess.

My parent nods again.

"I call him *Mercury*," she blushes more.

"Why '*Mercury*'?" My brows hitch as I scoff.

"Because he is lightning-fast and never misses his target," she explains with all seriousness. "Just like the Roman god, Mercury."

"Nice," I grin with newfound understanding.

"Ready to hunt for dinner?" Mom smiles brightly.

"Are you serious?" My eyes widen.

"Extremely."

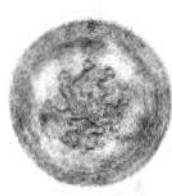

I have never seen anything quite like it.

Never in my wildest dreams could I have ever imagined what happened next.

My mother—Marina Marquez—and I are stalking something through the dense forest of Paradiso. On high alert, we slowly survey our surroundings, keeping a watchful eye for prey. Inside of my chest, my heart is beating a loud staccato and I pray that the errant organ does not give us away. With a gentle hand, my mother touches my arm and mouths:

"Be calm."

Immediately, I will my pulse to decrease, shocked that it listens.

Like Diana, the goddess of the hunt, Mom listens to the sounds around us: birds tweeting, leaves rustling, insects buzzing… *Wait!* Up ahead, movement catches our attention.

"What are we hunting?" I whisper, filled with curiosity. "Something tasty I hope."

Mom motions for me to stop speaking, nods her response, and then I hear her answer in my head.

'There are lots of wild boars, goats and, believe it or not, sheep on Paradiso, but today they are not our target.'

'What other animals live here?' I reply telepathically so not to startle our victim.

She thinks for a minute before answering.

'There are also rabbits, wild turkeys, pheasants, and quail. In the freshwater lakes there are catfish, crawfish, bass, and char. You've already seen all of the different varieties of sea life in the inlet.'

Suddenly, she stops in mid-step and points to a small clearing up ahead where huge bamboo stalks are growing in clumps. Their thick stalks are strong and a lovely shade of moss green. They are so tall that they almost disappear into the intertwining tree canopy.

'Do you see it?' my huntress mother inquiries, still in my head.

Quickly, I scan the area, disappointed that I have not noticed what she already has.

'What am I looking for?' I question psychically, not seeing her mark.

Slowly, Mom crouches low and pulls me down beside her.

'Focus on the area at the base of the largest trunk of bamboo,' she requests, pointing once more.

To my surprise, near the clump of bamboo, partially blending into the surrounding weeds and overgrown brush, stands a wild turkey. His feathers are the same shades of the foliage around him, and his gobbling almost sounds like singing.

'That's what we're eating for dinner?' I ask enthusiastically, ignoring my complaining stomach.

'Uh huh,' Mom replies. *'Now, shh!'*

Again, she motions for me to be still as she moves a little closer to her prey, her feet silent and sure. Steadily, she brings the bow up to her face, adjusts her hold on the weapon, and takes aim, all the while holding her breath. Next, she purses her lips and slowly exhales her breath as if she is a deflating balloon.

Without hesitation, she releases the arrow and as the fletching skims her cheek it leaves a thin scratch, but it heals as quickly as it was formed. Silently, we both watch as the handmade projectile whizzes through the air. All it takes is that one arrow directly to the turkey's brain to instantly kill the proud bird.

Amazing!

Never in my wildest dreams could I have imagined making such a sure shot, especially since the turkey's head is such a small target. To do that, my mother must be well-practiced. One day, I hope to be able to do it just as well, if not better.

No words are spoken as my mom recovers the arrow. With steady hands, she gives the used item a strong tug, pulling it out of her prize. The only thing left is to clean the shell-tipped point and the top of the shaft. She does this by washing it in the nearby pond then lays it across the thick grassy covering to dry in the sun. Effortlessly, Mom picks up the heavy fowl and calmly waves her free hand in the direction of the largest pieces of bamboo.

"Selena, get the thickest stalk that you can find."

I glance at her then back to the bamboo.

"Why?" I question, sounding like a curious child.

"We'll need it to cook the turkey," she replies confidently.

"How— "

"You'll see," she cuts me off.

Leisurely, she turns to head back to the beach when I stop her.

"Mom?"

"What is it, sweetheart?"

I pause.

"Do you have a machete?"

Again, she laughs, but this time her cheeks heat.

"No need for a machete," she prompts, nodding to my hands and feet. "We have built-in knives."

"Oh yeah!" I blush.

Then without further delay, I call the talons on my right hand and strike with one determined swipe against the thickest piece of bamboo. The entire stalk comes crashing down. Instinctively, I move in the direction that it is falling and catch it before it can hit the ground. With a pleased grin, I follow my mother out of the woods.

Watching her hunt is both impressive as well as terrifying. I am in awe, and I want to be just like her when I grow-up.

Back on the beach, I study intently as my mother plucks, cleans, and prepares the large, plump turkey. Lost in her own thoughts, she stands and begins walking back to the forest.

"Where are you going?" I yell after her quickly retreating form.

"Come with me," she entreats with a steadfast grin. "We need some seasonings."

"Is there a grocery store in there that you're not telling me about?" I tease playfully. She does not answer, so I chase her rapidly moving body. As we traipse through the thick forest floor she slows to ask:

"Do you remember what wild ginger smells like?"

"Of course, I do," I nod and grin. "We use it a lot when we make Asian dishes."

"Yes," she smiles. "We do."

"Do you want me to smell for ginger?" I ask just to make certain.

This time, she nods.

"I'm going to find some wild onions, garlic, and tapioca leaves," she reveals as I smell for the uniquely pungent aroma of the exotic spice.

After several minutes of foraging, we exit the wooded area with handfuls of the ingredients we will need to make dinner along with a few more things that my mother did not mention.

"What's all that other stuff?" I point to all of the extra items she carries.

Mom smiles as she looks down at her edible treasures.

"As luck would have it, I managed to find a few morel mushrooms, rainbow carrots, and a couple of good-sized potatoes," she informs, gleefully.

It is impossible not to laugh at her obvious enthusiasm.

"How are we going to cook all of these things?" I cannot help but wonder out loud.

"You'll see," is all she utters.

Then just like a professional butcher would, she uses her talons to carve the carcass into smaller more manageable pieces, and then heavily seasons the meat, before giving it ample time to marinade. As it sits on a large wooden plank soaking up the aromatic flavors, Mom cuts the large bamboo stalk in half, and then cuts out the soft, edible insides using her razor-like talons. Afterward, she squeezes the end close with her bare hands. At last, she fills the hollow stalk with all of the ingredients including the now cut-up raw pieces of turkey, and without breaking a sweat, she seals the other end and lifts the entire heavy trunk onto her left shoulder.

"Can you start a fire, please?" Her question aimed in my direction.

"Umm," I hesitate. "How do I do that?"

"Gather up as much dried tinder you can find," she tutors. "There's a large flat stone a few feet away near that coconut grove, stack them in a neat pile then rub your talons together to get a fire started."

The thought that I can create fire just by rubbing my talons together makes me giggle.

As fast as I can, I run to make the fire following Mom's instructions to a tee, but for some reason the easy sounding task, is giving me trouble.

"I can't get it to light," I huff in exasperation.

"Don't be discouraged," she sympathizes with a warm smile. "I couldn't do it the first few times either."

Searching for something, she scans the area.

"See those two rocks?" she points in the direction.

"Yes."

"If you can't get it lit strike those together to get a spark then light the fire," she advises.

'But that's giving up,' I reply telepathically.

Mom nods.

'Then keep trying,' she adds with a cheeky glower.

Determined to complete the undertaking, I continue to clack my talons together and by the eleventh time, a spark strong enough for the task ignites the dried twigs and leaves. I squeal my excitement, and soon it becomes bigger, brighter, until we have impressive flames.

"I knew you could do it," my mother compliments, giving a mischievous wink then begins the next step.

Using two larger rocks, Mom creates an elevated platform where she lays the bamboo cooking vessel over the roaring fire. She then steps back to admire our work and seems genuinely pleased with our accomplishment.

"Terrific job!" she praises, making me beam.

"When will it be finished?" I hear my stomach growl loudly.

"It will take about forty-five minutes or so," she answers as her tummy begins to protest too.

"What about a swim to help us pass the time?" I peek around her body to get a glimpse of the sapphire lagoon several yards away.

Suddenly, Mom grins then turns and jogs toward the inlet leaving me to stare after her.

"Last one there is a rotten egg!" she shouts acting like a kid.

Yup! That's my mom!

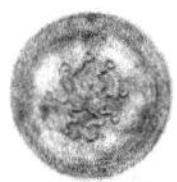

Just as promised, the succulent medley of seasoned turkey and vegetables tantalizes our taste buds as we sit under a large palm tree enjoying our food along with the wonderful scenery and pleasant company. If Ando and Dad were here, it would be even better, but being with Mom in such a relaxed setting is truly priceless. I want to stay this way forever.

"How is the food?" Mom questions nervously. "Alright?"

"Uh huh!" I manage to answer as I lick my fingers of the delicious roasted meat juices.

She laughs as she gnaws on a tasty leg bone.

"Mom?"

"Yes, Selena?" she responds, looking up from her meal.

"Was that *'The Calling'*?" I quiz. "I mean, was that all there was to it?"

Mom glances away, her features lined with concern.

"Not completely," she finally answers.

"What else is there?" I press for more information.

"There is a ceremony that has to be completed in order for you to be truly connected to the aunts and me," my mother informs, her volume almost inaudible.

Instantly, my imagination goes to a dark place.

"Should I be worried?" I frown.

"If I survived it then you certainly will," she reassures me with a small smile that makes me feel a little better.

"Will it be painful?" I grill then change my mind about learning the truth. "Never mind, I'll wait and see."

At a loss for words, my mother says nothing, only smiles again.

"Thank you," I convey changing the subject as I wipe my mouth with the back of my hand.

Mom peers at me with a confused expression.

"For what?" she asks, wiping her mouth similarly.

Acapella

Overwhelmed by the moment, my chest tightens, and I memorize the current scene.

"For being the most incredible mom ever!" misty-eyed, I whisper.

CHAPTER TWO

Massive rainclouds are coming in from the east, covering the sky like cotton balls rolled in fireplace cinders. The not-so-distant horizon once decorated a powdery-blue is now dampened with varying shadows of gray. In the distance, a flock of pelicans diving for lunch several yards offshore have now flown back to the protection of the rocky coastline to wait out the storm. My brother, Ando, and I, on the other hand, sit comfortably on the terrace watching the sailboats entering the safety of the *Marina Piccolo* below.

"Lena," he sighs, tugging at the hem of my plain, white t-shirt. "You actually went there?"

I nod and smile remembering the few hours Mom and I spent on the island together. It was the most incredible time of my young, uninspiring life. I wish we could have stayed longer.

"Seriously, Lena?" Ando questions as he points to the darkening horizon. "And you and Mommy hunted and swam there?"

For the second time, I nod.

"Cool!" he grins.

No longer afraid, we watch as the bluish-black shape that protects and hides the Siren Grotto, shifts and squirms between the sea and the sky. It always reminds me of when the television's satellite signal gets distorted when it rains, but as usual, this signal seems to be alive.

"How was it there?" he pries, longingly. "Was it nice? I bet it was nice."

"I didn't want to leave," I admit sheepishly feeling that longing, that emptiness deep in my gut.

"What's it called again?"

Once more, I feel that all too familiar tightening in my chest.

"Mom called it *Paradiso,*" I exude, feeling proud. "It means 'Paradise'".

"Paradiso," he repeats like a parrot as he leans back into the comfortable lounge chair at our family villa.

Unfortunately, we only have another month of our vacation left. That fact makes me sad. Granted, I miss Isla Flora, but I will miss Capri even more.

"Isn't Capri gorgeous?" I ask no one in particular.

As many know, the four-mile-squared island situated in the Tyrrhenian Sea, on the south side of the Gulf of Naples is one of the most incredible islands in the Mediterranean. According to various members of my immediate family, it has been a travel destination since the time of the Roman Republic. Our vacation home is located in the *Belvedere of Tragara* which is a lofty, panoramic promenade lined with amazing homes overlooking the *Marina Piccolo*.

The villa is constructed around a breathtaking quarter-of-an-acre garden and is only a brief ten-minute walk from the *Piazzetta*. As you enter the grounds, guests are welcomed by an ornate gate that, according to our groundskeeper, was wrought in the early nineteenth century by a local ironsmith. It is a single-level structure comprised of hand-made tiles, whitewashed walls and barrel-vaulted ceilings enhanced by cypress beams. A polished marble foyer accesses the great room which is centered around a marble fireplace. The house is entirely decorated with classic Italian furnishings including a collection of original artworks, a large, fully equipped, modern kitchen, three bathrooms, five bedrooms, along with a small laundry room.

Everything about the property is truly breathtaking, but with all of its lovely architecture and décor, it cannot hold a candle to the natural beauty of Paradiso.

"What are we talking about?" Dad questions as he brings out a tray of ham and cheese sandwiches.

"I bet, I know," Mom states, following her husband with a pitcher of homemade lemonade.

"What's it called again?" Dad asks for the umpteenth time in twenty-four hours.

Mom, Ando and I all answer: "Paradiso."

Dad chuckles.

"Ok, alright, Paradiso," he reminds himself once more.

For some unknown reason, the man cannot seem to keep that one word in his mind.

So very strange.

"Come and get it," Mom whistles like a chuck wagon cook calling for the cowboys.

"Mmm," my six-year-old brother exclaims exuberantly as he takes his first bite then hums as he takes the second bite of the thick sandwich.

"That must mean it's good," I playfully tease.

"This is so yummy!" he confirms using his words.

Practically starving, I take two sandwiches and some potato chips from a bag that Ando has been munching on. I thought I was always hungry; my brother is worse. He reminds me of a bottomless pit that never gets full.

"When can we take Ando to Paradiso?" I query right before biting into the nearest sandwich.

Mom glances at Dad who glances at me.

I glance at my plate.

My brother glances at everyone.

"I'm a Siren," Ando reminds, holding up his sandwich in mid-bite.

"Part Siren," I remind him.

"It is my *birthright*," he pouts, biting into the bread like a ravenous shark.

"Where did you hear that word?" Dad smiles, obviously impressed with my brother's newly found vocabulary word.

"From the aunts," he grins.

"The water in the Siren Grotto is poisonous," I add, feeling a bit superior.

"If you can survive it, so can I," he states with determination.

"I don't think you can," I tease.

"You're a brat!" he huffs.

"You're a bigger brat!" I huff back.

"Mom," he whines. "Tell Lena to leave me alone."

Already knowing whose side she will take, I respond, "Fine… go to the Siren Grotto. When you wake-up dead, don't come running to me."

Everyone looks at me strangely.

"What in heaven's banana does that mean?" Mom finally speaks up.

Dad snickers while pouring lemonade into his glass and then into Mom's and Ando's.

I feel my cheeks heat.

"I heard it somewhere," I admit, holding back a snicker of my own.

"Interesting," Dad chortles. "Very interesting."

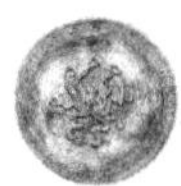

At a leisurely pace, I walk to my bedroom toward the back of the bungalow overlooking the sea. The room is simple, but elegant and is completely white with soft sheer white curtains, an ornate cypress canopy bed dressed with white linen sheets that feel as soft as air.

'I wish I could go back to Paradiso,' I think to myself, longing to enjoy the peace and quiet the island offers.

'We'll visit again soon,' Mom answers my unguarded thought.

I start to complain, but before I can release my introspection, she counters with: *'We'll take your brother next time.'*

'But Mom—'

'But Mom nothing,' she replies with finality that warns me not to push my luck.

'Fine, I'll wait,' I reluctantly concede.

Why can't I go back to Paradiso alone? I have asked Mom and Dad, but they just shrugged and said, "Because we say so."

And that was the end of our extremely one-sided conversation.

So, for the time being, I have held my tongue, but I am positive that I can get them to change their minds. One day, I intend to win that battle.

Still thinking about the black shape at sea, I settle into the window seat in front of the opening. From my perch, I can observe the entire harbor, along with *the Faraglioni* which are limestone formations that jut out above the sea, just like the ones on Paradiso. The view from my window even allows me to see further out into the bay on clear days, but not today. Today, thick clouds cover everything.

However, regardless of the oncoming rain, I am quite happy for the moment. In my peaceful state, I close my eyes and begin to hum, the same low tune with those few varying octaves, uncomplicated and comforting. Something to do to keep my mind occupied until we go out to the movies later this afternoon. As usual, the need to sing comes over me, like it often does. So, I oblige the need, like I often do.

Se la vie.

"Hmmmmm… mmmm… laa… laa… lee… la… la," I play with the sounds; letting them fade at some points then letting it grow at others. Again, my brain drifts to Paradiso and I imagine how divine it must be there during rainstorms and how much I would like to be there, right now.

And then I hear it. I hear the most beautiful tune, but it is not in my head. It is coming from outside, down below, where angry waves thump against the coastline. The male voice sings to me; *calls* to me.

"Follow me… into the sea… in the ocean waves we'll play," he sings in perfect pitch.

He?!

Wait!

Amphitrite could mimic human voices as well as Sirens.

Then… *Wham!*

Just like before, my stupid lungs have locked causing my stupid gills to kick in!

I can't breathe!

Fortunately, this time, I know exactly how long I writhe without oxygen on the white-washed floorboards trying to crawl back to the window. Twenty-five seconds to be exact. I counted each painful moment; however, it seems more like an hour before Mom, Dad, and Ando come running to my aid.

"Not again, Selena!" Dad reaches me first. "What's wrong now?!"

Mom's face is flushed, and Ando is trying to help me to my feet.

"Are you kidding me? Your lungs? *Again?*" Mom screams. "This is ridiculous! Concentrate on activating your lungs, sweetheart!"

I do. I try with all of my might. I try and… *They kick in!*

Then just as quickly, they switch off!

"Can you pick her up?" Mom shouts at Dad who is mumbling obscenities in Spanish and is completely covered in sweat.

I feel sorry for him. He is a marine biologist who has no clue how to cure his fish-daughter. In his defense, I am a conundrum. I can admit it.

"Are we throwing her out of the window again?!" he barks, but this time, he is already opening the window.

"Yes! Throw her out!" My mother orders like this is a commonplace occurrence. "She'll be fine!"

"You got it!" my stepfather agrees. "One *Flying Wallenda*, coming up!"

"Go faster!" his wife barks, and then grabs hold of my legs and helps to throw me out of the open window.

Without a parachute!

Without a life preserver!

This is so freakin' cool!

Just as before, I feel the rush of air as I plummet past the cliffs toward the seawater below. Unexpectedly, I flashback to a few short weeks ago when Mom and I had to jump from the same bedroom window into the Tyrrhenian Sea to save my life. At first, I thought that was bad. Now, it's amazing!

Almost there.

Finally, I hit the transparent surface…

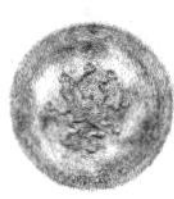

The world around me suddenly becomes a loud, low rush of muted currents in my ears. Immediately, I started breathing in the salty brine of the sea. It is refreshing and hits the spot.

Whew!

When I come to my senses, I discover that I am not alone. Several feet away two pairs of eyes stare at me from behind an outcropping of seaweed, a long leafy stalk still being held between their teeth. Surprisingly, I have not seen this type of fish before. These two are approximately two feet in length with bodies that are adorned with large scales. The upper parts of their bodies are gray, but their lateral sides are silver and covered with several rows of horizontal black stripes.

Filled with curiosity, I attempt to converse with them.

"What type of fish are you?" I ask in Siren.

Curiously, they glare at me then finally, they speak.

"We are *Qualos*," both answer together.

Not understanding, my brow furrows which earns me another strange expression.

"Humans call us striped, red mullets," indignantly they educate.

Eager to know more about them, I study their small heads and triangular-shaped mouths crammed with teeth that are miniature, compact, and arranged in several rows on their lower spade-shaped jawline. These two particular fish have stocky, torpedo-shaped bodies with short pectoral fins and unique forked tails.

My gravy!

I am turning into my stepfather. Soon I will be ordering textbooks about marine habitats and how they affect the longevity of the planet. *Ugg!* To my dismay, I am becoming a nerd.

"Unlike most fish, you do not have lateral lines." I blurt with fascination.

They glance at each other then back at me.

"Huh?" They both respond at once.

I smile before clarifying.

"That's an organ which detects changes in the water currents."

Both fish look at me strangely, their bodies hovering weightlessly in the warm depths.

Getting nowhere and hoping to hide my embarrassment, I apologize for startling them with that clickity-clackity language of the Sirens, and they slowly return to their task of pulling long strands of seaweed from the densely packed sand completely ignoring me.

"How's it going—" I begin, but the two turn up their fins in disgust.

"Human?" the bigger fish clicks to the smaller one then before I can say anything else they start to giggle.

"What's your problem?" I snap, more than offended at their rudeness.

"Are you a surface dweller?" the small one asks, eyeing me up then down.

"I'm a *Siren*," I inform with an indignant harrumph.

"If you are a Siren, where is your webbing?" They inspect me from head to toe then back again.

Instantly, my temper rises, and I give them a *Mr. Spock* one eyebrow up the other down which translates from teenager-looks into *Rude little bugger!*

Wanting to calm down, I take a few more deep breaths then motion to the surface.

"If you must know, I had to be thrown from my bedroom window when my gills activated."

Curiously, they continue to glare at me.

"What is a wind-o?" the larger fish queries just like the aunts would.

"A window is an opening in a home," I explain in simple terms.

"I see," the fish replies, seeming content with the explanation.

"Has that ever happened before?" they ask in unison.

"Well… yes," I meekly admit. "But in my defense, I'm a young Siren."

"Obviously," they snicker.

"Hey!" I chastise. "It's not as easy as it looks!"

"Apparently," the smaller fish states with a more pleasant tone. "I hope you get the hang of it, young one."

Glad that the tension has been lifted, I smile back.

"Usually, it just takes several seconds for either my lungs or gills to kick-in, but lately I can transition almost immediately," I boast.

"Good for you!" the female fish compliments sincerely. "I am Stripes."

"Very nice to meet you, Stripes," I express, taking her fin and gently shaking it like I would someone's hand.

She smiles sweetly at the odd gesture.

"I am Hunter," the male fish offers me his fin as well.

"Hunter?"

He blushes.

"I am great at finding food scraps," he informs with a puffed chest.

"Good to know," I grin. "May I ask a question?"

"Sure," they concur.

"Did you hear singing?"

"Nope," they reply, returning to the gathering of seaweed.

"Oh," is my only response.

"Well," Hunter begins. "It has been nice chatting, but we have got to get back to work."

"What do you need seaweed for?"

"We're decorating our home," Stripes answers proudly.

"I see," I respond, not realizing that fish decorate.

"We are newlyweds," Hunter smiles at his lovely wife.

"Our cave is right over that ridge, near the red coral," Stripes waves her tail in that direction.

"I'll bring you a cave-warming present when I'm back in the neighborhood," I promise the adorable couple.

"How sweet of you," Stripes grins her appreciation.

"It was great meeting you!" I declare, waving goodbye.

"Do not be a stranger," Hunter flicks his fin in response.

"Be careful out here," Stripes warns. "Lately, after sunset, strange things have been happening."

"What sort of strange things?" My eyes widen.

Hunter swims in close to my ear as he states: "Whirlpools churning up the sea, explosions, sinkholes suddenly appearing then disappearing, and hordes of jellyfish and eels attacking."

"All sorts of witchery," Stripes whispers sheepishly.

Instantly, my face reddens with the knowledge that I caused a lot of those events.

"Wu-well," I stammer, "I'm sure it was just a fluke."

"I hope so," Hunter clears his throat. "I would hate for this neighborhood to go sideways."

"Me too," Stripes nods in agreement. "We want to start a family soon."

Hunter glances around.

"Where is your family, young one?" he questions.

"Please, call me Selena."

"Se-le-na," they repeat it slowly then giggle. "That is a strange name."

"I was named after the moon goddess," I educate with a chuckle.

"Ahh! Then I am sure you will do the name proud," Hunter praises.

"I'll try," I beam.

"See that you do," Stripes pats my wrist with her fin.

"Where are your people?" Hunter asks again.

I motion to the surface.

"Then make sure you tell them that you are alright," he encourages, just like a father would.

As they watch, I pause, cock my head to the side then close my eyes. A slow smile creeps over my face before I inform, "It's done."

"What is done?" both fish ask.

"I just told my mother and brother that I'm going exploring and will be back soon."

"Oh," they whisper, appearing to be a bit confused, hoping I do not have brain damage from the lack of oxygen during my journey down the side of the cliff I suppose.

I laugh, shaking their fins one more time.

"Are you sure you are alright down here by yourself?" Stripes inquires, surveying the area.

"I promise. I'll be okay," I answer to the best of my knowledge.

Not sure that I will be alright, they glare at me. Suddenly feeling uncomfortable, I decide to say my goodbyes.

"Good luck with your decorating," I state, hoping that they will be safe too.

"See you around," Hunter wiggles his fins good-naturedly.

I, in turn, grace him with a playful wink.

"I hope so."

"Visit anytime," Stripes utters with a large grin.

"See you soon." I giggle, swimming away. "You've made my day."

CHAPTER THREE

The swim from Capri to wherever my wanderlust is taking me is a scenic route. Overhead, subdued sunshine dissects the aquatic barrier separating the human realm from the oceanic one. As I leisurely swim along the rocky seabed, admiring the multicolored coral clusters and the gracefully swaying clumps of seaweed, I feel that blanket of contentment wrapping me in its strong arms.

"Where should I go?" I ask aloud, trying to make up my mind.

Unfortunately, nothing comes to mind.

"Should I go back to the Siren Grotto?" I hum, tapping an agitated finger against my bottom lip.

Now that I know how to find it, it is definitely a possibility, but without Mom or Ando, I would be lonely.

Next time, I want to show my brother the land that is truly our home.

"I haven't been to the Blue Grotto in several weeks," I ponder the destination once more.

Forget it.

The last time I was there, Amphitrite trapped Ando and me inside the cave using an invisible barrier, a barrier so strong that it took Mom, Ligeia and Leukosia's powers to destroy it. Nope! I think I will steer clear for the time being.

Clearing the disturbing memory from my brain, I try just enjoying the marine habitat, but my mind keeps wondering about my final destination. I need to make a decision before sunset, or I will be forced to return to the villa. Mom and Dad would definitely be upset if I stay out after dark.

'You're absolutely right about us getting angry with you if you're out too late,' I hear my mother's voice as she uses her telepathy.

'Mom,' I whine. *'I can take care of myself.'*

'There are too many unknowns here,' she reminds parentally. 'I don't feel comfortable with the idea of you out when it's dark.'

'I can be killed in the daytime too,' I add then grimace, hating myself for planting that seed in my already paranoid mother's mind.

Silence.

Mom clears her mental throat.

'Be home by sundown,'

Her clipped tone makes me shudder.

'I'll be home on time,' I promise, giving in.

'If you need any help… any help at all…' she continues, softening her blow.

Her worry makes me smile to myself.

'I'll call,' I state firmly. 'I swear.'

'Your dad is grilling tonight,' Mom cleverly entices, knowing that the way to my heart is through my stomach. 'The ribeye steaks are marinating as we speak.'

My stomach suddenly growls from that tempting knowledge.

'Then I definitely won't be late.'

ACAPELLA

'See that you aren't,' that is her last proclamation then my mind grows quiet.

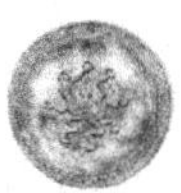

When I am certain that my mother has tuned out, I turn toward the open ocean, but before I can resume my journey, I hear it: *The Chauffer* by the 80's pop band Duran Duran.

Raspy, yet sweet and soulful, he sings:

> *"Out on the tar plains, the glides are moving,*
>
> *All looking for a new place to drive.*
>
> *You sit beside me so newly charming,*
>
> *Sweating dewdrops glisten freshing your side..."*

Just like yesterday, those seductive lyrics beckon me to follow even though I know I should not, but I do anyway.

"Follow me, young Siren," the voice suggestively summons like the serpent to Eve, the promised fruit too tantalizing to resist.

It is the young man from the yacht! The one I tried to lure to a watery grave.

Guilt-ridden, my thoughts seize, and my esophagus tightens.

What do I do? Answer? Not answer?

Dear Father!

Okay, my mother wiped his memory of the 'incident', so as far as he is concerned nothing ever happened. Right?

Right!

Then I wonder if I can communicate telepathically with a Human.

Let's see.

Taking hold of the volcanic glass charm secured to my necklace, I concentrate.

'*Where are you?*' I ask through thought, trying to decipher the direction where the voice originated.

'*I am close,*' he playfully chuckles back inside of my mind with a voice not too deep, but not too high either.

Holy crap! It works!

'You have an exquisite voice,' I compliment, looking around, but seeing only vegetation and an occasional sea creature. *'Who are you?'*

Unfortunately, he avoids the question.

'Find me,' he confidently invites once more. *'You will see soon enough.'*

Instantly, warning bells go off inside my head and the hairs on my arms stand at attention, but still, I want to answer. Vacationing here has been a lesson in the fact that Sirens are not the only supernatural beings on Earth. In fact, the creatures we have encountered make Lucifer look like a squishy, loveable, round-bellied puppy. Realizing this, I still answer:

'Okay.'

I even frown, wondering why I am agreeing against my better judgement.

'I have heard many things about you,' he informs knowingly.

What the what?!

'Really?' I reply, finding humor in his admission. *'I find that hard to believe.'*

'The oceans are buzzing over you,' he educates, matter-of-factly.

Once more, alarms are screeching in my ears, but my curiosity takes over. Now I know that he is *not* human. I should end this conversation and swim home, but instead I ask:

'What are they saying about me?'

'Many interesting things,' he purrs, the sound music to my ears.

Stop swooning! I chastise myself. *Remember Andrew. Remember Andrew. Remember—*

'Find me,' he challenges in that all too confident way of his. *'I am dying to meet you, Selena.'*

I feel a guilty twinge in my chest because of my feelings for Andrew, but lost in the moment, I choose to ignore it.

'How do you know my name?'

'I told you,' I hear the humor in his voice. *'You are the newest and greatest craze in these parts.'*

'Be serious,' I condemn, blushing.

'Come to me and all of your questions will be answered,' he states excitedly.

Filled with embarrassment, I blush even more, hoping he cannot see my face.

'How do I find you?' I question, feeling like the world's greatest moron.

There is a pause.

'Close those beautiful eyes,' he commands, and I follow. *'Listen to my voice and my voice alone.'*

'Alright,' I agree, unable to fight against logic.

'Do you think you can do this?' he prods, challenging my competitive nature.

'I'll try,' I sheepishly respond.

'Good, girl,' he flatters, and usually anyone besides my parents or aunts would instantly get my dander up, but when he says it, I do not mind. Excited to meet the phantom voice, I keep my eyes closed and concentrate on dissecting each sound currently adrift along the seabed.

I hear the waves above my head and quiet them until they are almost motionless.

I hear the wind as it rushes across the water and still them to barely a breeze.

I hear the underwater currents as they glide across my skin and slow them until they have almost stopped.

Within seconds, the entire sea is perfectly still.

'Impressive,' he praises. *'Quite impressive.'*

Again, I concentrate, listening to what remains.

'Find me yet?' he teases.

'You're encased in something,' I realize from the echo. *'Concrete maybe... No—'*

'Come now, Selena,' he sneers. *'Should I just tell you?'*

'Wait!' I clack in Siren.

'What was that?' he asks. *'I am not fluent in Siren.'*

'Oh!' I exclaim, understanding that it might not be Amphitrite in disguise.

'Perhaps I will tell you—'

Before he can finish his sentence, I hear the resonance of sunlight as it hits the sea. It has an extremely distinct crackle as the salt heats up just a tad. Also, the unique sound of wind tunneling through a narrow passage then hearing as it grates against limestone. Finally, I hear a heartbeat, strong and steady.

ACAPELLA

'I know where you are!' I beam, heading toward the Blue Grotto.

'Do not be long,' he requests impatiently, making my own heart race.

Then out of the blue, a vision of Andrew appears in my mind, but I brush it away, not caring at the moment. I must meet the man behind the voice.

'I'll be there in a flash,' I proclaim confidently as I kick my legs allowing water to get trapped against the folds of my webbing.

Like a torpedo, I speed through the still sea toward the opposite side of the island. Eager to meet the source of the vocals who can sing like a Siren, who might be a demon or something just as scary, but for some reason it fascinates me.

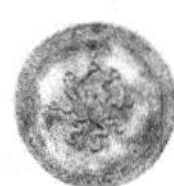

It takes only fifteen minutes at my current warp speed to arrive in Anacapri. However, I have now had enough time to second guess my decision to meet 'the voice'. Several times during my trek, I have imagined it being Amphitrite, but since our previous encounter, I have seen neither hide nor hair of that demonic goddess.

'Are you close?' the foreign male voice inside of my head startles me.

'I can see the entrance to the Blue Grotto,' I nervously respond, looking ahead at the cave entrance.

There is a brief silence then the voice commends:

'You are very fast, Selena.'

'Not as fast as my mother or aunts,' I admit, gaging his reaction. *'But soon I will be.'*

'I like your confidence,' he states, admiringly, not showing any concern or fear.

'I like how you sing,' I grin.

'Stop!' he snickers. *'Now, I am blushing.'*

That knowledge makes me blush too.

What about Andrew? My arms stop in mid-stroke. *I shouldn't be doing this.*

'Have you changed your mind?' the smooth voice questions, sounding disappointed.

'I'm not sure this is a good idea,' I mentally whisper, knowing he can hear me.

There is another uncomfortable pause.

'I am not going to hurt you, young Siren,' he reassures, and I believe him for some odd reason.

Then I hear several voices to my left about a quarter of a mile away.

'There is a boat of tourists heading this way,' I add, but he either does not hear me or does not care if we are found.

'Hurry then,' he answers at last.

Without further hesitation, I make my way toward the cave. No longer afraid of the outcome. No longer afraid, for now.

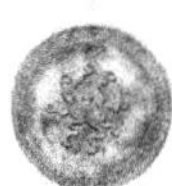

It does not take long to slow my speed in order to maneuver through the narrow entrance into the grotto. Calling my scales just to be safe, I slip carefully past the six feet wide by three feet high opening. It is just as I remember.

Inside the famed cavern, rays of glorious, midday sunlight, passes through a subaquatic opening in the limestone and shines through the seawater. Magically it creates a vibrant blue reflection that irradiates the whole cavern. The sight always takes my breath away.

"Hello?" I call then hear my voice as it echoes back when it hits the stony walls. "Are you here?"

Silence batters my senses, so I dive down to the bottom of the cave thinking it will be safer there although being in an enclosed space with a stranger is not the *'safe'* thing to do regardless.

When I think I will lose my senses, he finally responds.

"Come to the surface," the masculine voice answers.

More cautiously, I venture to the air-filled pocket near the ceiling.

"Show yourself!" I order as my head pops out of the water and my gills retract allowing my lungs to activate.

"Are you nervous?"

"No," I admit with a shaky tremor to my voice. "But tourists will soon be here."

"Then fix it so they do not disturb us," he challenges, roguishly.

"How do you suggest I do that?" I query placing both hands on my hips as I tread water, tone irritated.

"Did you subdue the sea and the wind?" He laughs.

"Guilty as charged," I pompously come clean.

"So," he expresses blankly.

"So, what?" I huff with growing agitation.

"*So*, reverse your will," he smirks. "Put the sea back to the way it was before."

Ahh! Makes sense!

Taking the black, volcanic glass pendant on my chain between my palms, I focus. Focus on moving the sea. Focus on agitating the air. Focus on all of the intricate calculations that need to be manipulated in order to make a small storm and not a deadly monsoon.

"Let it be as it was," I order the sea and the wind, and it does what I command. The winds begin to blow stronger, harder. The once docile waves begin to agitate like a washing machine on the bulky-items cycle. For added spookiness, I move the clouds to cover the sun and to show off, I create a mild thunderstorm.

From outside of the cave's entrance, I hear an unfamiliar voice announcing in a rough, thick Italian accent:

"Sorry, ladies and gentlemen, but it is no longer safe to go inside of the grotto. My sincerest apologies."

Suddenly, I feel guilty. Guilty that the tour guide will not be able to make his wages or tips today. Guilty that the tourist will not be able to see such an amazing natural wonder. Guilty in general for causing a storm so strong that I hear the boat's hull scrape against the limestone.

Closing my eyes, I turn the storm into a slight drizzle, but leave the waves choppy enough to keep the people out for another hour or so.

"Like I said… *impressive,*" the masculine tone tickles my eardrums like wisps of smoky tendrils meandering off of flickering flames.

"We don't have much time," I advise, not wanting to miss my curfew. "Show yourself or I will leave."

"Here I am, young Siren," he speaks, but the sound keeps shifting within the space.

"Are you moving around?" I question with a frown. "You wanted to meet, *sooooo* let's meet."

"Are all Sirens so rude?" he asks, and I hear the smirk in his tone. The sound causes my pulse to race and not in a good way.

"Amphitrite?" I gasp, activating my talons to their full length. "If you want another fight, I'll be more than happy to oblige!"

He chuckles before declaring, "I am definitely *not* that pathetic creature."

"Are you a man?" I grill, feeling braver.

His sudden burst of laughter startles me.

"For all intents and purposes," he mumbles. "Yes, yes, I am."

"What does that mean?" My eyes narrow and my pulse quickens.

"I have all of the parts," he reveals cheekily, definitely making my face turn a bright shade of scarlet.

"That's good to know," I remark as I dive down to the bottom to examine the area from below just in case I need to get out in a hurry.

When I am confident that I can escape, if necessary, I swim back up.

"Then who are you?" I enquire again as I resurface.

"Do you really want to know me?"

I think for a few seconds.

"Yes," I mumble, searching for him, but seeing nothing except limestone and shimmering blue light.

"Your wish is my command, young one," he announces and before my eyes, as if all of the molecules in the grotto start to separate then reconfigure into a twinkling shower of brilliant light, he appears.

A golden-haired young man, probably nineteen—twenty at most—stands before me with eyes the deepest shade of amethyst I have ever seen. Those eyes, surrounded by thick gold lashes that capture the blue light of the grotto and glow emerald, pierce my very soul. He is tall, at least six-feet-four-inches of lean, tanned muscle and a smile more dazzling than diamonds. His perfect form is clothed in a pair of shorts and a polo-shirt.

"You are beautiful," I blurt without thinking.

His face reddens and his smile broadens.

"I believe you meant handsome, but thank you," he chuckles. "You are spectacular too."

"You already know who I am," I remind, feeling heat creep all over my body, but I do not care. "How?"

"You, my girl, are *legendary*," he informs sincerely.

"Then your sources are misinformed," I admonish, completely taken aback by his comment.

All he does is stare at me, lancing my spirit with those sparkling orbs of amethyst. This being looks at me and I melt. Then at last, he speaks.

"Selena Antonius Thermopolis Marquez of House Melpomene," he bows low like he is addressing royalty. "Granddaughter of Parthenope, daughter of Marina, sister of Fernando, child of the sea, *a Siren*, shall I go on?"

Again, he bows.

"Stop bowing!" I order with a scowl. "You're making me uncomfortable."

"That was not my intention, my lady." He gazes at me so sweetly.

"You have me at a disadvantage," I prompt, changing the subject.

"I do?" he grins, impishly.

"Tell me your name or I'll leave," I boldly assert, admiring his strong rugged features.

"Apologies, sometimes I forget my manners," my companion admits, shaking his head. "Please, call me *Ares*."

CHAPTER FOUR

Enjoying the view of my new acquaintance, I continue treading water as I watch him watching me. He seems much older, wiser and has an aura of quiet strength surrounding him. I can imagine everyone he meets wanting to throw themselves at his feet.

Myself included.

"Ares," I repeat, liking the sound of it. The name sounds familiar, but I do not remember the source.

Smiling, he pushes a lock of blonde hair away from his eyes.

"I like your name," I praise like I am five.

"I like that you like it," Ares reveals looking down at his bare feet.

"It's unique," I commend, unable to look away.

'Ares... Ares,' I keep repeating in my head as I skim through my memory banks looking for something to jump out at me.

Where have I heard that name?

"It is alright," he grins shyly, bringing me back to reality.

"Is it a family name?" I counter, trying to diffuse the awkwardness of the moment.

"My parents thought it was fitting," he pompously divulges, still studying the space.

Unexpectedly, my upper lip begins to sweat, and I am glad that the water droplets clinging to my scales hide it.

"I'm named after the—"

"The Moon Goddess," he whispers like it is top-secret. "I know."

I grin at his response, but then he adds:

"Actually, her name is *Selene*."

My eyes instantly widen.

"How did you know that?" I probe, wanting to know more about this mysterious stranger.

Ares laughs wholeheartedly; the kind of laugh that travels down your spinal cord and settles in the pit of your stomach where they transform from awkward caterpillars into beautiful butterflies. All of my extremities begin to tremble, disturbing the water around me so that it ripples outward as though someone has thrown a pebble into it.

At least I know he is well-educated. In my experience, not many people know about the ancient Greek Titan goddess of the Moon with so much detail. The only reason I know about this bit of information is that my Aunt Ligeia once went on a fifteen-minute rant about that very subject. She scolded my mother for changing the last 'e' in the goddess' name to an 'a'.

I am not prepared for what he mentions next.

"The true Selene—" Ares scans me up and down, and then adds as he points toward the heavens. "—was not as stunning as you."

Giddy, my mind is racing, and I am glad that he thinks I am attractive.

"You have lovely scales," he beams, irises sparkling like moonbeams. "They shine like polished beach glass, and you are just as impressive as the other females in your family."

"Thank you," I accept with a tummy full of nervous knots. "Are you some sort of *creature* disguised as a Human?"

There is another long pause.

"Umm—" He runs a nervous hand through his golden strands.

"I'll take that as a *'no'*," I add, palms sweating in the water which is weird. "Do you live here?"

"Here?" he motions around the grotto which makes me laugh.

"On Capri," I quickly clarify.

"No, not here," Ares blurts, nervously. "Not Capri. Not usually."

"Are you from the mainland?" I ask, hearing a slight accent when he speaks.

He shakes his head.

"I am not of this place," he mutters below his breath, making me strain to hear his declaration.

"Not of this place?" I question with confusion. "Explain."

"One day soon, I will explain everything," Ares says, looking back at me. "I promise."

And I believe him completely. Truly, I believe.

Again, I hear voices from outside the entrance.

"We should leave before the weather clears enough for the tour groups to come inside," I encourage, not wanting to explain how we got inside the grotto.

"Do not go," he pleads. "Not yet."

"I think I should."

I am about to switch to Siren-mode when he stops me.

"Wait!"

Taken by surprise, I stop.

"What's the matter?"

Slowly, he kneels on the rocky edge surrounding the water.

"When will we see each other again?"

I grin not knowing the answer, but hoping it is soon.

"I'm not sure," I reveal sadly.

"Hopefully soon," Ares winks and takes my hand without permission. Gently, he kisses it. Just once. One perfectly placed kiss along the knuckles.

"Soon."

Dinner tonight does not have the same carnivorous *'Zing!'* that it would normally have. Instead of being overjoyed by the perfectly grilled steak sitting on my plate, my attitude is one of indifference. That is a rare event, especially for someone like me who could eat ribeye three times a day, every day, for the rest of my life and be extremely content.

"Lena!" Ando's voice snaps me out of my stupor.

"What?" I murmur, returning to my meal.

"Why aren't you eating?" my brother demands as he takes another bite of his already cut beef.

"Huh?"

"Can I have your steak?" he asks, ready to reach over with his fork and take the unsuspecting piece of meat.

"No!" I snap, knocking his fork away with a snarl.

"Fine," he growls retrieving his eating utensil from under the dining table. "But you didn't have to be so mean about it."

Of course, he is right.

"I'm sorry," I apologize with a falsely placed grin.

"Are you feeling alright?" Dad queries, right before taking a sip of his iced tea.

"I'm fine," I answer too quickly, earning a Vulcan eyebrow raise from my mother.

Uh oh! Her 'mom-senses' have been activated due to my vain answers. I have awakened the beast.

Mom starts her own series of questions.

She opens with: "How was your adventure?"

"What adventure?" I spew, uneasily.

At my tone, she stabs a broccoli floret with the force of *The Incredible Hulk*. Without warning, beads of perspiration appear along my forehead making me look guilty before Mom's trial even starts.

I am not off to a good start.

"Your swim in the harbor," she continues. "How was it?"

Needing additional time to formulate an acceptable response, I take a long gulp of my drink in order to get the right wording, one that does not raise doubt. That would be disastrous.

"Good," I do not elaborate.

"Anything exciting or unusual happen?" Mom grills, cutting a piece of her steak.

"No," I reply, returning her eyebrow arch and raising her a wide-eyed expression. "What could have happened?"

Immediately, my mother stops eating and rests her utensils beside her half-eaten plate of food. In typical fashion, she clasps her hands and rests them in her lap. In this position, she reminds me of a female version of *Oliver Twist*, asking for more without saying a word. Next, she looks me dead in the eyes which automatically make me sweat even more.

When I cannot stand the scrutiny any longer, she finally asks:

"Why are you being defensive?"

Unable to stop it, I feel heat fill my round cheeks and spread outward until it reaches my ears and neck. If I did not look uncomfortable before, I really look like it now.

"I'm not," I sulk, continuing to eat.

"Hmm," she sounds, further irritating me.

At last, I make eye contact. Even though my mother's ability to draw out information is done with military precision and concise interrogation, I still attempt to confront her. All I need to do is keep a well-placed poker face. If it gets brutal, Dad will step in as usual and defuse the situation with his suave and soothing Latin accent.

Attempting not to blink, which is one of my 'tells' that I am trying to hide something, I cross-examine.

"What does that mean?"

"Nothing," Mom responds nonchalantly then returns to eating the remaining broccoli on her plate.

My stepfather seems entertained by our back-and-forth banter. He resembles a chair umpire judging a spirited tennis match. Ando also sits quietly observing our battle of wits as he gnaws on the bone of his ribeye.

"Selena," Dad speaks, entering the ring.

"Yes, Dad?" My eyes never leave Mom as I respond.

"You're leaving something out, aren't you?" he interjects with a broad grin which throws off my concentration.

Like a defeated athlete coming in last at the finish line, my gaze returns to my plate as I sit staring at my food. Wanting to avoid suspicion, I decide to play dumb and hopefully, she'll buy what I am selling. For good measure, I cross my fingers for extra luck under the table.

"I met two fish today," I remember with a chuckle.

That should throw them off of my trail.

"What kind?" Ando perks up with the bone still clutched in his small hand.

"They were a pair of newly wed striped, red mullets," I describe, enthusiastically.

"Did they have names?" he asks, reaching for his cup of water.

I nod.

"The husband's name is Hunter, and his wife is Stripes."

After she swallows, Mom is back in the conversation.

"Were they nice?" My mother appears to be interested in my new friends.

"They were so sweet—"

"You ate them?!" Ando gasps, and then squeals. "How could you?"

I gasp too, only much louder, but with more mortification and disgust.

"I… did… not… eat… them," I annunciate, indignantly.

Believing me, he releases a long-held breath and begins to load his fork again.

"Good," he answers with an uneasy grin. "Will you introduce me to them?"

"Maybe," I tease.

"C'mon, Lena," Ando whines like a puppy. "Take me with you tomorrow."

"We have plans tomorrow," Mom interjects.

I look at her inquisitively.

"We are visiting Naples for a few days," she informs with a grin.

"Why?" I snap, and Dad scolds me with a look.

"It will be nice to experience life on the mainland," my father suggests, ending all debate because he holds the mantle of *Dad-Supreme*.

"I wish someone asked me if I wanted to go to Naples," I grumble rudely.

Mom glowers at me.

"By the way," Dad interjects after wiping his mouth with a napkin. "Andrew called this afternoon while you were out on your swim."

Startled by the news, I accidentally drop my fork and it clanks against the plate.

"He did?!"

Dad nods his head.

My imagination goes on high alert. Suppose he felt *'a disturbance in the force'* and knows about Ares. No. He cannot be that in tune with my emotions.

Can he?

"What did he want?" I interrogate, chewing on my bottom lip. "Is everything alright back home?"

Dad and Mom glance at each other and then at me.

"He just wanted to see how you were doing," Dad responds, suspiciously.

Nervously, I play with the unused napkin currently covering my lap, completely aware that my hands are not only sweating, but also trembling. It would be detrimental to let my parents see that. Then they would know I am not telling the whole story.

"What did you tell him?" I probe, concentrating on remaining at ease.

"That you are well—" Dad replies with an easygoing tone.

"What else?" I interrupt.

"I told him that you went for a swim." His eyes narrow as he attempts to figure out why I am tense.

"Is that all?" I add, needing more information, and it takes all of my self-control to resist the urge to bite my nails which I sometimes do when I am under stress.

My father observes me, waiting, sizing me up in his head I suppose.

"I told him that you would call him back," he relays with a slight frown.

"Oh," I mutter on an exhale.

"Are you?" The intuitive male still glares at me.

"I'll call after dinner," I reply, picking up my fork.

Even Ando stops eating and joins the staring competition. I feel like a fly under a microscope. All eyes are on me.

"Selena, what's going on?" Mom interrogates, placing her napkin on the table beside her empty glass.

"Nothing," I babble too quickly.

"What happened on your swim, Selena?" Mom sits straighter.

"Nothing," I whine, repeating myself. "Absolutely nothing."

"Are you sure?" Ando comments with a wary expression.

"What's with the third degree?" my voice rises an octave.

"You're acting so strangely." My stepdad jumps back into the fray.

"May I just eat my dinner, please?" I sigh.

"Go ahead," Mom and Dad both answer.

Ando responds with a snarky, "Hmm."

Feeling my cheeks redden, I begin to consume my steak and vegetables with gusto. I do not look up until my entire plate is clean, spotless actually.

Ugg!

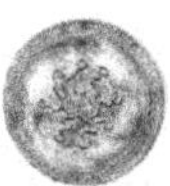

After such an edgy conversation, I retreat to the sanctuary of my room. Right now, I stand looking out of my bedroom window into the surrounding darkness, too lazy to switch on my Siren vision in order to see the lovely harbor. Instead, I stare at the blinking light on my cellphone notifying me that there is a message awaiting my reply. In my gut, I know that Andrew has left the voicemail.

Wearily, I play it.

"Hey, Selena! This is Andrew. Just wanted to hear your voice and let you know that I hope you are having fun on your vacation. Give me a call when you can. Talk to you soon. Bye!

Oh! I'm in Sitka, Alaska! Lots to tell you! Ok!
Call me! Btw… I miss you!"

Filled with nervous energy, I pace back and forth debating if I should call him, all the while my footsteps almost wear a path across the immaculate bedroom floor. Anxiously, I glance at the bedside clock and calculate the time difference. It is ten o'clock at night here in Capri, so it is twelve in the afternoon in Sitka, Alaska.

Determined to get it over with, I hit his preprogramed cell number and wait.

The phone rings. Once. Twice—

"Hey!" Andrew answers, his tone dripping with excitement.

"Hey!" I repeat, feeling my heartbeat accelerate.

"How's Capri?" He sounds peppy.

"Wonderful," I pause then continue, adding, "but odd."

"*Siren* odd?" He laughs.

"Of course," I snicker. "What are you doing?"

There is a short pause as he asks me to hold, then I hear a soft feminine voice in the background asking for his lunch order. I giggle as he requests: a bison burger with cheddar cheese only, double order of French fries, and a small side salad with bleu cheese dressing. My entire body convulses as I clasp my free hand over my mouth so I will not burst into riotous laughter, but Andrew hears me anyway.

"I haven't eaten since six o'clock this morning," he chastises with a smile that I can hear over the cell phone.

"I see," I giggle.

"I am a growing boy," he reminds with a chuckle.

"Yeah, growing *out*," I jokingly rib then clear my throat.

"Ha! Ha! Ha!" he mocks. "Very funny."

There is another halt in our conversation when his father asks a question, but he returns after a few more seconds and apologizes for all of the interruptions. Then I hear his dad teasing him about maybe now he will be in a better mood since getting to talk with me. Totally embarrassed, my cheeks fill with heat.

"What was I saying—"

My eyebrows hitch at his lack of focus.

"You must be incredibly tired, Mister Barnett?" I state, feeling sorry for my cute… umm… *boyfriend?*

Andrew has never formally asked me to be his *'girlfriend'*. It was implied a few times, but never confirmed. The only fact that I know is that he likes me, and I like him. For now, that is good enough for me. My life is complicated enough at the moment to add another variable to the extremely complicated equation.

Unexpectedly, he releases a loud yawn just as I make my observation.

"Why are you so tired?" I probe wondering what he and his father are doing so far away from Isla Flora.

"I'm helping my dad for a few weeks," his tiredness instantly dissipates, and my curiosity awakens.

"What's your father doing up there?" I query, wanting to know more details about their trip.

"He's a photographer for National Geographic," Andrew downplays it like it is no big deal when it obviously is a humongous deal.

I have always loved that magazine and now there is a *The National Geographic Channel* on cable. It is one of my family's favorite television stations, next to *The Food Network*. Dad usually has it playing on the flat screen in his office when he works from home. When Ando and I were much younger, Mom says he would read articles to us instead of children's books. Sometimes, he would even turn them into lullabies.

"I was born off of the coast of Anchorage," I inform proudly.

"I know," the teen snickers.

"What city are you at again?" I add as several more text messages flood my cell phone.

"We are at a seaside fishing town called Sitka," the teen reveals. "It's beautiful, peaceful."

My device vibrates notifying me that I have received several more annoying texts.

"Hold on, Andrew," I quickly check my device thinking they are advertisements, but instead I see a selfie of Andrew and his father sitting at a quaint sidewalk café with a delicious meal on the table in front of them, along with snapshots of the local scenery and wildlife. I snicker as I rapidly swipe through them. He and his dad are adorable.

Andrew looks like an exact replica except younger and with dark hair instead of blonde. Both are extremely handsome.

"I was going to ask if you are you having fun, but I can see that you are," I giggle as I lay on the bed to continue our conversation. "How's the bison burger?"

"Mmm," he moans. "Awesome!"

"You must be having a great time with your father," I smile and roll my eyes.

"Kinda." He laughs.

I laugh too, enjoying our easygoing banter.

"Why only *'kinda'*?"

"I'm his assistant," Andrew reveals on a blush.

"Really?" I snort. "What's your job description?"

"Carrying bags of camera equipment, learning about the various lenses and filters and making sure Dad has everything he needs when he's on location," Andrew sighs again.

From his explanation, I can envision them hiking through rugged terrain as they aim to find the perfect location as they track a migrating herd of moose or a pack of wandering wolves. I smile at the image of Andrew handing him different lenses as his father strives to capture the perfect pictures to enhance their story. To tell the truth, I would not mind doing that job.

"It's a lot of work, up at dawn," Andrew continues. "Bedtime at midnight."

"That still sounds amazing!" I exclaim, almost jumping out of my skin from the excitement.

"Yeah," he grows quiet. "I miss you though."

Bringing up his selfie, I smile as I gaze longingly at Andrew's handsome face and even more handsome personality. Suddenly, I need him to know how I feel about him, but for some reason the only words that come out is:

"I miss you too."

CHAPTER FIVE

It is gorgeous here, and all around are black spruce, paper birch and alder that appear to grow up into the violet sky until all you see are hefty trunks. Moss covered trunks that I can barely wrap my arms around. Below my feet, a dense carpet of drying leaves intermingles with dark, fertile soil and wild mushrooms littering the forest floor that crunch as I traipse through a narrow pathway. The woods are so dark that it is difficult to trace which direction I came from or where I am going.

"Where are you?" I ask the surrounding darkness, hands outstretched like a blind person searching for something familiar.

"I am right here, my love." His angelic voice floats around me confusing me further.

Bewildered and afraid, I glance to my left, then to my right, and still, all I see are trees. Trees to the north, trees to the south, and there are no distinguishing markings to use as a guide. The surrounding sounds are foreign too.

ACAPELLA

Naturally, I am used to the whooshing of the currents as they dissect the oceans. The soothing songs of humpback whales and the muffled hum of the creatures that make their homes in the many inlets, estuaries and gulfs. Sadly, I cannot identify with land mammals and their habitat. Here, I am out of my element.

I am lost in more ways than one.

"I don't see you," I whimper, on the brink of tears, lost and alone.

At last, he answers in a hushed tone.

"Follow my voice," he compels.

In that too familiar way, my chest tightens then retracts, then does it once more. Against my wishes, my palms start to perspire, and I wipe them angrily on my faded blue jeans.

What am I doing out here at this time of evening?

I should be snuggled in my bed all toasty warm, sipping on a cup of hot cocoa as I study the aurora borealis in all of its glory. Instead, I am cold, hungry and damp stumbling around in the dark.

"I am trying," I sigh anxiously.

"Try harder," the male voice instructs without compassion.

Suddenly, I feel tears rolling down my face.

"Do not cry," he admonishes firmly and without pity.

Darkness is everywhere and the void it creates suffocates me as if it was a living breathing entity, and I wish with my everything to flee, but the need to see him is stronger than my fear. Yes! I *need* to see him. I need to hold him in my arms, press my head to his chest and listen to his heart beating.

Without that, I will remain lost.

"Show yourself!" I demand with a sniffle, clinging to the last bit of my resolve.

Finally, he takes pity on me and reveals his location, confidently stepping out of the shadows. His thick, onyx tresses blowing in the breeze, wild emerald irises gleaming under the starry skies as his smile shines even brighter than the Moon Goddess' rays.

"Andrew!" I chirp, running toward his outstretched arms.

Without thought, I leap into those arms knowing they are the safest place to be. Instinctively, he tightens his embrace, pulling me against his muscular chest. This is where I belong.

"Have you missed me?" the teen questions, gazing down into my weepy eyes.

I wish I could lie to him and tell him that I do not need to be with him, but my soul would hurt too much to do so. Never have I been so desperate, so out of control than in this moment, with this man. Every waking hour is filled with thoughts of him… thoughts of *us*.

Taking a deep breath, I profess.

"More than you'll ever imagine."

He smiles, holding me securely.

"Kiss me," I implore as his head descends to mine.

Everything is moving in slow motion, even him. The wind rustling the leaves reduces to a gentle breeze. Animal noises become muted, and every moment becomes more intense… more vivid. Holding my breath, I wait for his next move.

"*Shh!*" he speaks softly, and I feel his minty breath against my cheek, warming my chilled skin. "Not yet."

"I love you!" I express as his lips brush tenderly against mine.

At my confession, he smiles which activates those adorable dimples that make me lose my train of thought.

"I love you more!" his voice trembles.

Finally, we kiss, and it lasts for an eternity, starting soft… then hard… then even softer than before. The intensity of it makes my toes curl within the confines of my sneakers, and I want the moment to last an eternity. Let the world fade into oblivion just as long as we remain, *here,* in this endless embrace.

As if he has done this hundreds of times, his arms encircle my waist while his mouth moves ravenously over mine. Almost predatory, his tongue sweeps across my lips, urging me to allow him greater access.

"You taste like strawberry-flavored lip gloss and sinful things," he moans into my mouth.

Dear Zeus! This can't be really happening.

Instinctively, my lips part in silent reply and he takes the invitation to slip past. Completely lost in the moment, our tongues seek each other out, dancing against one another in a passion-filled Samba, discovering responsive nerves and caressing them with velvety licks.

Unable to think clearly, I groan before pulling away, ending the most devastating kiss I have ever had the pleasure of experiencing. With my eyes still closed, I open my heart. I open my mind. I open my soul to him, to my dearest Andrew.

"Selena," he whispers while his hands caress my face then are replaced by one finger that traces my lips. "You are mine."

"I am yours," I repeat, tightening my embrace around his narrow waist.

Gently, he kisses my forehead allowing the faint scent of cypress mixed with heady notes of bergamot, oak moss, labdanum and a hint of patchouli sooth my frayed nerves. When combined, they create a warm, mossy-woody fragrance that contrasts with the bright citrus topper touched by a trace of bitterness.

Wait! This is not Andrew's regular cologne.

He must have decided to try something new, but it does not matter. It smells wonderful.

"Will you love me forever?" he implores on a whisper.

I nod, enjoying the sound of his heart beating against my cheek.

"Forever," I reply, wishing he would take my lips again.

Time stands still and all the other sounds fade away as we stand wrapped around each other.

"Please, open your eyes, my love," he pleads sweetly.

Leisurely, I open them, more in love than I could have ever imagined possible.

Shocked into silence, I stand staring up at the man before me, amethyst orbs glisten down, a mischievous smile playing upon full, sexy lips.

Ares!

"Lena!" Ando's voice wakes me, and I glance around the bedroom trying to get my bearings, perspiration still lingering on my brow.

"What?!" I bark, pushing him away.

"You're talking in your sleep again," he tells as he fixes his teddy bear, Alfredo, between us, making sure he is not squished. According to my little brother, Alfredo is a tad bit claustrophobic. How Ando knows that word is totally beyond my comprehension.

Annoyed by the interruption, I grunt.

"Why are you in my bed?" I huff.

With sleep-rimmed eyes, he glances at the window as a bright flash illuminates the bedroom. Obviously terrified, he snuggles closer and takes my hand in his as he closes his eyes. With my anger quickly dissipating, I throwing my arms around his small form, and hold him close.

"There's a bad storm and the lightning and thunder woke me," my brother confides.

"Why don't you sleep with Mom and Dad?" I inquire sleepily, wanting to resume the dream.

Thunder rumbles in response, making me feel guilty.

"Please?" he begs, and I agree without further argument.

"Fine, you can stay," I approve. "But no more talking; is that clear?"

"Yup!" he beams happily. "I won't talk anymore."

"One peep and you're going back to your room," I remind, adjusting my head on the pillow.

"Uh huh," he responds with a big yawn. "Goodnight, Lena."

I smile at him, closing my eyes once more.

"Goodnight, baby bro."

A few seconds later, I hear, "Lena?"

"Grrr!" I growl like a rabid dog. "What now?"

Ando props up on his elbow.

"Can you make the storm stop by using your Siren powers?" he questions innocently.

I shake my head.

"I've tried before, but the aunts said that we can only control what we have created," I imitate Aunt Ligeia like an expert.

There is a pause before Ando probes, "Who is Ares?"

Suddenly, my eyes fly open.

"H-huh?" I stammer, my cheeks reddening.

"Ares," he repeats. "Who is that?"

"I don't know," I fib. "Go back to sleep."

With heavy eyelids, he yawns again, and I yawn with him.

"Were you fighting?" he questions, determined to get an answer.

"No!" I snap. "Why do you ask?"

"Because you were making a lot of weird noises," he reveals. "Are you sure you weren't beating Ares up?"

"Just go to sleep," I respond, avoiding the question.

Obeying my demand, he fixes Alfredo under his neck and closes his sleepy eyes.

Within a few minutes, he dismissively releases my hand and turns away to find a more comfortable sleeping position.

"Sweet dreams, Lena," he whispers.

"Sweet dreams to you too."

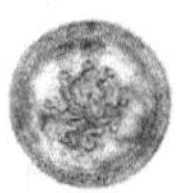

The next morning there is no evidence of the terrible storm. Once again, outside, the sky is a soft cornflower blue with wisps of fluffy white clouds. A multitude of seabirds are flying out to the harbor to catch their breakfast while we sit in the kitchen consuming ours.

"Pass the bread, please," I vocalize in Dad's direction.

"Would you like some more scrambled eggs?" he asks with a broad smile.

"Mmm... yes... thank you," I answer with a wide smile.

"You're in a great mood this morning," Mom confirms warmly as she butters a slice of toasted whole wheat bread.

Why shouldn't I be in a good mood?

Acapella

Andrew and I had a wonderful discussion and we got caught up on everything important. We laughed a lot and when we got off of our call, I felt lighter than air.

I smile back, but do not respond.

"How is Andrew?" My stepfather interrupts my train of thought.

"He's terrific," I swoon, trying to forget the dream I had of Ares.

"What is he doing this summer?" he continues.

"Right now, he's in Sitka, Alaska with his father," I add, reaching for another sausage link and a spoonful of diced tomatoes.

"That's cool!" Ando gushes, offering his empty plate to Dad for some more breakfast.

"He's helping with photography stuff," I add, knowing they will ask sooner or later.

"Alaska is a beautiful state," Dad grins as he glances over at Mom who takes his hand in hers.

I find it adorable that they still look at one another like they are seeing each other for the first time. That is the kind of love I want. Love that still feels new even after decades, or in my mother's case, most likely centuries. Sadly, David is mortal and their time together, from her perspective, will be brief, but according to the old adage: it is better to have loved and lost than never to have loved at all.

"Mom?" Ando pops their love bubble.

"Yes, my dear?"

"When will you take me to the Siren Grotto?" he wonders, exuding excitement.

"How about tonight?" she gleams.

"Yippee!" He almost jumps out of his seat. "Can Daddy come too?"

All three of us look at Dad who has his *'please take me'* expression.

"I would love... love... *love* to see the Siren Grotto!" He sounds just like Ando all bubbly and boyish.

"Honey," Mom exhales. "It's too dangerous for humans."

"I'll wear my scuba gear," Dad insists boldly. "I'll follow all of your directions. I promise."

Mom, however, is having none of this. Straightaway, her face darkens, and her aquamarine eyes transform to a menacing sapphire. This only happens when she is too angry to discuss things. I guess Sirens are not the best communicators. Truth be known, I have seen her almost rupture a blood vessel when confronted. Right now, I am glad I am not Dad.

"No way," she sulks, standing quickly, almost knocking her chair over.

"Marina—"

"I said *'no'*, David!" she admonishes. "I'm not taking any chances with your life."

In a whirlwind of hair and hand motions, my mother grabs a handful of dishes and disappears into the kitchen. Several minutes later, we hear the clanking and clamoring of items as they are loaded into the state-of-the-art dishwasher. With our enhanced Siren hearing, Ando and I can hear Mom mumbling curse words at the room in general. Stunned at her reaction, we glance at one another then look down at our plates, pretending not to have overheard her agitated rant.

Silence… incredibly loud silence expands throughout every crevice of the formal dining room. It is so silent that it is deafening.

"Selena," David waves toward the door. "Can I see you in the other room?"

I nod and follow him out of one room and into the adjoining formal living area.

"What's up?" I ask, knowing what is coming next.

"I need a huge favor," Dad begins.

Those words make me shudder. Whenever my stepfather wants to perform unsanctioned science experiments, ones that might get him in trouble with Mom, his face becomes very animated, and his eyebrows hitch up to his hairline. Everyone in the family knows this fact and tries hard to avoid him when he gets this look.

"Umm," I look up then quickly away. "Are you going to ask me to get a sample of the water in the Siren Grotto?"

Intently, he studies my face.

I chuckle before adding, "You would also like samples from the freshwater on Paradiso."

He blushes and chuckles at the same time knowing that he has been caught.

"I need a few more samples too."

"Dad?" I ask, shaking my head.

"Yes, sweetheart?" The suave Latin scientist smiles broader than usual.

"Am I going to get in trouble with Mom?"

He sighs and before answering, he searches over my shoulder to see if my mother is still in the kitchen.

"Be discreet," he advises with a childlike expression that reminds me of Ando.

All too familiar with my stepdad's tenacity, I give in to his wishes.

"I cannot believe you," I pretend to be disappointed so to make him feel guilty, but he does not! "You want me to be your own personal spy."

"Am I that transparent?" he frowns playfully, causing me to giggle.

Both Ando—who is now standing in the doorway nibbling on a crust of bread—and I nod.

"You're a Marine Biologist nerd who is married to a Siren and has two fish-children," I tease with a wink. "You are as transparent as glass."

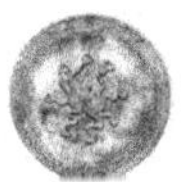

Shortly after finishing breakfast, Ando, Mom and I set off on our trek to our familial homeland.

"Hurry, Ando!" I click then sharply clack. "Your arms are too stumpy."

"Well… well… your butt is too big!" he clacks back caustically.

"Mom! Talk to your son!" I *click-clack-click* loudly. "He's bothering me!"

Mom rolls her lovely eyes.

"Ando."

"Yes, Mommy?" he responds too sweetly.

Recently, my brother only uses the word 'mommy' when he is in trouble. He is really good at appearing innocent when he is usually the perpetrator of most of our sibling strife. Luckily for me, Mom and Dad have figured out his dastardly ways.

"Please, I beg you," the woman who gave birth to us puffs, shaking her head. "Can you leave your sister alone?"

"Bu-but she started it!"

"I don't care who started it," our mom sighs as if she is exhausted.

"That's not fair," he pouts.

"Life isn't fair, my dear," Mom reminds with a frown. "All we can do is make the best of it."

With that fact acknowledged, our mother resumes her swim in silence.

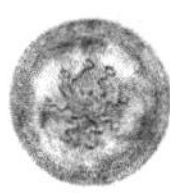

Thirty minutes later, Mom informs, "The blackness should be here, right about… *now.*"

Just ahead, in the water that same inky substance ebbs and flows, meandering around the multicolored coral and the gently swaying seaweed. It looks like an alien lifeform slithering closer and closer.

"Is this what I see from the veranda at the villa?" Ando gasps as he reaches out to touch it.

Mom and I nod.

"It smells like octopus' ink," he coughs when he inhales some of it.

He is correct about the awful stench that the barrier exudes. It almost makes you wish that you did not have a nose. Also, the substance has a tar-like texture that sticks to you as if you are a duck trapped in an oil slick. If you stay long enough in the strange *goo,* it could do serious damage to your respiratory system. Of that I am certain of.

"Hold hands," Mom commands. "We can't stay in this *'stuff'* too long or it will paralyze us."

I didn't know that.

"Let's go," I decide, suddenly feeling vulnerable.

Mom glances around.

"Keep watch for the—"

'Sharks!' Ando shouts inside our heads almost deafening us.

"Crap!" Mom yells in Siren.

"But we can control sharks!" I remind, wanting to stand my ground.

"Not these sharks," she educates with a frown. "They are special sharks that were created to be sentinels and protectors of the Siren Grotto."

"Cool!" Ando shouts, causing Mom and I to stare at him.

He blushes.

"Well, it is," he mumbles below his breath.

"The only ones who can control them are Melpomene the Muse and the aunts… *The Originals.*"

"Oh!" Ando kicks his legs faster. "That's not cool!"

"Ando!" Mom shouts. "Get on your sister's back!"

Immediately, I help him into place, waiting as he locks his arms and legs around me like a baby koala.

"Ready?" I ask, my breath quickening to match my accelerating heartrate.

Frantically, he nods.

Acapella

Needing no further prodding, I blast off toward the area where the entrance to the Siren Grotto is. Behind us, Mom kicks and punches our pursuers, and in my brain, I hope her kung-fu is strong because the last time she got bitten, and I had to tear off one of my scales to save her. Needless to say, it was not fun.

'I heard that, young lady,' Mom admonishes telepathically.

It is at that moment that my vision briefly clears and locks onto our salvation.

"I see it! Dive down!" I clack pointing to a small cleft in the rocky seabed. *"Now!"*

"Where?" Ando looks around.

"Don't you see it?" I chastise in Siren. "It is to our left… over there… near the red coral!"

Keeping my lightning-fast pace, I glance down and see more darkness, darkness that is trying to hide the entrance.

"I can't see anything, Lena!"

"Try adjusting your eyes!" I request, just like Mom did to me on my maiden voyage to the Siren Grotto.

He tries, but nothing happens.

"I still see nothing!" Ando huffs.

"Don't worry," I soothe. "I couldn't do it the first time either."

"Less talking!" Mom clickity-clacks loudly from the rear. "More swimming!"

"We're here!" I shout as I unwind my brother from my body and shove him inside the cleft as I follow closely behind.

"It's too dark," he whimpers, treading water, his breathing loud in the space.

"Not for long," I pacify, knowing about the secret light source. "Be patient."

In the surrounding darkness, I feel Mom touch my shoulder and I turn.

"Are you alright?" I ask, hoping she is not hurt.

Unlike the last time, she laughs.

"Never better!" she clarifies with a broad grin. "Sometimes a good fight is all you need to let you know you're still alive."

I giggle.

'Mom, it's dark in here,' Ando notifies in our heads. *'Can we get some light, please?'*

'Command your eyes to see beyond this plane of existence,' our mother petitions with a toothy smile.

Without hesitation, my brother does as he is told, and to both of our amazement, he succeeds on the first try.

"I see it!" He beams, glancing around.

Figures.

Mom laughs as I frown.

"Great job, son!"

Show off!

"Breathe in the water, Ando," Mom implores wanting him to become accustomed to his new surroundings. "It's better to let your body slowly acclimate to the sediments."

My brother, of course, follows her instructions, breathing slowly as he allows the particles in the grotto to enter his bloodstream. Only once did he begin to cough and complain about a strong burning sensation in his chest. However, his eyes did turn a sickly yellow and stayed that way for several minutes.

After an hour or so, Mom finally questions, "How do you feel?"

My brother takes several deep breaths then smiles.

"I feel great!" he informs with a grin. "Strong."

Mom hugs him, relieved that her son is adjusting well.

"Let's swim down," she continues in Siren-speak, motioning toward the bottom of the cave floor. "Selena will lead the way."

More than willing, I do. I lead our party of three into the bowels of the grotto, our hands clasped tightly together. Calmness begins to filter through my veins, and just as Mom had done on our first visit, I hunt the nearest wall. After a few minutes, my fingers touch a lever protruding from the rocky surface. Shrugging, I pull the mechanism into what I hope is the 'on' position, and overcome with excitement, I let out a wail so loud, so blood-curdling that both Mom and Ando release my hands to cover their ears.

Like before, the sea around us begins to glow and heat, and the Siren Grotto walls illuminate as if thousands of tiny multicolored lightbulbs have suddenly been switched on. We all smile when we see the sea life drawn on the rocky walls, along with the other unique objects and shiny metals that guide our path further down into the mysterious cavity.

Ando and I shut our eyes and I 'feel' my way instinctively through the Siren Grotto.

"Too bright!" he complains like I had. "I can still see the light through my eyelids."

"Keep them closed," I implore, giving his hand a gentle squeeze. "I'll tell you when to open them."

When I think my brother and I might truly lose our sight, I hear our mother's voice inside of my head encouraging us.

'You can look now.'

On pins and needles, we do, and the sight that greets us will always be overwhelming. It will always take my breath away. Of this, I am certain.

"This is the Siren Grotto?" Ando's tone is awe-filled as he takes everything in.

Mom nods.

"It is," I whisper, suddenly on the verge of happy tears.

In my peripheral vision, I see Mom's eyes fill with tears of joy too.

She mumbles, "It is good to bring my family home."

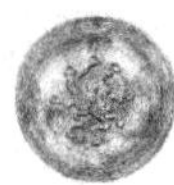

The slow journey through the grotto, past the cave paintings and lights into the lagoon is always spectacular. Strange sea life and even stranger vegetation renders you speechless, and even without our Siren vision, the colors underwater glow with a vibrant neon hue that is almost indescribable. Truthfully, there is nothing more incredible than right here, right now.

"I've seen this place before," my brother informs as his hands glide along the limestone wall. "My dreams bring me here."

I turn toward him to reply, but this time I can only stare. His powers are truly astonishing and sometimes scary. He may not have webbing or scales, but having the power to see the future is pretty darn incredible.

"The Siren Grotto is only the entrance that leads to Paradiso!" my brother practically yelps as he points toward the island. "It really exists!"

Filled with unfettered jubilation, he takes off at full speed with a huge grin plastered to his youthful face.

"Wait up!" I call after him.

Crazy kid brother!

"Hurry, Lena! Hurry, Mom!" he squeals excitedly. "We're almost there!"

Mom and I glance at one another and smirk.

"I can't wait to climb the fruit trees and drink coconut water right out of the husk!" his words escape in a rushed jumble of Siren.

Showoff!

"There are animals on Paradiso too," he educates. "Did you know that, Lena?"

"I do," I nod and smile at his enthusiasm.

"There are wild turkeys, pheasants, boars, goats… I think there's even—"

"Ando, take a deep breath before you faint." I interrupt his rambling.

"I can't wait to explore," he grins, ignoring my comment.

Mom speaks, at last.

"We'll look around first then we'll make some dinner."

"I can't wait!" he claps as his speed increases.

Hastening my pace, I follow him toward the land mass. Several minutes later, all three of us break through the surface. This time, I ignore the pressure in my ears.

Immediately, I feel at peace. Like nothing can harm us here. It is ours.

It really is home.

CHAPTER SIX

We decide on a quick dinner of striped sea bass accompanied by island-grown fruits and vegetables, simple, but delicious.

"This fish is *ah-ma-zing!*" my brother declares, licking his lips.

"I totally approve." Mom breaks off a piece of roasted breadfruit that is keeping warm on the glowing coals of the firepit we constructed.

"How long have we been here?" I ask, glancing at the dive watch on my wrist.

Our mother stretches lazily with her arms above her head. Gracefully, she moves. I am always jealous.

"Six or seven hours, I think," Mom states drowsily.

"I'm tired," Ando announces with a yawn and a stretch of his own.

Unlike my family members, I am wide awake.

"Can I explore?" I question Mom.

"Of course," she smiles. "Paradiso was created specifically for us. Have fun."

"Are we camping here tonight?" Ando's aquamarine eyes sparkle.

"Yes, we are." Mom hugs him tightly making him giggle.

"I hope Dad won't be upset," I add, wondering if David is lonely back at the villa.

Before we left for Paradiso, Mom made him a light pasta dish for dinner along with a fruit salad for a healthy dessert. My stepfather has been complaining that he is developing a potbelly due to all of the rich Italian foods he has been sampling. I have not noticed a 'belly,' but come to mention it, he has been wearing baggier clothing lately, mostly sweatpants and t-shirts.

"He won't," Mom continues. "We discussed it earlier today."

"Good to know," I smile.

"Go on, Lena," my brother urges. "I'll go exploring tomorrow."

I nod in agreement.

"Mercury with you," Mom adds, getting more comfortable.

"Why?" I gulp. "I thought you said we are safe here."

"We are," she reassures. "But it never hurts to be prepared… just in case. These are strange days after all."

Then they both yawn.

"Rest well, you two," I kiss them on their foreheads like parents often do. "See you in a little bit."

"Have fun," Mom says, closing her eyes. "And be careful."

My brows automatically arch with confusion.

As my mother has said many times, Paradiso was created just for our family. Nothing here will harm us. It is the one place on the Earth that we can be who we truly are, yet she still remains in her traditional parental role and insists on treating me like a human teenager. Even though this makes no sense to me, I obey her instructions.

Half-heartedly, I gather up the bow and one arrow, just in case—God forbid—I need to protect myself or my family.

"I will."

Acapella

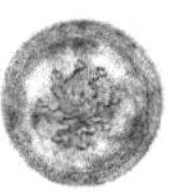

Why did I ever agree to my stepfather's request?

"Rock samples, soil samples, water samples, plant samples… all types of samples," I mumble as I fill the plastic *Ziploc* bags with all of the materials that Dad has entreated me to gather.

What am I? His personal Siren-shopper?

After a half-an-hour more of gathering, I begin to feel tired. Looking around, I spy a small, flat clearing. Needing to lie down, I quickly arrange clumps of soft grass and scattered leaves into a neat pile. Carefully, I position myself as I would on a regular bed, all the while being careful of protruding sticks and 'whatnots' that may be in my sleeping area. Lighthearted, I stare up at the stalagmite ceiling filled with phosphorescent materials that resemble stars. Overhead, I listen to the calls of the mockingbirds and watch the movements of the small creatures in the canopy of the various trees. Thankfully, tonight the air is cool with a hint of salt and jasmine.

Without much effort, my eyes begin to close, and the welcomed arrival of sleep slowly drifts over me.

"Selena!"

Startled by the unfamiliar voice, I jump up from my horizontal position on top of the makeshift bed.

What in the name of Zeus?!

"Selena!" it calls again.

Unnerved, panic-stricken, and frightened to death, I grab the bow and the one lone arrow I brought; ready to stand my ground.

"Who are you and what are you doing here?" I probe the night.

Silence.

"Answer me!" I bellow, wondering if Mom and Ando can hear me.

"I have been waiting for you," says the enticing hypnotic female voice floating on the wind.

"Huh?" I gasp, heart in my throat. "Why?"

"Follow me," it compels.

Why do these things keep asking me to follow... and why... why the hell do I listen?

Learning from past mistakes, this time, I stay perfectly still.

"Who are you?" I demand again in a more menacing tone.

"Do not be afraid, young one," the pleasant voice lures me like a worm to a fisherman's hook. "I am Gaia."

"Gaia?" I scoff. "The Earth Goddess?"

It laughs and the sound is glorious.

"Actually, I am the Goddess of Nature which includes naturally, no pun intended, the Earth and everything on it."

"Yeah, right," I mock, backing away from the direction that the voice is coming from.

"I will not harm you," the feminine voice states calmly.

"Why should I believe you?" I blurt, glancing to my right and then to my left.

She pauses.

"Because it is through me that you get your strength, your power."

My brows hitch.

"My power comes from the sea," I clarify in my most steady tone. "I am *Siren*."

There is another pause.

"May I show myself?" she asks, throwing me off balance.

"Umm," I ponder. "I… guess… so?"

The soft breeze strengthens.

"Do not be afraid," she advises pleasantly.

"O… kay…" I mumble and my palms start sweating.

As I wait, the earth starts to tremble. Not hard like an earthquake, more like when a massive vehicle rolls over the ground. Above my head there is a loud crack of electricity accompanied by several blue sparks then with a life of its own; the smell of ozone becomes thick in the air. Suddenly, the soil below my feet is now stacking on top of itself creating a mound that is as tall as my dad. Grass steadily begins to grow out of the heap then transforms into a long, olive gown. The foliage at the top of the mass continues to sprout until it resembles beautiful dark-brown tresses adorned with a wreath of broom flowers with specks of jasmine blossoms.

Before my eyes, the entire thing becomes a *woman*! The most stunning mocha-complexioned woman I have ever seen. Slowly, she opens her eyes, and amber irises blink at me.

Oh! My! Goddess!

"Gaia?" I swallow the lump in my throat.

"The one and only," she grins with perfect teeth.

"I don't understand why you're revealing yourself to... *me*," I wave at my trembling body and face stained terrified-red.

"You are of *The Three*," she flutters, her voice similar to hummingbird wings.

I study her demeanor, and then meekly ask, "Of '*The Three...*' you mean The Sirens?"

She nods, smiling brightly.

"Unlike your mother and brother, you are blood-bound."

What?

"Blood-bound," I repeat, not liking the sound or the implications of that description.

Gaia holds her right arm out, and within seconds it is covered with native birds that not long before were high in the treetops. She speaks to them in a language similar to Siren, and the birds seem to be speaking back.

Nervously, I begin to shift my weight from my left leg to my right.

"Shall we sit?" she asks politely.

"We can sit on the ground, but it probably won't be too comfortable," I reply glancing around.

At that, she smiles and with a nod of her head the ground starts to shake again, but this time it transforms into two throne-like chairs with cushions made of soft grass.

"Sit," the goddess orders sweetly, and I do.

"Wow!" I gasp, running my fingers over the cushion.

"Do you require sustenance?" Gaia questions in her naturally regal manner.

Eager to see more, I nod, holding my breath in anticipation.

With a snap of her fingers, a tree trunk rises from the ground and as I gawk, out of the stump grows a large bunch of red grapes, several orange kumquats, and a golden pineapple.

"Help yourself," the goddess encourages, so I do.

Without hesitation, I take a few grapes and one of the brightly colored kumquats. Tentatively I take a bite of a grape, and almost moan my delight. So juicy. So sweet. So, satisfying.

"How does it taste?" Gaia questions with genuine interest.

I giggle.

"It is the most delicious fruit I've ever tasted," I answer honestly.

"Water?" she graciously offers and instantly a brook of clear spring water bursts from the Earth like a fountain. "Have a drink."

Cupping my hands to create a bowl-like shape, I take a sip… then another… and finally a long gulp.

"Oh my gosh!" I exclaim. "This tastes just like the spring I drank from the first time I visited Paradiso!"

She smiles that mysterious smile and all I can do is smile back.

"We do not have much time, Selena," she admits, from out of the blue.

"Do you have to be somewhere else?" I wonder aloud.

Acapella

"I must return to the Earth," she frowns slightly, but even that expression makes her look even more beautiful.

"Why?" I probe not wanting our visit to end.

"I am a part of the Earth," she explains. "When I am away for too long, it will start to whither and eventually—"

"—it will die," I finish her sentence. "Then why did you leave the earth now? Just to meet me?"

She nods.

"Why?" I query again. "What's so important about me?"

"You are of *The Three*, yet so much more."

"*More?*" I gulp my embarrassment. "Why does everyone say that?"

"As *you* grow, your powers will grow," she frowns again.

"Is that a bad thing… my powers growing, I mean?"

She exhales.

"When you tap into sea," the goddess continues. "How do you feel?"

"Unstoppable," I glow.

"Every time you channel the sea you tap into my strength," she educates without a smile. "The strength that holds the world together; *literally*."

Unable to answer, I stare at her filled with confusion.

"Power is addictive," she warns. "It can lead you down a path that you do not wish to travel."

Immediately, I feel a migraine growing between my temples.

"I don't understand, your majesty, umm… your highness?" I respond, pressing my fingers where the pain emanates.

This time she smiles.

"Just Gaia," she states humbly with a twinkle in her eyes.

Speechless, I continue staring at the intimidating goddess before me.

"Sometimes things that appear to be good are not—" she pauses then continues, "—Sometimes things that appear to be bad are not."

"I still don't know what you're trying to imply," I whine.

"Remember who you are, Selena," the ancient being reminds with a reassuring hand against mine. "You are a descendent of *The Three*. Your greatest strength is love."

Huh?

"What do you mean by that?"

"Your great-grandmother once told you that your *Aria* is your true strength. Use it and it will never lead you astray."

The ground trembles again and I know she is returning to her rightful place.

"I must go," Gaia informs sadly.

"Wait!" I cry out. "Don't go! I have so many questions. Please, don't go."

"Be well, young Siren," Gaia gleans with a sparkle in her eyes as the objects she created along with herself retreat back into the ground. "You are of *The Three*… never forget."

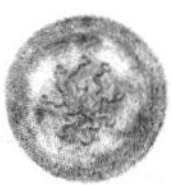

The next morning, I wake beside Mom and Ando, who are both sleeping soundly. Unfortunately, I have been awake since last night when I was visited by Gaia, only getting to slumber a few minutes at a time. The goddess's words continuously haunt me no matter how much I try to forget them.

Beside me, Mom stretches which causes my brother to stir, but not wake. He resembles a cherub, sweet and endearing. I just want to pinch his cheeks, but I decide against it.

"Good morning," she slowly opens her eyes and smiles lovingly. "You're up early."

"I couldn't sleep," I admit, staring at the calm lagoon a few yards away.

"Is something wrong?" my mother asks, immediately fully awake.

"Gaia," I murmur.

"Mother Nature, *that* Gaia?" she blinks in bewilderment.

I nod, looking up when I hear the first roll of thunder.

Cocking her head to one side, she questions, "What about, Gaia?"

Unwilling to stall anymore, I answer.

"She paid me a visit last night."

Several bolts of lightning stain the sky and I hope that they do not 'accidentally' strike one of us, especially, not Ando who is still asleep. That would be a horrible way to wake-up: tingly like a lightning rod with your hair sticking straight up, even though it would be really funny.

Mom scoffs, hearing my thoughts, but says nothing regarding the inappropriateness of them.

"No way," she rolls her eyes, ignoring the sudden change in weather.

Still in shock, I can only stare at her, my expression sincere, eyes welling with tears.

"*Holy crap!*" she whistles coming to a sitting position. "What did she want?"

"To talk," I profess then clear my throat.

The wind strengthens causing our curls to twirl above our heads as if they are caught in an invisible cyclone.

"To talk?" My mother's eyes widen. "To *you*?"

"Yup!" I reply as I grab a handful of sand, enjoying the feel of it between my fingers, but release them to see the particles get sucked into the whirlwind.

Mom's body straightens.

"That can't be good," she mutters to herself as the first raindrop lands on her face.

Slightly offended, I pout.

"Why?" I add. "What are you holding back?"

"Well," my mother adds. "Gaia traditionally appears to warn of impending doom."

Shocked, I blink, unable to form a thought. My brain torn between the implications of what Mom is saying versus being one of the two people being rained on. The rest of Paradiso is rain-free, including my still slumbering brother.

"She counsels those who she believes will bring about..." Mom's words trail off, disturbing me even more.

"Bring about *what*?" I feel goosebumps form even though it is warm.

Mom places both hands on my shoulders, her features burdened.

"Tell me," I order gruffly, then huff, "Mom?"

"What is it?" she huffs back and places her hands on her hips.

"The rain," I smirk with a slow blink that I know she dislikes.

Her hands immediately leave her hips and this time fold across her chest.

"What about the rain?" she answers my question with her own.

"Could you stop it, please," I request politely, suppressing a snort.

Quickly, she glances around with a cheesy grin.

"Oops!" she blushes with embarrassment. "Sorry."

And just as quickly as it started, it ends.

"Could you do something about us looking like wet rats?" I grumble, allowing myself to grin.

Mom blushes again.

"Wind," she orders, and the wind suddenly increases. "From the four corners."

This is new.

Unexpectedly, from all directions, gusts of different kinds of winds reveal themselves. There is a frigid stream coming from the north, a smothering smoldering stream from the south, a more temperate stream from the east and a stinging one from the west.

Holy crap!

"Close your eyes," Mom commands and I listen.

With my eyelids tightly shut, I start to feel the various winds intermingling, twirling, rushing faster and faster, whipping against my body, almost painfully they slash at my exposed human skin.

'Mom!' I shout in her mind. *'It stings!'*

'Call your scales!' she reminds, and I immediately do.

After a minute, I hear my mother's voice again.

"Scatter," she whispers, and I hear her over the din then it goes deafeningly silent with no breeze at all.

I want to open my eyes but hesitate.

"It is safe. Open your eyes," she states, so I do.

I open them to see that both she and I are completely dry, our long curly hair resembles tattered bird nests piled on top of our heads.

"How did you do that?" I gasp, my mind completely blown away.

Mom blushes.

"Practice," she replies with a mischievous wink. "Let's wake your brother. He hasn't seen the island yet."

"Mom?" I pause her motions with a gentle touch to her left arm. "What aren't you telling me?"

"Aren't you hungry?" she questions, changing the subject as she attempts to smoothen her hair and brush the particles of sand and dirt off of her.

"Surprisingly, no," I inform bluntly, glaring at her.

Suddenly, her right foot begins to tap.

Oh no!

Then she starts biting her lower lip.

Not again!

Next, she looks around and I know that the pacing will soon commence.

"Tell me," I order harshly. "Please."

Then she says the words that no one wants to hear… *Ever*.

"Gaia only reveals herself to those who she believes will end the world."

"*Oh!*"

CHAPTER SEVEN

With my mother's world-stopping admission, I pace the length of the floor, almost tripping twice over my trembling legs and knocking knees.

"I think we should leave," I tell my parents as we all gather in the living room watching an English-subtitled family movie attempting to forget Gaia's foreboding appearance.

"What?" Dad looks up from the bowl of popcorn we are all sharing.

"We need to leave Capri," I boldly repeat. "As soon as possible… if not sooner!"

"Selena," Mom intercedes on Dad's behalf. "I'm sure you're overreacting."

Stunned, I glare at her with wide eyes.

"The Goddess of the Earth made it a point to introduce herself to me. *Me!* And you tell me, '*Oh! By the way, you will destroy the world.*'"

Everyone stares as I continue pacing, biting my bottom lip, while twirling a curl until it is almost completely straight.

"Your mother said *'might'* destroy the world," Dad tries to comfort, but does a horrible job of it. "Not *'will'* destroy it. There's a big difference."

Rolling my eyes, I respond.

"Destroyed is *destroyed*," I add with all finality.

"Are you sure it was Gaia?" Ando speaks up, and then shoves a handful of the buttery kernels into his mouth. "Maybe it was another evil creature tricking you."

"No other deity can access Paradiso without an invitation except Gaia," our mother interjects. "*Oh!* And of course, Melpomene the muse… and the sisters… and us."

"Are you certain?" I probe.

She nods.

"Gaia created Paradiso by request of Zeus, and before you ask, no, not even the ruler of the gods can gain entrance to the island without Siren consent."

"What should we do?" I groan, holding my stomach.

"The full moon is in two days," Mom reminds. "We will perform the actual ceremony for *The Calling* and then you will be in more control of your faculties."

"Ceremony?" Dad probes with confusion. "What ceremony? There's a ceremony?"

"Yes," his wife answers.

"I thought Selena only had to be exposed to the waters of the grotto in order to complete *The Calling*?" he blinks.

"*The Joining* ceremony is always done on the night of the full moon," Mom reveals.

"What does '*The Joining*' ceremony entail?" David interrogates wearily.

"It's exactly as it implies," my mother sighs. "It is when all of the Sirens join their powers for the first time."

"Why?" Ando asks.

"In order to seal our bond," she explains.

"*We*—Ligeia, Leukosia, and I—will channel the power of the moon as well as the sea through Paradiso in order to balance and complete *The Siren Calling*."

"Huh?" Dad glares at her as if she is speaking in a foreign language.

"*The Siren Calling* is our true nature. It is the predisposition that allows us to tap into our underlying humanity and compels us not to follow our natural instincts as predators. Basically, it suppresses our need to kill."

"I see," he chokes on Mom's explanation.

"Completing *The Joining*, combined with exposure to the high concentration of black volcanic ash on Paradiso, will fuse itself to the subject, in this case, Selena, and become a part of her."

"In other words," I interject. "The glass will become a part of my body? Even more than it already is?"

"Yes, the obsidian will physically fuse to your bones." My mother tries to sound positive but is failing miserably. "Its particles will join your bloodstream and will become a more significant part of your DNA."

"It sounds painful," Ando interjects with a grimace. "Will it hurt?"

Mom stays silent which tells me that it will hurt. Probably hurt a lot.

"But afterward, you will be able to control these urges," she reassures. "You will also be able to pull energy from the moon, as well as the sea, and even from other Sirens."

"What did you say?" Dad questions blankly. "I thought she could already tap into other Sirens. Isn't that why you are able to communicate telepathically?"

His spouse thinks for a moment.

"Yes, it is like that, but *more*," she continues. "When necessary, Selena will be able to funnel power *directly* from the aunts as well as her brother and me."

Her words are meant to comfort, but it sounds horrific to me.

Horrified, my stomach starts churning.

"I'm going to be sick," I announce, slapping my hand over my mouth as I race to the bathroom.

My life keeps getting worse and worse.

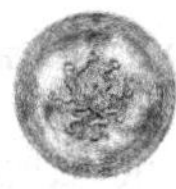

Knock… knock… knock!

"Lena?" My brother calls from outside my bedroom door startling me.

"What?!" I bark, swiping away the tears that refuse to stop.

There is a pause.

"May I come in?" he begs.

I think for a second before answering.

"If I say no, will it stop you?"

There is another longer pause.

"Probably not," he giggles, making me smile.

"Come in." I shake my head.

Slowly, he opens the door and peeks inside. He looks so cute with his gray and blue stripped pajamas with the smiling penguin wearing a scarf and galoshes on the pocket. This time Alfredo is not with him. I assume the intelligent teddy bear wanted to stay in bed.

Not saying anything, my brother makes his way towards me and plops himself on the bed, all the while watching me with bewilderment.

"Lena?" he asks at last.

Nervously, I wait to hear the bad news.

"Did you have another bad dream, Ando?"

He waits.

"Well…" he begins then stops.

"Just tell me," I huff, trying to brace myself for what is about to be said.

"Melpomene, I mean Melody, wants to see you," he informs with a strange expression.

"How do you know this?" I reply, sitting up, wishing that this drama would just end.

"I can talk to her through dreams," Ando discloses guiltily, avoiding eye contact.

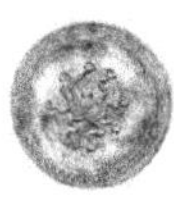

My stomach is a ball of undulating, squirming, knot of serpents writhing around inside of me. Try as I may, my anxiety refuses to subside, and it is all I can do not to throw up again. Even Ando's reassuring words cannot help calm my soul.

"I can't believe I let you talk me into this," I grumble, glancing around the darkening road. "Why couldn't this wait until morning when *things* can't blend into the shadows?"

My brother shrugs.

"Melody wants to see us tonight," he huffs on a loud exasperated exhale.

My pace slows.

"I thought she was dead," I blurt without thought wishing I had not dared say it out loud.

"Like I said," he reminds. "Melody talks to me in my dreams. I knew she was alright. I told Mom and Dad when it happened."

I smile.

"I see," I respond below my breath. "Why didn't you tell me?"

Ando shrugs.

"I didn't tell you because you were busy freaking out about what Gaia said," he admits, protectively.

"Did you tell Mom and Dad that we're going to see her?" Ando grills for the third time as we continue walking out of the well-lit *Belvedere di Tragara*.

"Yes, I did," I respond honestly as we make a left at the 'mom-and-pop' grocery store at the corner of our street. At a steady pace, we head toward the rugged hills above the town, my palms unusually dry as we follow the now unlighted path.

Why are we doing this?

It is gloomy out here away from the glow of the settlement. Thankfully, tonight the sky is clear and the almost full moon shines softly; its bright rays diffusing the shadows. The hike would actually be enjoyable if I had not been told earlier that I could possibly destroy the planet.

Twenty minutes later, we stop in the middle of the dusty, unpaved, tree-lined path high above the town of Capri, wondering if we have come to the right place. At night, everything looks the same.

"Usually, the narrow path that leads to the clearing in the woods is here, right?" I consult my brother.

"I think so," he manages, but does not convince me or himself.

Where is the path?

"I think it's in here," I claim, taking my sibling's hand and cautiously venturing into the heavily wooded area where the bushes are taller than both of us.

Wait! Is this the right spot?

"*Melody!*" I shout not caring about anyone passing by. "Melody, we're here to talk!"

I think for a second or two.

"The mosquitos are biting tonight!"

Still there is nothing.

"I'm serious!" I yell again, smacking a mosquito that bites my neck like a vampire. "Great-grandmother!"

"My gracious!" a silky voice startles me. "So loud."

I smile, relieved to hear her, even if I am being scolded.

"Where are you?" I query, glancing around the woods.

As we watch, the clearing in the woods appears as the cottage emerges out of the mist in a fog of shimmering sparkles and static electrical currents. In the darkness, all I see of the Muse is her short, plump silhouette draped by a hooded jacket.

Thank heavens!

Without thought, we hug her, tight!

Right away, I notice the lovely scent of wildflowers and baked goods wafts around her while that slight tingling of inspiration builds inside of me until it is almost a painful sensation. However, at this most perfect moment, elated to hold the ancient Muse in my arms, I choose to ignore it.

Great-grandmother Melody!

Finally, we let her go, still enwrapped in her spell, and cheerfully, she grins at us.

"Come inside, my dears," she invites with a warm caring smile. "I have missed you."

Then graciously she steps aside, beckoning toward the small *Hobbit*-sized door leading into the even smaller home. The structure itself is quite appealing. It reminds me of a house you would read about in a fairytale.

"Shall we stand out here for the entire night?" Melody questions mockingly as she removes the cloak revealing her stunning face.

Shaking my head, I pout.

"By the way," she begins. "Do your parents know that you two are here? I do not want them upset—"

"They know," I interject.

Ando nods in agreement.

Not quite convinced, Melody cocks her head to the side.

"I am surprised they decided to let you come here by yourselves," she worries.

"We can be very convincing," I admit, confidently with a blush.

Melody laughs, and as usual, the sound is light and airy like the clinking of wind chimes on a gentle breeze. It is the most pleasant sound I have ever heard.

"I am sure you are," she agrees with a smile, motioning us indoors.

Thrilled to have found her, we enter, my defenses now at rest. Melody's presence always puts me at ease. I know that she loves us… without a doubt… I just know.

Inside, the adorable cottage smells of the comforting aroma of baking cookies and warm chocolate. As before, our great-grandmother is a delightful and gracious host, feeding us as only she can as she flutters to and fro refilling our dainty floral teacups.

"How have you been?" I ask, trying to keep from smiling, but failing miserably.

"I am well," Melody replies with a mixed accent that I cannot place.

"I thought we lost you," I admit shyly, wanting to hug her once more, so I stand and do just that.

Our family Muse grins and blushes.

"I am a tough old bird," she snickers. "Plus, I am stronger than I look."

She winks playfully making us giggle.

"You, Miss Selena, have been extremely busy."

Feeling guilty, I remain silent until I cannot help blurting.

"I don't want to talk about it," I blush, knowing that she is referring to me defeating Amphitrite as well as almost killing the young man on the yacht and temporarily killing the museum tour guide in Anacapri. Thank goodness Mom was able to revive the tour guide and *The Three* saved the guy—*Ares*— before he drowned.

Patiently, she listens as I explain all that had happened since the night Amphitrite attacked during our family reunion. In true Melody-form, she grins and nods with no judgment and complete understanding.

How she does this?

I have no idea, but I am glad she does.

"You will find your way, Selena," she comforts. "I know you will."

My insecurities suddenly disappear. Our great-grandmother is so different to the rest of the women in our family. We have clearly got height where she is a much smaller entity. She does not even have aquamarine eyes—

"Actually," Melody speaks up. "My eyes change color depending on my mood."

"Huh?!" I gasp, shocked and embarrassed. "You can read my mind?"

Melody beams.

"It is one of my gifts as a muse, remember?" she discloses. "Actually, I am more *empathic* than *telepathic*. However, with family I can sometimes hone-in to thoughts."

Ando giggles.

"I wish my eyes could change colors too," he announces loudly as he crosses his eyes in an attempt to modify them.

"It is an overrated skill, believe me," the Muse pacifies, making him stop from fear that his eyes will stick that way. "No need to be jealous."

Melody sighs and even that sound is heavenly.

"You are perfect the way you are," she continues with a broad grin. "Never forget that."

I smile at her loving comment.

"I think that it's amazing that your eyes are like a mood ring," I compliment, feeling more and more at peace here. I am not sure if the feeling comes from Melody or from me. Either way, it makes no difference.

"Thank you, Selena," Melody speaks with that alluring tone.

After consuming several treats, Ando immediately heads toward the backyard in hopes of seeing Belen while I stay inside with our hostess.

"We can't stay long," I mention, remembering Mom's instructions not to dilly-dally.

Melody pauses as I scan our surroundings. Just like before, I suddenly hear the faintest tune in my head as I stand in close proximity to her.

"I understand," she says longingly, and I am certain she is thinking of her Siren daughters and my parents. "Would you like some homemade borscht?"

I chuckle at her offer. She always offers us food. I think it is one of her ways to put people at ease. I enjoy it because she is an amazing cook.

"Great grandma, there's a lot you need to learn about teens these days," I tease respectfully. "Beet soup is *not* as tempting as pizza."

"You and Ando will have to teach me more about teens of today," Melody challenges in a playful voice that makes me relax even more.

Happily, I nod.

"Did I hear you right?" she continues. "What would you like to know?"

"I have a few questions," I confess.

"Ask me anything," she encourages.

"Tell me more about where the Sirens were born," I insist, needing clarification even though my heart already knows the truth.

Her eyes close as she reminisces.

"Ahh… yes!" she sighs. "I have not been back to Paradiso for eons."

I smile. Of course, she knows the island's name. After all, she raised her daughters there.

"It is the most incredible place in the entire world," she educates with a nostalgic gaze. "My children and I placed each jewel in the walls of the Siren Grotto with our own hands. It took centuries to get enough to light the way to the island."

I smile at her vivid memory.

"Lena?" I hear my brother's voice coming from the kitchen.

"What?" I query, wondering why he is not outside. "What are you doing in there?"

"Looking for cookies," he informs innocently as we hear a chair being pulled across the kitchen's wooden floor.

"There are some sugar cookies on the top shelf of the pantry in a white airtight container," our Muse directs with a slight grin.

"Want some, Lena?"

I pause for another second knowing that Melody, like me, always has a hidden stash of chocolate.

"Get me something with chocolate," I request.

"There is a dark chocolate torte in the refrigerator," Melody informs with a hearty chuckle.

Politely, she turns back to me, giving me all of her attention. Relaxed, I snuggle into the comfortable floral sofa and lean back to admire the space. I give an approving nod.

Acapella

It always amazes me that the cottage looks rather small from the outside, but it is incredibly spacious with oversized, rectangular windows encircling the entire circumference of the home that allows the picturesque cypress grove to become the main focus. The walls are stucco and painted a soft, powder blue decorated with several famous landscape paintings which are original pieces of art.

The living room has a floral-print sofa and loveseat combo with a tree stump base glass-top coffee table anchored by a handwoven multihued carpet that must be worth a small fortune. To my left, there is a small dining table surrounded by four hand-carved, mahogany chairs. Currently, Ando is in the cramped yet tidy galley-style kitchen sporting open shelving and a slew of 1950's era appliances next to a long row of windows overlooking a lush garden of fruit trees and vegetables, many of the plants not native to the Mediterranean.

"Did I pass the test?" Melody questions with concern. "Are you certain now that I am not some trickster?"

"With flying colors," I grin.

Suddenly, Ando appears from his foraging carrying three dessert plates, three forks and the chocolate torte on a silver tray he found in the pantry. Carefully, he sets everything on the coffee table then sits on the opposite side of Melody who is now between us.

"Let's eat!" he blushes, diligently distributing the goodies he has procured.

Melody slices the flourless torte and serves us, all the while, cheerfully chatting and reminiscing on times long past. Without restraint, the Muse shares stories of the original *Three*, stories that I am certain would make them blush, if in fact they could blush. Ando giggles as if he has lost his senses completely while I continue to smile with reddened cheeks at the heartwarming recollections.

"And that is how Ligeia almost burned down the barn," Melody guffaws uncontrollably.

Ando and I both snicker as the vivid picture of a five-year-old Ligeia attempting to cook a red snapper and instead almost causing a catastrophe.

Melody dabs the corners of her eyes with the edge of her apron.

"Aren't you lonely here, in the woods, by yourself?" I blurt, taking another sip of steamy Oolong tea.

"Sometimes," she admits with a frown, reaching for the teapot. "But I have been alone for eons now."

"That's sad," Ando pouts, his eyes welling with tears. "You can come live with us."

Melody laughs, the sound is like stars twinkling in the heavens on a cold night.

"I am certain your parents would not like that idea," she smirks.

"Yes!" he claps merrily. "Come live with us! You can have my room."

Sweetly, she smiles and pats his hand.

"Where will you sleep, Fernando?" she probes in all seriousness.

My brother thinks for a moment before informing, "I can share Lena's room."

"What?!" I exclaim, choking on my beverage.

"Yeah!" he continues.

Immediately, I shake my head.

"We can get bunkbeds. I've always wanted bunkbeds. Lena can sleep on the bottom bunk. I'll get the top one," he rambles.

"Wait a minute," I groan. "Let's not get ahead of ourselves."

"C'mon," he pouts. "I don't want great grandma Melody to be alone anymore."

I sit in silence contemplating his words.

"Neither do I," I concur. "Neither do I."

Melody, on the other hand, shifts uncomfortably, her eyes filling with unshed tears as she clears her throat.

"Ando said you wanted to speak with me?" I say, changing the subject.

She nods, turning to face me.

"When is *The Joining* ceremony?" she questions, abandoning her dessert for the time being.

"The night of the full moon," I educate with a dry mouth and sweaty palms.

"Tomorrow," she whispers, gazing out of the window at the darkness.

Nervously, I nod.

"Have you prepared for it?" she queries with all seriousness which stumps me.

"I didn't know I had to prepare for it," I admit meekly, my hands immediately clasp together on my lap in order to hold down the need to tap my feet. "Mom didn't say that I need to prepare for it."

Melody shakes her head.

"Normally, you would not need to, but we live in complex times," the ancient being begins. "The world we live in is no longer black and white; instead, it is many shades of gray all blending together."

"I don't understand," I respond, truly mystified by her comment.

"The powers inside of you will triple, perhaps quadruple," she tells bluntly. "In Sirens, the push and pull between the human world which you are a part of, and your true nature will always be in conflict."

"Mom says that after *The Joining* I will be more balanced and able to pull power from the elements and other Sirens," I proudly reveal.

"You will have more of a choice," the Muse clarifies. "Your body will no longer rebel against you, that is fact, but never forget that immense power comes with increased accountability and power can corrupt, even the purest of heart."

"It won't corrupt me," I promise, exhaling as I reach for one of the forks and dive into my heavenly slice of chocolate torte. "I won't let it."

"*The Joining* does not take away your innate instincts," Melody continues as she too cuts into the moist concoction. "It simply allows you the ability to choose which side to follow.

Whether it be Siren or human, it is still up to you to make the wise choice."

"But Melody—"

"You are a teenager," she interrupts, her eyes swirling until they morph into an icy shade of silver. "You are already a giant ball of raging hormones, my dear girl."

I smirk, relishing our 'chat' as well as the densely rich slice on my plate.

"I know this too well," I chuckle.

"During the ceremony, focus on your Aria," my great grandmother pleads. "Remember all of the things it represents: family, love, honor, and loyalty. Those are your real strengths, your real power."

"Can you come to the ceremony?" I ask, filled with hope.

"For reasons I am unable to share at the moment, I cannot venture to Paradiso," Melody confesses with a heavy heart. "But I will be there in spirit. Watching over you. Inspiring you."

Unable to stop myself, I embrace her. My mind begins to race as the Aria she inspired springs into my mind. It plays softly in the background, but I hear it, nonetheless. It is a part of me, and it is the best part of me.

"I will miss you, but I'll be back soon," I sniffle, holding back the tears. "I will."

"And you will still be my Selena," she giggles, twinkling irises now a lovely light lavender.

"Yes," I grin, inhaling her naturally enticing fragrance. "I will always be *your* Selena."

CHAPTER EIGHT

It is early and I cannot sleep. Restlessly, I lay in bed for almost an hour before deciding to get ready for the day. Wanting to begin the day, I take a quick military shower and eat a bowl of cereal before venturing out onto the verandah to watch the sunrise.

Unfortunately, the sun never rises. Well, it did rise; I just cannot see it due to the poor weather conditions. Today, there is a fog so thick that describing it as pea soup seems appropriate. I am not sure what caused it, but as far as the eye can see it covers the surface of the water, stretching out toward the bleak horizon.

Then I hear *him*.

Out in the harbor, I hear his sweet voice calling to me.

"Selena."

But I cannot see him through the unnaturally dense fog that sits atop the *Marina Piccolo.*

Then, as if responding to my thought, the fog thins just enough for me to make out a vessel. It is a large ship, shiny and new, at least one-hundred-ninety-seven-feet of *Fincantieri* brand yacht. Squinting, I recognize the vessel by the painted name on the bow: *Anna-Sofia.*

It is him! Ares!

As if an MP3 player has been turned on in my head, a rhythmic beat begins. The sound starts low and then expands when it meets the air. Heavy-laden with bass and percussion, it pounds a rhythmic song just like the sea.

It calls me.

Completely plugged in, I concentrate. With practiced perfection, my mind segregates every exquisite note from the world around me.

It is definitely him!

Slowly, my eyes open and like before, his exquisite voice—his angelic voice—accompanies the music with perfect precision, and without trying, I recognize the song. The lonely lyrics speak to my soul. They speak to the Siren in me.

Then that familiar voice starts to sing:

"… and the sun drips down bedding heavy behind

The front of your dress, all shadowy-lined

And the droning engine throbs in time

With your beating heart."

It is!

Duran Duran's ballad, *The Chauffeur.*

What's happening?

My hackles suddenly rise as the unsettling feeling of *déjà vu* slaps me in the face, hard.

'Turn your ship around,' I project my thoughts so only he can hear me. *'It's not safe for you to be around me. Leave and never come back.'*

Unaffected, Ares continues to sing, ignoring my warning.

He can't be this stupid!

In the middle of the harbor, the same *'young man'* that I compelled to follow my Siren-song, and the very same one that revealed himself to me at the Blue Grotto, sits on the upper deck of his parents' silver yacht. This time dressed in dark-washed, denim shorts, a white *'Salt Life'* t-shirt, and white boat-shoes. Gold-highlighted, blonde locks wave accosting shimmering amethyst irises.

Acapella

Wait! Amethyst irises!

My mind struggles with the realization.

Leukosia once told me that only the Olympian gods have amethyst eyes!

Concentrating while grasping my obsidian charm, I project to only him.

"Which god are you?!" I bark, voice a bit shaky.

Shyly, he smiles showing teeth that are straight and bright white which only enhances his sun-tanned skin.

"Have you missed me?" he inquiries, ignoring my question, voice raspy yet pleasant.

At a loss for words, I stand on the verandah, staring at him, unable to move. Unable to formulate another thought that does not end with me diving off of this cliff and swimming out to him.

No!

As difficult as it is, I will myself to stay where I am.

"I have missed you," Ares declares, his smile replaced by a lonely frown. "Swim out to me, Selena."

Realization dawns as I reprimand.

"You tricked me!" I snarl, speaking at a normal volume. "You've already shown me that you're not human, but you aren't some *'lesser-being'*, are you?"

"No," he states unapologetically. "I am not, but neither are you."

Stumped for the moment, I contemplate my next comment.

"I don't know what game you're playing, but—"

He cuts me off in midsentence, saying, "Hey! You tried to kill me, remember?"

I pause, looking away then back at his unrelenting stare.

"I will never forget," I reply, wracked with guilt. "Why are you here?"

"To see you," he grins, melting my heart.

"I still don't know what type of creature you are," I remind, staring back across the fog-covered harbor.

Casually, he runs a hand through his soft tresses.

"I am *Ares*," he states, chest puffed like a peacock.

"I still don't know what that means," I huff, almost ready to send a rainstorm at him and dump him into the sea.

"Swim out to me," he compels. "And I'll explain."

"How do I know that you won't try to hurt me?" I interrogate boldly.

He thinks for a few seconds before answering.

"We have met before and we seemed to have hit it off," he pompously reminds. "Did I try to hurt you then?"

"No," I reply abruptly, then—

Hold on!

"'*Hit it off*'!" I growl. "I almost destroyed you… wait, tell me who and what you are, now!"

Obstinately, he shakes his head.

"I will explain in person, and I will not harm you," he counters, and I know that he is telling the truth; however, still upset with him, I mock.

"And that should mean something to me?"

"If you forgive me for not revealing my true self, I will forgive you for almost sending me to the Underworld," he states convincingly, making me smile against my will.

Stop flirting with him!

"I'll think about it," I respond at last.

"I want to see you again," he tries to convince, but I stick to my guns. "Come to me and I will explain all."

"That's not wise," I comment with a half-hearted chuckle.

Ares frowns.

"Nice boat," I praise smugly.

He blushes.

"Thank you," he smirks.

"Who is *Anna-Sofia?*" I demand with a raised eyebrow. "Are you even old enough to own such an expensive ship? Does it belong to your parents?"

With a hearty laugh he shakes his head.

"Not exactly," he grins. "Come on. I have delicious snacks onboard, purchased them myself."

"I'm not swimming out to talk or eat," I inform harshly as I turn back to the villa. "Goodbye, Ares."

Suddenly, my cellphone rings. The sound is brash and jarring in comparison to the placidity of the morning. The shrill sound causes me to jump out of my skin. As usual, my entire body tenses. Filled with annoyance, I glance at the screen, but do not recognize the number that is calling.

"Hello?" I snap, uncaring of who I offend.

"*Ciao, bella!*" the seductive male voice greets in Italian.

I can hear my heartbeat accelerate.

"Ares?" I swallow the remaining saliva in my mouth. "How did you get this number?"

A couple seconds of silence pass as I wait with the device pressed against my ear. I am not sure how to react, to be terrified or flattered. Is it possible to feel both emotions at once?

"I want to see you," he requests, voice smooth as molten metal and just as dangerous.

"No... ok... I can't!" I respond looking back at the yacht apprehensively.

He laughs, and the sound goes directly to my spinal column and travels south.

"Why not?" he questions sweetly; much too sweetly for my liking. Naturally, my right foot begins to tap against the tiles, and before I can answer, he adds: "I feel extremely exposed out in the open like this."

What?

"Why?" I sigh.

As we continue our awkward repartee, a light smattering of cumulus clouds that are hovering about a quarter of a mile away sweeps in. Quickly, they descend, concealing his location.

How strange.

"Because it looks incredibly bizarre us talking to each other this way," he snickers. "What do you think?"

Wanting him to return to the conversation at hand, I agree with a nod, a huff, and a roll of my eyes.

"Can you please stay on subject?" I chastise with a groan.

He nods back.

"For one thing, my parents would kill me," I educate with an exasperated huff. "Secondly, I don't know you from Adam. You could be a crazed serial killer."

Ares chuckles and I am taken aback that his cheerful disposition is unoffended by my insinuation.

"I could be," he jokes with an audible smirk. "But I am not."

Still staring in his direction, I realize he is now completely hidden from my view.

"Are you causing this fog?" I interrogate, placing my free hand on my hip in defiance.

There is another gap in our conversation as he formulates an answer.

"Yes," he confesses at last. "If you swim out to the yacht, no one will see you. The mist will conceal you."

Completely conflicted, I weigh the consequences of following his request.

Not knowing how to respond, I retort, "My parents—"

"Will not know anything if you swim out to me... right... now," he encourages and for some idiotic reason I hang up, stand atop the verandah railing, mutter a quick prayer and... jump!

Great Father in Heaven!

Like a lead weight, I fall.

Fall past the gray cliffs that guard the island.

Fall past the clumps of green foliage that brighten the jagged rocky terrain.

Fall until I elegantly pierce the liquid surface with only the smallest splash.

Temporarily, the rushing current accosts my eardrums, but then rapidly fades.

"I can't believe I'm doing this," I mumble to myself in Siren as I swim with determined strokes toward the *Anna-Sofia*.

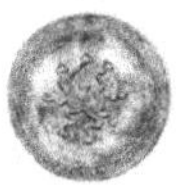

It takes only a few minutes to reach the vessel, out of breath, but intact. On deck, Ares puts the cellular device back in his pocket and strides to the side of the ship where I tread water, waiting for him to let down the ladder. He gazes down at me, and I can see his joy that I am here, *with* him.

"Are you going to help me up or...?" with trembling lips, I demand.

He blushes unexpectedly making me giggle.

"So demanding," he teases, red faced, but just as handsome as he extends a hand.

Not wanting to slip and fall, I grasp it as I climb the final rung and he lifts me like I weigh nothing at all onto the deck. He grips me firmly, but not too hard. My pulse is racing once more, and I pray he does not hear my 'tell-tale' heart.

"I will get you a towel," he states then disappears inside the cabin.

Nervously, I glance around. Wondering what possessed me to do this, and why would I risk my parents' wrath? Honestly, I have no clue.

"Here you go," the young man says as he hands me a plush towel. "Would you like some tea?"

Needing desperately to warm up, I nod.

Once more, he hurries to the cabin. Keeping occupied, I wander around the deck admiring the brass accents, immaculate hardwood floors and high-tech nautical devices. Everything is as it should be, sleek and modern.

"Sorry it took so long," Ares apologizes as he reappears. "I could not find the sugar. I hope honey is sufficient."

Again, I nod.

"Your ship is impressive," I remark, running a hand over the smooth steering wheel.

Gallantly, he motions to a small seating area, and I am obliged to sit. Not knowing what to do with my hands, I anxiously play with the hem of my soaked floral romper. Ares, however, does not seem to notice my disheveled state as he pours two teacups of the steaming brew then adds a squeeze of lemon to both, then finally, a generous stream of golden honey to each cup.

"I hope you like golden raisin scones with Devonshire Cream," he announces, avoiding my gaze.

"I do," I reassure, admiring his graceful movements and his polite mannerism. "My Mom makes incredible scones, so does my great grandmother."

Ares chuckles.

"I am positive these are not as good as Marina's, but— "

"*Stop!*" I jump to my feet and take a step back. "I never told you my mother's name!"

Taken aback, he closes his eyes realizing his mistake.

"Who the hell are you?" I probe, hackles up.

Deliberately, he straightens to his full height of six-four.

"I am Ares," he starts, expecting his admission to clear the air, but it does not.

"I know your name—"

"I am Ares," he repeats with more confidence. "Son of Zeus and Hera, one of the original Olympians."

With this new bit of information, I feel my temples throbbing hard.

"But that would mean you are—"

"—the God of War," he reveals, bowing low.

Holy! Crap!

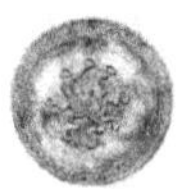

The World begins to spin faster, or at least it seems that way to me. My vision blurs and my stomach lurches warning of my stupidity. Hopefully, I can make it out of here alive.

"I'm leaving," I growl like a rabid dog, keeping my gaze on the *thing* in front of me while steadily walking backwards to the railing.

"I will not harm you," Ares comforts from a safe distance, and I believe him.

"What do you want?" I snarl, hating that I let myself be tricked.

"I want to get to know you better," he states sincerely, dimples showing.

"Yeah, right," I jibe, glancing over the railing. "You probably want the location of The Siren Grotto too."

His worried expression softens.

"Why would I want the location, when I already know where it is?" he answers with a question, which I hate.

"How is that possible?" I respond in kind.

"My father is *Zeus*," he smiles as if that explains it all.

I guess to him that makes sense.

"For argument's sake," I ponder aloud. "Let's say that I believe you, then what other information do you need?"

"Absolutely, none," he educates with a firm tone.

"Why should I believe you?" I frown, weighing my escape plans.

"I am Ares, *God of War*," he repeats. "If I wanted you dead, you would be."

I consider his words, before replying.

"I guess that's true," I reluctantly agree, taking another glance at the sea.

"Please stay," he begs.

Unsure, I still agree, but remain at high alert, talons drawn.

"You will not need those," he smirks, staring at the two-inch weapons on both hands.

Suspiciously, my eyes narrow.

"We'll see."

This makes him laugh.

"Would you please sit at least?" he requests in that same regal manner that is difficult to resist.

Against my better judgement, I do.

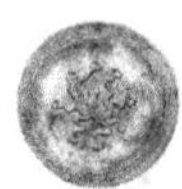

For at least a half an hour, the mysterious Ares and I make small talk over tea and scones. We tell each other about our lives and our goals. Obviously, he has a much more fascinating past than me. All the while, the hanging fog hides us from prying eyes. There is no breeze coming off of the sea, but the morning is remarkably cool and humidity free.

"You know who I am?" I question awkwardly.

He nods.

"You are a *Siren*," Ares reaches for a second pastry.

"And you are a *god*," I repeat, practically chocking on the words.

"I am."

"So, you traipse around pretending to be a college student now?" I ask, trying to figure out my host and why he has taken an interest in me.

"Gods never '*traipse*'," he snickers.

"Uh huh," I respond with raised brows.

"But yes, I have attended many fine higher learning establishments," Ares wryly divulges. "But never as a student.

"I have mentored great warriors like Genghis Khan and Sun Tzu; tutored the genius minds of Plato and Socrates and was consul to conquerors like Hannibal and Alexander the Great, to name just a few."

"Impressive," I mock playfully, earning a stern glare.

"Not to brag, but I have matriculated from Oxford, Harvard, Yale and Annapolis," he continues proudly. "Currently, I am a sophomore at WestPoint—"

"I get it," I snort. "You're a badass in every way possible."

"Correction… the *original* badass," he mocks himself.

"Why do you find me interesting?" I question in a rush of words.

"You are special," he answers without hesitation.

Before I can protest, he reaches out and caresses my cheek and then tucks one lone curl that has separated itself from the others behind my ear. Boldly, he leans closer and kisses my forehead, but then stops. With an unknown expression, he watches me, studies me.

Finally, he speaks.

"I am here because you captivate me, young Siren."

His admission makes me choke on my saliva.

"Umm, that's not a real answer," I tell, hoping not to break a smile.

"I thought you were a mere high school student," he teases playfully. "Not Selena Antonius Thermopolis Marquez, attorney at law."

Leaning back in my seat, I provoke him saying, "Do you need a lawyer?"

"Do I appear to be the type of bloke that needs a barrister?" His brows hitch upward.

Enjoying the upper hand, I take a sip of tea, before responding.

"Yes, you definitely are the bad-boy type," I add without a smile, but his laugh is so contagious that I start laughing too.

"How old are you, really?" I blurt when our laughter finally subsides, wanting, no... *needing* to know the answer.

"Does age truly matter?" he probes, leaning forward, his mouth too close to mine.

Fighting the urge to taste his lips, I stand quickly, bump into the table that thankfully is bolted to the floor and immediately feel like a fool.

"I have to go before my parents wonder where I am," I remind, wishing I had never agreed to spend time with the beguiling gentleman.

"Of course," Ares stands too, but much more gracefully. "Thank you for spending time with me, Selena."

I nod and without so much as a goodbye, drop the wet towel and race toward the edge of the deck, diving outward without hesitancy into the placid waters of the Tyrrhenian Sea. As I enter my domain, the harbor sheds its tranquil manner and instantly turns choppy, even the fog starts to lift and disperse.

As I swim toward the coastline, I hear *The Chauffeur* playing again from the direction of the vessel; the song's instrumental accompanied by an ongoing orchestra of thrashing waves and roiling currents. Blustery fingers pluck a sharp bass against the rough cliff side, their beat hard and fierce.

Unable to stop myself, I look back and it is the biggest mistake of my life.

There he stands. Looking like the original sin. Golden hair blowing in the wind while perfectly shaped brows furrow above thick, extra-long lashes highlighting hypnotic amethyst orbs.

"See you soon, Selena!" he shouts against the wind, the sound slightly muffled.

Steeling my nerves, I resume my swim back to land, but my heart is not in it. My heart is back on the *Anna-Sofia* with Ares, the God of War.

CHAPTER NINE

My mother enters the kitchen just in time to see me push away my full plate.

"That's a first," she states with a confused expression on her face.

"Huh?" I blurt, not truly paying attention.

She nods toward my lunch.

"You've never turned your nose up at fried chicken, mashed potatoes, and corn on the cob."

Exasperated, I sigh.

"I'm not hungry," I mumble, my mind still on Ares and our 'chat'.

Mom immediately sits on the seat beside me. Her brow furrowed as if she already knows what is bothering me. Knowing that she once was me, to a certain extent, she probably already guesses what is wrong.

"Talk to me," she encourages in her motherly way.

Reluctantly, I turn to face her, needing her counsel.

"Explain what will happen during *The Joining*," I request.

Mom smiles, but it does not reach her eyes.

"I have explained several times," she tweaks my nose playfully.

Taking a cleansing breath, I respond.

"Please, tell me one more time," I plead, concerned at what may or may not happen.

Tenderly, Mom wraps her arms around me and pulls me close, so close I can smell her fragrance against my heated cheek. Like I did when I was a little girl, I wrap her curls around my fingers, gently playing with them. For some reason, it has always comforted me.

"As you wish," Mom agrees then places a kiss on my forehead. "Where shall I start?"

As is customary, I answer.

"Start at the beginning."

Amused, my mother chuckles; the sound is like soothing balm to my tattered nerves.

"Very well," she begins. "When the moon is at its pinnacle and the seas are at their calmest, *The Three* will draw power from the sea and the moon—"

"I know how to draw power from the sea, but how do you siphon it from the Earth and each other?" I interrupt.

"We channel," she explains freely. "Just like when you use your volcanic glass charm to do the same."

"But how do we channel *each other*?" I press with fascination. "Or will I automatically know how to do it 'cause it's a *Siren-thing*?"

"Correct," my parent beams proudly. "It's a *Siren-thing*."

"Then the next part is…" I press, desperate to know more.

"Then through Ligeia, Leukosia and me, you shall be christened in fire and in ice." Obligingly, Mom continues.

"Fire and ice?" I grimace, suppressing the horrific vision in my head.

How in the world will there be ice? *We're in the Mediterranean!*

"That's the part that troubles me," I reveal, feeling that tightening in my chest and my tummy lunge at the same time.

"If I can survive it," she smiles. "Then it will be no problem for you."

Gently, she smooths my hair away from my eyes, but the fear inside of me doubles then triples.

"It will be quick," she comforts. "I give you my word."

Although I am not convinced, I nod.

"Here," Mom says placing the plate in front of me once more. "You'll need your strength. Eat."

Fighting against the nausea, I take a bite of the flavorful chicken breast; the meat melts in my mouth, but instead of enjoying it, it makes me queasy.

"Mmm," I pretend to like it, so not to hurt my mother's feelings. "You are the best cook."

"I accept that commendation." She grins.

"I'm still afraid," I confess under my breath.

"It is okay to be afraid." My mother winks. "I was afraid too."

"You were?"

It is her turn to nod.

"I don't understand why you are being so vague," I respond, trying to keep down my bite of chicken.

Trying to be helpful, Mom cuts the remaining meat into bite-size pieces like when I was younger. I am not sure why she does it, but if it makes one of us feel better then so be it. Who am I to object?

"It is difficult to explain is all," she confesses, concentrating on her task.

"Can you try please?" I insist.

Acapella

"The gist of it is," Mom's eyes glimmer proudly. "At the end of *The Joining* you will be stronger, faster, hopefully wiser, and more connected to who you are and who you are meant to be."

Self-doubt stifles me as I ponder that concept.

More connected?

"Will I be more Siren than human?" I ask, needing to know.

Mom kisses my left cheek and then my right.

"You will be whoever you wish to be," she answers cryptically. "It will be your choice."

"Explain," I beg, losing patience.

"For example, Ligeia and Leukosia chose to be completely Siren," Mom patiently explains. "They are guardians of the oceans and all lifeforms in it. Even though they are technically in this world, they are apart from it."

I stare at her not quite comprehending.

"Before finding us on Isla Flora, they didn't care about the human world," Mom continues.

I am still so confused.

"Then why did they save Nicole's life when she was a little girl and almost drowned?" I interrogate.

Mom smiles.

"They're not monsters," she reminds. "They have compassion, to a degree."

"I see," I reply not knowing what else to say.

"Plus, they had seen Nicole and her grandfather fishing together for years," Mom emphasizes. "They knew that they were good people."

At last, understanding dawns on me.

"So even Ligeia and Leukosia can love humans," I respond.

"Without a doubt," she mumbles. "They're quite fond of David."

I laugh.

"Too fond of him, if you ask me," I mock with a saucy wink.

My mother playfully slaps my arm.

"Mom?"

"Yes, sweetheart?"

"Will Ando be with us for *The Joining*?" I ask, wanting my brother to attend.

"Would you like him there?" She grins.

"I'd love for him to be there," I confess, needing his level headedness.

"Okay," she agrees. "Your brother will be there."

"Dad too?" I add optimistically.

My face lights up, but then changes when I see Mom's face darken.

"That won't be possible, Selena."

I loudly exhale before pleading, "I need him."

"It is dangerous," she stands unyielding.

"He can wear his Scuba gear," I reply, ignoring her protest. Suddenly, my mother stands.

"No, Selena."

"He'll be fine," I continue with a hopeful lilt.

"I'm not willing to take that chance!" she barks sharply.

Silently, I sit with my hands folded in my lap wishing I had never pushed.

"I'm sorry, Mom," I whisper, feeling awful.

"He'll be there in spirit," she soothes taking my hand in hers.

As the tension grows, Dad suddenly appears in the doorway, an all-knowing frown on his handsome features, dark hair still damp from his shower.

"Are you ready?" David asks as he enters the kitchen where we are currently waiting for Ando.

"Not really." I pout.

His devoted wife stands and gives him a quick kiss on the lips.

"I'll check on Ando," she relays, leaving the room.

As expected, Dad takes her seat at the dining table. He is trying to be upbeat but is failing horribly. I give him credit though for at least attempting to be convincing.

"It's going to be fine, *mija,*" he comforts me in Spanglish, making me giggle.

"I'm sure it will be," I fake a brave face.

"Are you having second thoughts about this whole *'christening with fire and ice'* thing?" my human stepfather verbalizes my worry. "Let me talk to your mother. Maybe we can postpone it or forget about it altogether."

Meekly, I shake my head, feeling alone even though I am in a house filled with people who love me, who I love.

"I wish so badly that I could be there for you, honey," David declares, giving me a tight hug. "What can I do to help?"

"Nothing," I sniffle, wishing I could wake up and all of this would be just a nightmare.

"C'mon, little *fish-girl,*" he teases trying to lighten the mood. "There has to be something I can do to make you feel better."

I study him.

My Dad.

The only father figure I have ever had. The man who would fight a hundred Amphitrite's to keep me safe. I watch him and I feel even worse.

"Tell Mom not to make me complete *The Joining*," I plead in a flood of almost unintelligible words, and in the distance, we hear the first loud roll of thunder.

His forehead wrinkles with pity.

"Do you think something horrible will happen?" he quizzes, trying his best to appear optimistic.

"Remember when I tried to kill the young lady at the museum?" I meekly admit.

Instantly, the blood drains from my stepfather's face.

"Yes," he swallows hard, averting his eyes for a quick second. "I will never forget that."

"Did Mom tell you about the guy on the yacht?" I add, sheepishly.

I shake my head already knowing the answer.

"Of course, she did," I grumble, sarcastically.

"What's the point, Selena?" Dad fidgets.

Wishing I could disappear, I take a deep breath, but unfortunately it does not help.

"After the christening, I will be more powerful than I am now," I vocalize, shamefully. "The only change will be my ability to choose. *To choose!* That's ridiculous! Suppose I choose wrong and end up like the aunts?"

Dad frowns.

"What's wrong with Ligeia and Leukosia?"

Where do I begin?

"They chose the sea instead of intermingling with humans. They have been stuck with each other without anyone else for eternity," I ramble like I am on medication, and without fail, the tears come accompanied by an unexpected thunderstorm outside which I pull myself together, will it to disappear, and it does.

"What's the matter with their choice?" David grills.

"I don't want to be alone!" I feel my eyes getting misty again but force the tears to stay where they are. "I want to live among people. I want to get married and have children. Dammit! I want *not* to hurt people just because they piss me off, pardon my language."

Dad smiles before speaking.

"Take a breath," he encourages. "Think about who you are."

"I don't know who I am anymore." I start to sob, the droplets soaking my shirt and I hear the raindrops mimicking their tempo against the glass panes of the windows.

Sympathetically, Dad rests his hand on my shoulder.

"You are the most compassionate person I've ever known," he sincerely explains. "You always put other's feelings above your own. You have never hurt another living being—"

"But I have lately," I remind, looking away.

He shakes his head.

"That was a fluke," he states firmly and without hesitancy. "You are the most caring person... *Siren*... you know what I mean... I've ever had the pleasure of knowing."

I finally wipe the tears away and the rain stops again.

"Thank you," I give him a much needed second hug. "I still wish you could be there."

He becomes quiet and a strange glimmer appears in his expressive eyes as he rubs his hand over his clean-shaven chin.

"What are you thinking?" I murmur, nervously.

He snickers.

"Maybe there is a way."

CHAPTER TEN

The swim from the *Belvedere di Tragara* on Capri to the Siren Grotto is a lovely swim. Above our heads, diffused rays of moonlight penetrate the liquid barrier separating the sea from the air. The topography of the Tyrrhenian Sea surrounding Capri is fascinating, beautiful and mysterious, and along the rocky seabed, orange *Alcyonacea*, pink sea pens, and copper-colored six-fold branches of *Hexacorallia* sway softly as the current flows past their branches. Darting in and out of them are several multicolored fish of various species and a cuttlefish moving unhurriedly through the watery domain. To our amusement, we also spy a pod of dolphins playing with a discarded beach ball a few yards away from the coastline.

"What's in that?" Ando grills, tugging on the waterproof duffle bag on my shoulder.

"Nunya!" I snap anxiously in Siren, my mind on *The Joining.*

"What does *'nunya'* mean?" His brows hitch.

"None-ya business!" I chuckle then snort.

"Mom? Lena's being mean again," he tattles.

"No arguing tonight," Mom states firmly dissolving our sibling strife.

"Are you nervous?" Ando probes as he quickens his pace to keep up with me.

I glare at him for a long while before answering.

"What do you think?" I bark then quickly apologize.

He looks back at me, sympathy in his bright eyes.

"I know you're nervous," he sighs, the sound heavy with concern. "But it will be okay."

"Selena!" I hear my name being called from a few feet away near the reef.

Looking in that direction, I see a pair of striped, red mullets waving their fins. It is Hunter and Stripes, alive and well! Excited to see them again, I clickity-clackity my Sireny greeting. Then I notice the school of tiny red mullets swimming behind them.

They have a family!

"Congratulations!" I exclaim while rushing toward them.

"Thank you!" they answer in unison.

"How many are there?" I question Stripes, who is grinning from ear to ear (if fish had ears).

"There are four hundred and twenty-two!" Hunter clicks happily.

Excited for them, I smile watching his expanded family swimming about as their parents guard them.

"It must be dinnertime," I articulate while observing their offspring feed on algae, plankton and a variety of aquatic vegetation growing on the sea floor. Several little ones swim over to inspect us. Energetically, they click and clack all at once making it extremely difficult to understand them. My mother grins but taps her waterproof watch reminding me of our own schedule.

Before I can say my goodbyes, one of the newly hatched mullets, exuberantly exclaims, "I can jump really high!"

"That's wonderful!" I give my sincere approval.

"Today, I skipped across the surface of the water," another boasts. "Mommy and Daddy told me that this increases the amount of oxygen in my body so I can swim really fast."

A third gets my attention by slapping my leg with its tiny fin.

"What kind of fish are you?" it probes, looking at all three of us one at a time.

"I'm a Siren," I inform with pride.

"What's a 'Siren'?" Another swims toward us and stops near Ando's right elbow.

"Umm," I hesitate, earning me a poignant stare from their brothers and sisters.

Impatient, they turn to Mom.

"Well," she begins, "Sirens are a type of—"

"You look funny," one of them snickers, earning it a glare from its mother.

"We're part fish, part human, part god, part muse, kinda," Ando click-clack-whistles.

"Oh!" Content with his answer, they all shout. "Okay!"

Spontaneously, we all start to laugh, even Hunter and Stripes.

"Se-le-na, is this your family?" Stripes questions.

Proudly I nod.

"This is my mother, Marina, and little brother, Ando," I introduce to the large crowd.

"You have an adorable family," Mom praises in Siren.

"So do you," both Hunter and his wife reply in harmony.

As we converse, a small mullet with a black dot near its right eye speaks up.

"Are you related to Ligeia and Leukosia?"

"Yes," Mom answers clearly, but cautiously. "They are our aunts, why?"

"They are nice," the fish says wiggling its fins at the same time.

"Especially, Leukosia!" the little one with the dot informs cheerfully as she does a flip.

All three of us stand at attention.

"Wait!" Mom blurts. "You've seen the other Sirens?"

The little fish nods excitedly.

"Yay!" my little brother squeals like a piglet. "C'mon! Let's go!"

In response, my body fills with anticipation, glee, and then a large amount of terror.

"We'll see you again, Hunter, Stripes, goodbye everyone!" I wave as I swim backward already on the move, Mom and Ando close at my heels doing the same.

"Goodbye!" Hunter clicks as his wife blows a stream of bubbles.

"Bye!" all four-hundred-twenty-two of their young ones click too.

"Be safe," Stripes advises corralling her babies, the task almost impossible like herding cats or squirrels.

"Scary things lay below the surface," her husband advises. "Keep your wits about you."

I nod my acknowledgement, giving a slight smile.

"We will, I promise."

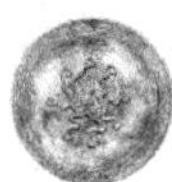

"So, they're back," I announce somewhat gleefully, thinking about seeing my grandaunts after several long weeks. I suppose they needed to recuperate after dealing with a murderous sea goddess and reuniting with their long-lost Muse-mother. It could not possibly get any stranger. Such is my life.

"Seems that way." Mom grins back after eavesdropping on my thoughts, her onyx locks streaming behind her as we swim at top speed toward the Siren Grotto.

Ando giggles excitedly.

"I can't wait to see them," he beams. "I've got two bags of Doritos— "

"*Shh!*" Mom puts her finger to her lips and stops in mid-swim.

Following her lead, Ando and I both stop too. Looking around, we realize we are in the very spot where we always encounter the inky poison that guards the entrance to the Siren Grotto. Unfortunately, it is also the same area where the sentinel of spinner sharks patrol.

'Do you see them?' I whisper in Mom and Ando's heads.

My mother shakes her head, but takes my brother by the hand. Nervously, she scans for danger, but nothing appears which is weird in itself.

Where is it?

"Where's the ink?" Ando verbalizes my concern as he floats closer to Mom's side.

"I have no clue," Mom admits wearily, her guard on high alert. "It should be right here."

"We should turn back," I try to convince. *"The Joining* can wait for another day."

Mom shakes her head once more.

"It is always here," our mother states firmly in Siren. "Always."

As we hover about three feet above the seafloor, we hear the first set of odd noises.

Thump! Thump! Grrrrrr!

"What's that sound?" Ando grips Mom's hand tighter, and instinctively Mom wraps an arm around his small shoulders.

"I'm not sure, son."

Boldly, I swim out a few feet to inspect the terrain and discern where the sound is coming from and who or what might be making it. Mom's right. I recognize the red coral that we use as a marker along with the unnaturally tall stalks of seaweed that grow only here in this spot. It is definitely the region where the ferocious sharks protect and where the wall of ink lurks.

Thump! Thump! Grrrrrr!

"We should go," I repeat with more urgency. "Something's not right."

Then the sound changes.

Slurp! Slurp! Slurp! Plop!

"What the hell is making that sound?!" I mutter too loudly and earn a *'watch your mouth'* stare from Mom. "Sorry."

Slurp! Slurp! Slurp! Plop!

"Mommy?" my brother's face turns ashen. "What's that sound?"

Slurp! Slurp! Slurp! Plop!

"C'mon," Mom starts swimming backwards, Ando's hand still in hers.

"Tsk-tsk-tsk," we hear to our left and freeze.

Slowly, we turn, almost afraid of what we will see.

'Aunt Ligeia!' Ando shouts in my mind deafening me.

"Tia Ligeia!" I join in the celebratory cheer. "You're here! You're really here!"

She blinks, bewildered.

"Of course, I am here," the stoic Siren frowns. "I must be here in order to complete *The Joining*."

Then she rolls her eyes like my brother taught her.

"Tia Ligeia!" Mom takes over. "Where is the barrier?"

Ligeia blinks again.

"I turned it off," the haughty, sarcastic Siren announces.

Surprised, we gape at her.

"We can turn the barrier off and on?" I probe with absolute fascination.

"Some of us can," the sassy sea nymph smirks, then fans her long eyelashes.

I see.

"How?" Ando interrogates as he takes our grandaunt's hand, and she allows him to.

"It is a secret that only my mother and *The Three* know," she reveals in Siren.

"Will you teach me the secret?" Ando pouts and Ligeia's frown deepens.

"The less who knows, the better," she says, and we all understand that that subject is now done.

Sirens.

ACAPELLA

"It is time," the redhead proclaims and turns to lead the way to the Siren Grotto.

"Do we have to do this, Tia?" I ask, hearing the desperation in my voice.

"What are you: *'a fraidy-catfish'* or a *Siren*?" My humorless aunt tries to joke but fails miserably. "No more swimming away. It is time for *The Joining*."

CHAPTER ELEVEN

Standing in the shallows of Paradiso's lagoon is the other sister. Of course, with Ligeia and Leukosia, there is no hugging. No sappy words. No loving terms of endearment. Just as it always has been, and probably always will be. I find it quite comforting actually, especially when everything else around me is wonky and unexpected.

"What is that *thing*?" Leukosia inquisitively touches the video camera equipment given to me by my stepfather. "Why is it here?"

I laugh at her disgusted, yet curious tone.

"It will let Dad see Paradiso and the ceremony without actually being here," I teach like I know what I am talking about.

"No human has ever heard of *The Joining*, let alone seen it," Leukosia informs. "I do not think this is wise."

"Why not?" I exclaim in Siren rather loudly.

"It is a *Siren* rite of passage," Ligeia adds indignantly. "Not a… what is it called?"

She thinks for a few seconds before adding:

"A soap opera."

"Where did you hear about soap operas?" our mother questions with a large grin.

Ando and I smile revealing our role in the matter.

"David is a Human." Ligeia chastises with a wave of a hand.

"We know this fact," Mom replies, rolling her eyes.

"We object to this '*vi-de-o*' thing," in unison the sisters reply.

"My husband is a scientist," my mother reminds firmly. "He would never betray you, *us*."

She points to herself, Ando, and me.

Unconvinced, the aunts simply stare at all of us.

"Marina?" Leukosia finally speaks.

"Yes, Tia Leukosia?"

"Do you have your medallion?"

At her prompting, Mom retrieves a thin ornate Byzantine yellow-gold chain from below her black swimsuit. Secured to it is a handmade triangular gold charm with a similarly shaped piece of volcanic glass nestled in the middle. At the ends, each tip swirls like a wave as it rolls toward the shore. It looks like an antique, an extraordinarily valuable antique.

"Mommy, where did you get that?" Ando gasps, his eyes fixed to Mom's necklace.

She grins.

"My father had it made for me," our mother touches the charm lovingly. "He gave it to me on my sixteenth birthday."

"It's breathtaking," I compliment, touching it too.

"Does this help you channel your powers?" Ando asks, still staring.

Mom nods.

"Mommy?" My brother reaches out to touch the invaluable piece of jewelry but pulls back his hand unexpectedly.

"What's wrong, son?" our mother notices his uneasiness.

"A couple of weeks ago, I had a dream about this medallion," Ando confesses self-consciously.

"Really?" the aunts and I speak as one.

"I saw this," he motions toward it. "Lying on the seabed in a tall thicket of seaweed."

Instantly, my stomach turns into a giant ball of knots. My heartbeat accelerates and my mouth becomes as dry as the Sahara Desert. This was the worst possible news I could have received.

"Did you see me?" Mom queries nervously.

Ando says nothing.

"It's alright, my love," she encourages. "Tell me."

Ando's eyes well with tears.

Still silent, he shakes his head.

"No."

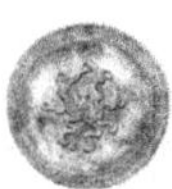

Powerless to alter my brother's visions, I cannot take my eyes off of our mother. I find myself turning in her direction, studying her expression, searching for chinks in her usually steadfast armor, but finding none. She seems to be just as strong, just as confident, as ever. Even more so if that is possible.

"Stop staring at me," Mom jokes, startling me out of my quandary. "You're making me feel like a circus freak."

Then she sticks her tongue out at me like a kindergartener on a playground teasing the new kid. I laugh and it releases some of my anxiety.

"Stop worrying so much," she orders with a wink. "You'll be the first Siren to ever get wrinkles."

Playfully, I make a funny face causing her to giggle. Ando, on the other hand, looks miserable. Sadly, I understand why.

"Don't be such a gloomy-Gus," I suggest, hoping his burden will be lessened if I make it seem inconsequential.

"How can I not feel bad, Lena?"

I shrug.

"I don't know," is the only response I can think of that does not sound like a lie.

Why do our lives have to be so complicated?

"I don't want this ability," he announces to all of us as we walk across the shifting sand at an unhurried pace. "I see things that I don't want to see. I know things that I don't want to know."

We pause briefly to consider his statement when the Sisters abruptly stop moving, only their *Rapunzel*-esque hair seems to be affected by their motion. Several seahorses swim between them brushing against their outer thighs and they do not notice when their rough exoskeletons graze their skin. I stare at them in awe.

"What is it?" Mom questions, her eyes dart from left to right then back again. "What's coming?"

"It is already here." They answer after a few seconds.

'What?!' I shout at their minds. *'What's here?'*

'Go back through the Siren Grotto!' they telepathically yell back. *'Now!'*

Without a second guess, Mom, Ando, and I swim as fast as we can down toward the lagoon bottom that leads to the exit of the grotto. Behind us, our ears are bombarded with loud squeaks, squeals, and squawks. The sound is so loud, so deafening that it literally batters my throbbing eardrums.

'Suppose they need help?!' my frantic question directed at Mom.

"They are the original Sirens!" Mom tries to comfort in Siren language. "They can handle themselves!"

Paranoid and scared, I dare glance behind me, but all I see is a thick cloud of sediment mixed with the black inky substance that protects the secret entrance. My hands automatically clench into fists as I fight the urge to turn around and help them. Mom's warning glare shatters that idea.

"We're not stopping!" she bellows with several clickity-clacks. "Look!"

Frantically, she points ahead of us.

"There's the cleft!" Mom directs. "Swim faster!"

But to our dismay, the sentinel sharks are poised right outside of the entrance. Angered at our presence, they attack with gaping mouths filled with anxious razor-sharp teeth.

"Turn back!" our mother barks like a general.

With no time to question, we follow her instructions and dive down. Terrified, Ando passes me and disappears back into the grotto. Right on his heels, I begin to descend, but hear Mom shout and turn. Instantly, I stop. Dread floods my entire being as I scan the murky depths for my mother.

"Mom?!" I shout-clack. *"Mom!"*

The echo of the churning sea taunts me as it bounces around the rocky space.

Dear Father! Where is she?

"Lena!" At last, I hear my brother.

"Get to Paradiso!" I command like General Patton leading the American troops at Bastogne during the Battle of the Bulge.

"I'm not going without you!" he rapidly clicks, clacks and whistles.

"Get moving or I'll kick your stubborn ass!" I snap, desperately needing to find the aunts and Mom.

Confused at our current situation, he stares at me for only a second then disappears into the sediment, and without losing a beat, I race back to where the cloud of debris is thickest hoping to find my family members. Hopefully, find them intact and alive. Right now, all I can do is pray.

"Mom!" I clack into the ink-laden water. "Ligeia! Leukosia!"

All the while, my heart thumps like the incessant jungle drums of some primitive tribe hunting its prey.

'Where the hell are you?!' I switch back to telepathy.

Unfortunately, no answer finds me.

No hope echoes against the sandy bottom of the sea…

Hope is about to leave completely when I hear *it*.

In the swirling water, I hear the faint calls of Leukosia's silky voice followed by Mom and Ligeia's more sultry tones. The dying embers of hope suddenly and miraculously reignite as I take-off at top speed toward the clamor. Readying myself for whatever is ahead, my scales burst forth almost tearing my delicate human skin. The webbing between my toes and fingers thickens to the point that they begin to itch, but I ignore the annoying sensation. Razor-sharp talons rip through my nails so fiercely that tiny droplets of blood tint the salty water around me, causing my quickly healing wounds to sting.

"Mom!" I clack loudly, and the sound actually rebounds off of the surrounding stony surfaces causing the seaweed to sway violently then uproot as if being ripped by invisible trowels.

"Over here!" My mother replies at last.

"I'm on my way!" I respond, filled with relief.

With a strong kick, my form cuts through the sea toward the sound of my mother's voice. Automatically, my Siren vision activates as the sediments floating around me thicken into something similar to a dense bowl of clam chowder. I do not know why my stomach growls, especially since I am heading toward danger.

I guess I am weird like that.

'Selena!' Mom shouts in my head. *'Hurry!'*

Finding new motivation, I switch to overdrive and every single muscle in my body explodes like pistons in a racecar's engine. The sensation is intoxicating, invigorating, and intense. I cannot help smiling to myself.

"Selena!"

Her voice is close.

Extremely close.

Right beside me, in fact.

"Mom!"

I come to a complete and sudden stop. All I can do is wait; wait for the pieces of sand and other particulates to settle back onto the seafloor. As the water around me clears a tiny bit more, I see them.

Acapella

My family.

My flesh and blood.

My everything.

Fighting each other!

To the Death!

CHAPTER TWELVE

Pausing briefly from their battle, they glance at each other with a strange look on their animalistic faces and then at me. Their normally expressive aquamarine eyes are completely black like the volcanic glass that makes up our DNA.

"What are you doing?" I ask, feeling the horror rising inside of me, choking me.

"Selena!" Mom shouts. "Find your brother! Leave now!"

Unfortunately, before I can retreat, Leukosia races toward me and shoves me with all of her Siren strength. I feel the sudden impact then the hard thud as my back slams into a heavy boulder resting on the rocky seabed. The force is so devastating that the stone leaves its resting place and rolls several feet to its new home where it resettles without complaint.

"Damn it!" I curse, feeling my scales buzzing as they soak up the vibrations. Instinct awakens as I leap out of the way as she comes around for a second attack, but this time I grab her by both wrists and hold her for a second or two before she breaks free. "Stop fighting me!"

She says nothing, only blinks then snarls. Leukosia, my aunt, the calm one, bares her teeth at me and growls like a rabid Rottweiler. Then she tries to bite me!

"I said: *Stop!*" the volatility of my voice slaps her like an extension of my hand, and she stops in mid-lunge.

As I restrain her, the blackness in her irises slowly fades and returns to the lovely aquamarine that I love so much.

"Aunt Leukosia?" I speak as calmly as I can. "Are you okay?"

She nods, quickly turning to see the punches being thrown between my mom and Ligeia.

"What's going on?! What's causing this?" the questions burst from my mouth. "Why are they fighting?"

Leukosia shakes her head, confusion reflects in her stare.

"I do not know," she gasps, pointing to the two Sirens in front of us. "One minute we were talking about the eerie silence of the water then *this!*"

"How do we stop them?" I snap harshly.

"I will take Ligeia!" my aunt clicks and clacks. "You deal with Marina!"

Nervously I nod, glancing at Mom who looks scarier than a ticked-off rhinoceros.

"I'll try!" I gulp, fearful for my life.

Just as I slowly approach my mother, I hear another.

"Selena!" a familiar voice calls to me. "Come to me."

Aunt Leukosia hears it too because she stops and looks around.

"Who is there?" she clacks but gets no response.

Ares!

"Selena," his voice softens to a whisper. "I am waiting for you."

Leukosia turns back to me, but it is too late, my body wants to flee. It wants to escape to a world where homicidal creatures are not bent on killing me or my loved ones. Unfortunately, all I can do now is think about myself. No matter what happens. I have to go to him.

Why?

I have no clue.

"*Selena!*" Tia Leukosia roars. "*I order you to stay where you are!*"

I cannot. I will not.

"I'm going!" I announce without hesitation, without shame.

Acapella

'Olympus help me!' the blonde Siren shouts inside of my head. *'We do not have time for this! Help me with your mother and Ligeia!'*

Not responding, I turn to leave. The voice still beckons me to it and for some reason I need to find it. I do not know why. I just do.

Something *else* has taken over.

"Do not move!" Leukosia commands in Siren and I feel my scales tense knowing that if she truly wanted to make me stay, she could. Thankfully, she has her hands full as Mom and Ligeia cease brawling with each other and fix their sights on her.

Logic shouts at me to help Leukosia. I do not think she can deal with two revved-up Sirens who seem to be determined to fight, but the voice returns.

"Selena, I am waiting for you."

"Ares?"

As though I am being pulled by invisible strings, I turn to the open sea, pausing briefly to stare at them, all three of them, hovering off of the stone-covered seabed. Their long hair fanning out around them like the flowing tails of Japanese betta fighting fish. They resemble battle banners waving against the onslaught of the increasing current. I study them, their similarities in particular. How their high cheekbones accent their flawless olive complexions. How every curve, every beauty mark, every aspect of their perfectly formed bodies is the same, and knowing they were formed from the same mold. Their only difference is the color of their shimmering locks and the pitch of their voices.

'Selena, I forbid you to leave! Do you understand?' Leukosia insists, cocking her head to the side mechanically.

"I'm sorry."

Baffled, Leukosia continues to glare at me until my mother grabs her from behind and Ligeia secures her hands.

"I am so sorry, but I have to leave," I repeat losing all of my willpower.

Before she can respond, I swim away. Not looking back for fear of what I will see. Somehow, I manage to steady my mind and block out my family's clicks, clacks, and mind-blowing thoughts as they begin fighting anew, but it does not matter.

Nothing else matters except finding *him*.

"Where are you?" I probe aloud awaiting a reply. "How do I find you?"

"Well," the masculine voice answers. "How did you find me before?"

I can't think!

"Ares?" I blurt still confused at my actions.

He pauses then finally answers.

"Have you missed me?" His voice is soft and charismatic. "I have missed you. More than I care to admit."

I feel my cheeks heat at his confession.

"Did you do something to my family?!" I furiously accuse as realization dawns.

There is an awkward hesitation that makes my skin crawl.

"Yes," he admits without a glimmer of remorse. "I did."

Instantly, my mind clears.

"What… *how*… why would you do this?!" I shout at him, moving my hands around like I often do when I speak. "You can make people fight?"

"I am the God of War, after all." He reminds, matter-of-factly.

"How could you do this?" I scold angrily. "To me, to my family!"

"Selena, you are wasting time!" he counters.

"Can you stop them from fighting?" I interrogate bluntly.

"Of course, I can make them stop," Ares grumbles.

"Then do it," I demand firmly, refusing to move.

"But they will come after you," he chirps.

"Do you want to see me?" I question knowing he does.

"Definitely!" I can hear Ares pouting like a disappointed teen.

"Then take your *'spell'* off of them and I'll find you."

"How do I know I can trust you to keep your word?" he huffs his frustration.

"You'll just have to trust me," I state with a no-nonsense tone.

There is another bout of silence as he ponders my request.

At last, he responds.

"Fine," the God of War snarls. "I will return them to their natural state."

Making sure Ares has done what he has promised, I lower my defenses, and allow my mind to open to my mother's thoughts. Her mind is clearing. The only thoughts she has now are those of confusion. Similarly, Ligeia and Leukosia also becomes placid, mellow. No longer are their ideas murderous, but contemplative and regretful. Suddenly, my mind is flooded by their questions, so I turn it off once more.

Where's Ando?

'Ando?' I reach out with my mind. *'Ando! Where are you?'*

A few tense seconds pass before he answers.

'I'm here, Lena!' he replies. *'I'm on Paradiso! I'm okay!'*

Thank goodness!

"Thank you," I say to the space around me knowing that wherever Ares is, he can hear me.

"You are welcome, my dearest Selena," he purrs like a cat stretching as he wakes from a long nap.

"Why did you do that?" more than a little curious, I ask.

"Do what?" he pretends to be clueless.

"Make my family members turn on each other."

He says nothing.

"Answer me," I nudge more aggressively.

When the silence becomes too much to ignore, he finally reveals his intentions.

"I need to show you something before you complete *The Joining*."

Utterly stunned by his knowledge of this extremely private Siren ceremony, knowing it is a heavily guarded secret, I quiz:

"How do you know about that?"

"I have been around for an extremely long time, Selena," resolutely, he boasts.

Staying in the same spot, skillfully, I tread water, debating whether to return to my family or go to him.

"I don't know if I can trust you," I spit like a cobra striking at an unsuspecting mouse.

"I would never hurt you," his words rush out making me believe him. Almost.

"Please, give me just five minutes," Ares begs.

All of my commonsense screams *'stay put'* but passion urges me to find him, to be with him no matter what the cost. No matter what the sacrifice. Whether it be my family or Andrew.

Dear Father! What about Andrew?

"Selena, just five minutes," he compels. "I need to show you something."

Steeling what is left of my dwindling resolve, I take several deep inhales of seawater into my gills. The invisible element fills my body and strengthens it… revitalizes it… clearing my head of all contradicting ideas, desires.

Before I can review the question, my mouth blurts:

"Will I be safe with you?"

Ares says only one word.

"Always."

CHAPTER THIRTEEN

t this moment, the Tyrrhenian Sea is warmer than it has been since I arrived in the Mediterranean. It feels like I am swimming in a bathtub rather than the sea. Somewhat timidly, I hold the god's hand, fearful of being without him. Shyly, I open my mouth to say something, but change my mind before I can speak my concerns. Instead, I swallow what little saliva I have left and almost panic as it gets stuck in my throat. Slowly, my breath ekes by as it slides down my contracting esophagus and into my lungs at last. Thank heavens my gills remember how to do their job because right now, I do not.

"Are you alright, Selena?" Ares questions, his silky voice tainted with worry.

I nod but tighten my grip around his warm palm.

"Are you having trouble breathing?" His empathy fills the space around him, and I smile.

"I'll be fine," I pretend, knowing that it is due to his close proximity that my entire body, from the roots of my hair to my talon-adorned webbed-feet, is affected by him, by this powerful timeless god.

"Where are we going?" I finally manage to ask.

This time he smiles, his amethyst irises practically glowing.

"I need you to trust me," the Olympian whispers, his sweet breath caressing my earlobe, making it even more difficult to keep my guard up.

"That doesn't answer my question," I tease, trying to continue my tough Sireny façade, but failing miserably.

My comment makes him chuckle deviously as he places his right palm on my cheek.

"I have waited for you for many years, Selena," he reveals tenderly, meekly. "You are special."

"Hmm," I huff. "I seriously doubt that."

Like a majestic lion, he shakes his golden mane as he removes his hand from my face. Immediately, I feel lost; lost like a song trapped in a composer's brain needing to be written, needing to be sung.

"I want to show you something, but I need you to have an open mind," Ares discloses, his expression sincere. "Can you do that?"

This time, I nod.

"Close your eyes and hold on tight," he requests. No longer able to resist his charms, I do as I am told, but before I can brace myself for whatever is coming next, I hear the sound of rushing wind in my ears and smell the salty brine of the ocean followed by the inability to breathe. Fortunately, my gills retract allowing my lungs to switch on, so instead of passing out, oxygen begins pumping through my form again.

Needing to see what is happening, I make the mistake of opening my eyes.

"What the hell?!" I squeal in Ares' ears making him wince. *"You can fly?!"*

Quickly, he tightens his grip around my waist, my back to his front, his muscular chest pressing against me. He smells of subtle cologne and sunshine. Eagerly, I inhale; memorizing its light woodsy notes mixed with hints of oak and bergamot. It is intoxicating.

"Do not look down," he orders, but for reasons unknown his words do not register.

"What did you say—" I glance down, and my brain seizes, and the sudden shock causes my talons to jab into his encircling arms. *"Oh my gosh!"*

"Ouch!" Ares bellows as a trickle of crimson appears on his forearms, the color actually quite exquisite against his naturally tanned complexion. "Would you please retract your talons?!"

"I'm so sorry!" I apologize as my cheeks redden. "I wasn't expecting *this*!"

Overwhelmed, I wave trembling hands at the clear sky around us.

Far beneath us, gently undulating waves continue their sensuous dance honoring the Greek Moon Goddess, Selene. Above, not a single cloud mars the heavenly violet-blue canvas speckled with sparkling stars like Dutch post-impressionist painter, Vincent van Gogh's *The Starry Night*.

Immediately, my talons return to their usual resting place beneath my cuticles. Thank goodness they are less painful retreating than advancing. I love that they are my own personal bayonets.

"Much better," Ares sighs as we both watch as the droplets of blood are reabsorbed by his skin.

"Wow!" I exclaim. "Not even Sirens can do that!"

"Do what?"

"Our blood doesn't go back into our bodies like yours does," I reveal then snap my mouth closed aware that I have let valuable information about my kind out to a possible enemy.

"Do you still need those?" the god quizzes as he glances down at my bare feet.

Following his downcast gaze, I notice my honey-colored webbing still remains along with my scales. Self-conscious about him seeing me in this condition, I blush again.

"I forgot about those," I admit. "I guess I have embraced my inner fish."

"Your inner fish?" he grins. "That is adorable!"

Completely embarrassed at my nervous condition, I stay quiet as we fly for at least a half an hour toward the distant horizon in comfortable silence. Looking behind us nothing can be seen of the rocky coastline of Capri or of the towering cliffs anymore; all that remains is obscurity and the seductive tune of a gentle sea. I cannot imagine anything better.

"You still haven't told me where you're taking me," I remind my pilot.

"I am taking you to the east coast of Sicily," he replies with a wry smile.

"What's there?" I interrogate, enjoying the cool night air.

"Be patient, young one," Ares requests with a crooked smile that makes me giggle.

Hmm, someone else calling me 'young one'.

"Over there," he points, bringing me back to the present. "We are almost to our destination."

Not too far ahead, I notice a dark, purple shape in the distance, and as we get closer, I recognize it is a mountain, an extremely colossal mountain jutting toward the on-looking moon. The sloping lands and surrounding plains are dotted with a few settlements around the base along with several wide-spreading vineyards and meticulously kept orchards. The air is scented with the fragrance of rich volcanic soil combined with dew covered foliage.

Skillfully and gently, he reduces his jet-like propulsion, slowing to a more manageable speed. Then, like a blonde *Superman* and I his *Lois*, we slowly descend, landing softly atop the mass' summit, sure-footed and precise.

Reluctantly, he releases me, but keeps ahold of my hand. Bravely, I move closer to the edge to scan below, and am not surprised that objects seem like doll's furniture from this height. The sight truly takes my breath away. It is both peaceful and eerie at the same time, but even though the setting is awe-inspiring, my thoughts race back to the family members that I have deserted.

Ares, sensing my reservations, tightens his grip on my hand and as if by magic, my apprehension vanishes, and curiosity replaces it. Now, all I can think about is *his* proximity and how incredible it feels to be free, free from Siren obligations and Human expectations.

Honestly, I wish it could last forever.

"It is extremely windy this high up," my travel companion informs. "Keep close. I do not want you to get blown off of the mountain."

"I don't want to fall off either." I snicker.

His expression remains blank.

"What is this place?" I ask in a whisper.

"This is Mount Etna," Ares, the embodiment of conflict whispers back, still holding my hand.

"Is this a volcano?" I probe, remembering the same smell in the surrounding waters of Ischia.

"Yes, yes, it is." He beams, impressed by my astute observation. "It is inactive at the moment. How did you know it was a volcano?"

"I can smell the volcanic glass," I blush.

"Impressive," he commends with a twinkle in his bright irises.

Breaking our connection, the gorgeous male points in the direction of the valley almost four thousand meters below. The height is overwhelming. Instantly, all of the hairs on my arms stand on end as visions of a strong gust of wind blowing me off accosts my mind; hopefully, Ares is fast enough to catch me before I go *'Splat!'*

Sensing my need to explore, he reluctantly releases my hand.

"Take a look around," he encourages. "But do not get too close to the edge."

With a slight nod, I acknowledge his warning, already missing the warmth of his grip.

"We're so high up!" I gasp, peering over the edge.

"Be careful," he warns more sternly.

But instead of listening, I ignore him for the moment, close my eyes and take a deep breath allowing large quantities of cold pristine air to fill my lungs. Instantly, I feel more like myself (there must be considerable amounts of obsidian in this valley). After doing this for several minutes, I cautiously begin to explore, staying within sight of Ares.

The lush valley is sparsely lit with subtle illumination coming from nearby homes, and even from this elevation my supernatural hearing picks out the soft neighing of horses, muffled cattle calls, the occasional barking dog, and the faint human voices that are still out and about.

"Why are we here?" I turn back to my companion.

Unhurriedly, he strides toward me, hand outstretched and I take it willingly, but this time I do not feel just warmth. I sense something else, something dark and ominous, something ancient and powerful. It startles me at first, but then I find it alluring, and then I notice it. The air around this man... *this god...* crackles like fireworks bursting forth as they reveal their strength. Everything about him exudes confidence.

"What do you see?" Ares probes.

I pause, contemplating his question.

"Farmland, breathtaking scenery, peacefulness," I reply, sheepishly, mesmerized by the swirling whisps of electric energy that surrounds his body like a tangible aura.

Cautiously, he guides me closer to the edge, but I am not afraid.

"Do you know what I see?" his tone hardens.

Taken aback by his sudden change in demeanor, I shake my head.

"Tell me," I implore, my interest growing.

The Son of Zeus inhales deeply, the motion causing his chest to expand.

"I see specks of lowly unevolved creatures that need guidance and purpose," his tone is cold, clipped, and no longer comforting.

"What?!" My mouth gapes at his confession. "How can you say that?"

"It is true," he states unemotionally like we are discussing the weather or vacation plans.

"You're wrong!" I fire back, releasing his hand.

"What have they accomplished in the brief time they have been on this earth?" he replies dryly. "Nothing, absolutely: nothing."

My body tenses and my palms begin to sweat.

"How can you say that?"

"I say that because it is accurate," he replies gruffly. "Look at them. Truly look at them."

With that statement, he touches one finger to my temple, and a wave of heat combined with anger and hatred fills my thoughts.

Visions of wars both past and present engulf me. The weeping of motherless children fills my brain. Brothers fighting brothers strike my senses, and all of the injustices for thousands of years fill my soul.

"What's happening?" I groan in agony, knowing that this is his doing.

"I am showing you the downfalls of humanity, Selena," he confesses.

"Why are you showing them to me?"

"Because you… *We* can fix them… fix humans," he states plainly.

"I don't understand," I simper, then remember who or rather *what* I am.

"Together we can rule this place, this world," he blurts unapologetically. "We can make this planet the paradise it was meant to be."

"I still don't under— "

"Truly look!"

Following his instructions, I stare at the valley once more, but this time I hone my senses so I can see and hear a local vintner beating his teenage son for accidentally tripping and thereby crushing a basket of freshly picked grapes. In another home, I hear a baby's hungry whimpers as it lies in its crib and my heart tightens.

As I continue, a disturbing smell creeps into my nasal cavity, and I realize it is the scent of human decay. Even with the wind, it pervades the entire valley floor. The odor is foul and repulsive.

"What is that awful smell?" I gag, already knowing what it is.

Ares pauses.

"You know what it is," Ares states, turning away from the edge of Mount Etna.

Compelled to know more, I sniff again. Immediately my Siren-senses decipher the decay as human in nature and that it has been decomposing for only a few short months. It is a woman, *was* a woman. The scent emulates from the barn on the vintner's property. I am positive. Suddenly, distress followed by pure unadulterated rage fills me and I grimace, disturbed at my newfound abilities.

"Why are you showing me this?" I growl, feeling sick to my stomach.

Again, Ares places a finger to my temple and that same energy zaps me, only this time, I feel as if it wraps around my mind and my heart. Disappointment dissipates allowing *something else* to bubble and ebb to the surface This time, I do not fight it. I just stand with my eyes closed allowing all of it to pour into me like a clay vase. It snakes through me, and I enjoy it.

This new sensation suppresses all of my worry, strife, and teen angst about being this supernatural being. The weight of the world no longer rests on my shoulders, bringing me down. No. For the first time since learning what I am, I feel *weightless*.

I feel free!

"Thank you," I say, placing my hands on either side of his face.

"For what?" He watches me through heavy-lidded eyes.

"For allowing me to see through your eyes," I sincerely thank.

"You were created for this, Selena," he reassures. "You are a Siren… a descendant of gods… you are worthy of this honor."

A smile spreads over my face as his compliment sinks in.

"This will be my gift to you," Ares, God of War promises, his tone overflowing with resolve.

As we stand with bodies pressed against each other, the wind blows stronger. Its icy fingers thread through my hair creating a whirlwind of dark spiral curls, but the cold temperature no longer bothers me. Even the faint sound of my mother's voice trying to contact me does not concern me. Ando tries to get my attention too, but I easily shut his thoughts out of my brain. The aunts try as well and it is a little harder to block them, but eventually I succeed.

"How do you feel?" Ares queries.

Immediately, I answer.

"I feel invincible." I smile confidently.

"I am glad," he praises as he lowers his head to mine and places a brief kiss on my lips.

Even when he pulls away, my eyes remain close as I stand enjoying this new freedom from human guilt.

"Open your eyes, Selena," his manly voice beckons. "Look at your kingdom."

Slowly, purposefully, I open my eyes and drink it all in.

The wonder.

The awe of this place.

It is everything I have ever desired.

"This is mine?" my voice wonder-filled at the gift he offers.

"It can be," his words swoon inside of my head. "All you have to do is want it."

I do want it.

I want all of it.

Acapella

I deserve it.

Seductively, Ares takes my hand, his fingers gently glide over my heated skin making my toes curl.

"Do you want it, dear… sweet… lovely, Selena?" he probes as he encircles my waist with sturdy arms.

As I stand watching the world below, it all suddenly becomes clear.

"Yes, I want it," I grin. "I want it all."

CHAPTER FOURTEEN

On padded paws, I sneak into the villa through my unlocked bedroom window, successfully avoiding my parents and brother.

Quickly, I race to the bathroom and shower, brush my teeth and comb my hair securing it in a loose bun to keep it out of my face. Awkwardly, I change into a pair of black sweatpants and a white and black baseball t-shirt. I manage to reach halfway down the hallway and almost to the sanctuary of my room before I am faced with all three of my immediate family members who stand wearing scowls and raised eyebrows.

It would be funny if I were not so tired.

"Where have you been?" David interrogates first.

"Out," is my only explanation.

"We've been worried sick," Marina speaks next, her right foot tapping silently against the hard floor. "Why didn't you answer my call?"

Being defiant, I shrug my shoulders knowing that my mother hates when anyone does that.

"I was perfectly safe," I educate with a lighthearted grin which only adds gasoline to the flame.

My parents stare at me without answering.

"Is there any leftover dinner?" I add, hearing my growling stomach.

"This isn't a joke," Mom reprimands as she continues to glare at me.

"Jeez!" I insult, maneuvering around each person, making my way to the kitchen.

Not appreciating my rude behavior, my mother opens her mouth to speak, but I interrupt without a second thought.

"There's no reason to be concerned," I state with a nonchalant hand gesture. "I can take care of myself."

Ando just frowns at me with that all-knowing expression he has developed.

"The aunts and I searched for most of the night for you," Mom reveals with a misty gaze. "We thought… we all thought…"

"I'm fine," I interject, annoyed at her overreaction.

"Selena—" David finally responds, but I cut him off with a raised hand.

"See?" I say turning around like I am modeling a new outfit. "Everything is intact."

After several minutes of avoiding further questions, we finally reach the kitchen. It feels like the longest walk in history. I imagine this is how death row inmates feel as they trudge down the long corridor to their doom.

Now starving, I head directly to the refrigerator and begin searching for something to eat. To my delight, I find a container with fried chicken and another covered dish of macaroni and cheese.

Just what the doctor ordered!

Famished, I grab a drumstick out of the bowl and take a large bite. I moan with pleasure when my taste buds register the perfectly seasoned meat. I do not even bother to heat the macaroni and cheese or to grab a fork, instead I opt for using my hand to break off chucks and shove them directly into my mouth. Shocked, my family stares at me for several long moments as I devour almost all of it.

"What is the matter with you?" David's expression is grave.

"Why are you being so disrespectful?" Mom shakes her head in disbelief.

"Where were you?" David repeats his previous question more sternly.

"I was in Sicily," I grin, remembering the night's events.

Mom's eyes widen.

"How did you get to Sicily?" she gasps.

I remain silent.

"Answer your mother," David tags into the ring like a professional wrestler during a match.

Stubbornly, I still refuse to answer.

Unexpectedly, Ando chimes in.

"She was with Ares."

Surprised he would tell on me, I glare at him wishing I could tear his throat out. It takes all of my self-control not to. However, in my mind, I have already done it, and it was vicious.

"What?" I snap. "How do you know this? Oh, wait, your dreams?"

With my fury barely in check, I step closer to him, but before I can reach him, David steps between us.

"Ares?" David's voice deepens. "Who is Ares?"

My brother watches me. The gears in his head turning as his thoughts are processing. I know that look well.

"That's none of your business," I say, trying to step around my stepfather's towering body, but he blocks my way.

Maniacally, I chuckle knowing that I could get past him if I really wanted to; his expression tells me that he knows it too.

"Ares is the God of War," Ando blurts. "She went to Mount Etna with him."

"Shut-up you freak!" I shout, making them all jump.

"He did something to her," he continues.

"I said, *shut up!*"

"I'm not sure, but I think he's taken her soul," my younger brother adds shakily.

"What do mean, he's taken her soul?" Mom probes with quivering lips.

Ando closes his eyes like he is accessing a distant memory.

"Like how he made you and the aunts fight each other," he mumbles almost at an inaudible volume.

The rest of us glare at him with wide eyes and wider mouths.

"You have to save her!" he shouts.

Without thought, I shove David away and lunge at the boy, striking him on the cheek, startling myself along with my observers. Mom's anguished cry hurts my ears and for a second, I regret my actions. Fortunately, the guilt disappears just as quickly as it formed.

"Selena! No more!" My stepdad bellows then lunges forward and grabs me, but I twist my body to one side and slip out of his grasp. My mother rushes toward me next, grabbing me by the shoulders. Ando stands perfectly still, unblinking, holding his cheek with both hands.

"*Stop!*" Mom shouts, shaking me. "This isn't you, Selena!"

"Selena, snap out of it!" My stepfather's voice sounds hollow and small.

Briefly, I struggle against their grip and eventually break free. From both sides, they attack, one holding my legs while the other secures my arms.

"Let me go!" I struggle hoping to escape.

"Stop fighting us!" David orders before turning to his wife. "Is this because of her not doing *The Joining*?"

Marina nods.

"*I'll kill you!*" I spit like a cobra. "I swear... *I'll kill you all!*"

"Marina!" Dad yells into the din. "Just let her go!"

"But David— " my mother protests, but she is cut off.

"*We have to let her go!*" Ando shouts at them both.

Instantly, my limbs are my own again, and without a backwards glance, I race to the verandah toward the balcony railing, pausing briefly to gage the distance to the sea, and the direction of the wind in order to avoid slamming into the rocks below.

"Don't you dare!" Mom's shriek startles me, but I resume my mission.

'Lena!' my sibling's voice manifests inside my head. *'You've got to fight him! It's the only way to break the spell!'*

"Get out of my head, Ando!" I snarl and my voice no longer sounds normal.

"Do you remember what Great-Grandmother Melody said?"

Huh?

"When we were at the cottage in the woods, she told you something," he continues, eyes misty. "Something about your Aria?"

My thoughts travel back to that time period. I can picture the entire scene: the quaint cottage surrounded by tall trees. The scent of cookies intermingled with Melody's expensive perfume. The extraordinary garden outback that grows so many eclectic produce and flowers. I can even recall the waves of inspiration that the beautiful Muse exudes.

Then I hear her words inside of my head, like she is right here with me, looking through my eyes at the beckoning water far below.

She repeats:

'That… my dear… is your Aria… This aria is made for only you.'

I think for a moment before replying.

'I don't care about the stupid Aria. I don't care if my soul is lost.' I reply, feeling my heart harden… *literally.*

"You can't mean that," Mom says from a safe distance.

"I don't care about family or friends or even Andrew," I brag with indifference.

"You don't mean that, Lena." My brother's expression grows sadder.

As if in a trance, I stare down at the beckoning waves *calling* to me.

"I do mean it," I reply with all sincerity.

"Think about what you're giving up." Mom jumps in, her face ashen and covered with rivulets of tears.

I hear David next.

"I know that you care," he reminds and for a tiny second, I come to my senses, but in a blink, it is gone. "Ever since you were a toddler, you've cared about everyone and everything. It's your greatest quality."

Again, the waves call me. It tells me to come home, to be free.

"This is too much," I whisper. "All… too… much."

Slowly, I shake my head, hoping to get his disappointed expression out of my mind. For as long as I can remember, David has stood by me when I have acted like a brat or have been overly *'teenagery'*. He has even supported me when I sprouted scales and gills, and turned into a *fish-girl*, but in the long run, does any of that really matter?

And just like that the decision is made.

Resolutely, I answer.

"I only care about shedding this mortal disguise, this unhappy existence being torn between two worlds. In this skin, I am unable to show my true nature, my true face, scales and all… for fear of retaliation—" I pause, wanting to block out everything that I was raised to believe, everything that was a lie. "—fear of *Human* retaliation."

"What about your Aria, Lena?"

I look at his darling face and respond.

"There is no Aria," I glare. "I'm going Acapella."

"Take that back!" he yells, becoming furious.

"Right now, all I want is the freedom to not care so much," I confess my true desire.

My experience has shown that Sirens carry the weight of the world on their shoulders. They feel everything more strongly than other beings. All of our emotions are amplified and eventually that takes a toll on our lives.

"Lena!" Ando shouts again. "It's Ares! He wants you to feel this way! He wants *You!*"

Tired of talking, I shake my head, trying to block out his words. My eyes well with tears, but I ignore them. My thoughts return to the sea and losing myself in its briny embrace.

Then I do it.

Without hesitation, I do it.

Do the thing that will change my life forever...

I jump!

ACAPELLA

PART TWO

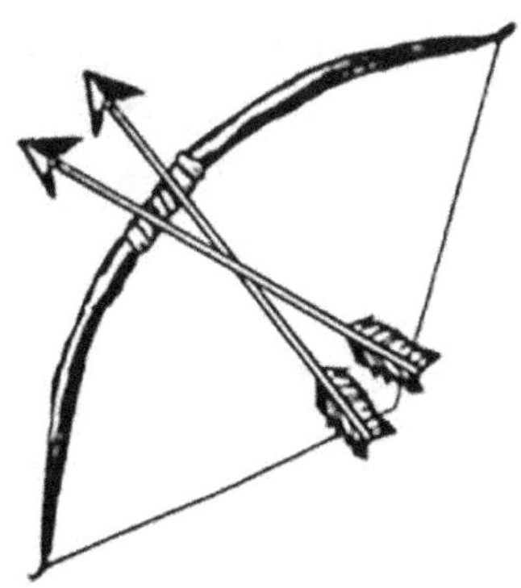

"THAT crazed girl improvising her music.

Her poetry, dancing upon the shore,

Her soul in division from itself

Climbing, falling She knew not where…"

—**William Butler Yates,**
The Collected Poems of W.B. Yates

CHAPTER FIFTEEN

The world is quiet as dawn approaches. Content for the moment, I sit watching another day emerge from atop my favorite stalagmite formation protruding out of the *Marina Piccola* harbor. Magically, the Mediterranean horizon transforms from deep violet to a moving pallet of vibrant streaks of golds, reds, and blues.

Normally, I would still be asleep in my room at the villa all snuggled in my bed as the sound of David's reverberating snores waft down the hallway while my little brother's baby snores follow. Mom does not make any sounds when she sleeps. It is like she is in a coma. I have never started a day without them close by, but today I begin it alone.

From high above, the cries of gulls and the flapping wings of pelicans making their daily journey to find food only causes me to covet their independence. Since I discovered that I am a Siren, my life has been filled with danger and uncertainty. Lately, especially,

I have found myself looking over my shoulder fearful of every shadow as I wait for the next villain to strike, but no more. It ends now.

Then, at last I hear it, or rather, I hear *her*.

"Selena," I hear Ligeia's voice coming from below the water's surface.

Immediately I look down, and at first all I see is agitated waves then her face comes into view as she hovers directly below the surface. She is stunning and scary at the same time, and almost looks like an expertly painted watercolor. Monet would have loved painting such a glorious subject.

"If my mother sent you to convince me to go back to the villa—" I answer before the request can be made, "—it's not going to happen."

"Marina did ask me to check on you," my aunt reveals in Siren language without guilt.

Searching for the blonde Siren, I scan the surface, but find no one.

"Is Leukosia with you?"

The redhead shakes her head.

"I am unaccompanied," she educates in that scholarly way she has.

"I'm serious, Tia," I blab. "I'm not going back."

"Why?" is her only inquisitive response.

"I'm tired of being pulled in two directions," I declare as I come to a standing position, being careful not to fall.

To my surprise, she studies me with sympathetic eyes.

"I can understand why you feel that way," her words are honest. "Fortunately, I have never had that conflict."

"You've never felt torn, *ever*?" I question with a frown.

Ligeia shakes her head.

"I have been married to the watery realm since I was born," she smiles revealing a flawless white smile.

Her comment inspired by my vivid imagination makes me picture a twilight wedding; her wearing a white dress holding a bouquet of pastel-colored water lilies *literally* marrying the sea, who is wearing a morning-blue tuxedo as Selene the Moon Goddess performs the ceremony. They swoon over each other as they exchange seashell wedding bands. The entire thought makes me chuckle.

"Tia Ligeia?"

"Yes?" her voice still comes from beneath the surface, making it more challenging to gage her mood.

I hesitate for a few seconds before asking, "May I tell you something?"

"Of course." Her attention is glued to me.

"I choose the sea too," I hear the words and they strengthen my conviction that I can be like my aunts and remove myself from humanity.

"I cannot fault you for that," the wise sea nymph replies, finally poking her head above the waterline.

"Ligeia?"

Solemnly, she listens. Listens as only another Siren can do. Hopefully, she will understand my dilemma.

"What is it, young one?"

"Exactly how long have you been alive?" I ask, hoping I have not offended her.

To my surprise, she laughs, loud and proud. When her laughter subsides, she speaks.

"I am older than you can fathom."

I giggle.

"Do you like being chained to your obligations?" I blurt. "I mean, are you truly happy being alone with only the sea and Tia Leukosia?"

Without losing a beat, she responds.

ACAPELLA

"It is my calling… my sole purpose. I am the bridge."

As she announces this, all around her, the seafoam capped waves sparkle like someone has just spilt a bottle of multicolored glitter over them. The vibrant color enhances her crimson mane making it resemble living flames. She looks so content, so at peace that it makes my heart ache that I still struggle with the choice.

Silently, we stare at each other until that familiar rhythmic bass combined with the steady beat of the percussion starts to mimic the pounding surf and immediately catches my attention. Like before, it begins soft and low then swells when it encounters air. There is no mistaking it.

"*Ares,*" I announce on a breathy moan, unable to control my outburst.

Ligeia turns to me and pleads.

"Do not sing, Selena!"

It is the first time I have ever seen her look concerned.

Ignoring her statement, I close my eyes and listen carefully. Masterfully, I isolate each note from the sounds of the morning: the calling gulls, the splashing of fish, the songs of whales, and the softly lapping sea. Immediately I recognize Ares' pleasant voice that already intermingles with the music in perfect synchronicity until it is impossible to distinguish it from Duran Duran's lead singer.

Knowing what I am about to do, Ligeia shouts, *"Selena! I forbid you to sing!"*

Unfortunately, I cannot not sing.

Caught in the moment, he sings the most mesmerizing rendition of *The Chauffeur* that I have ever heard and when Ares reaches the chorus, without hesitation, I begin to sing too, letting our voices serpentine and intertwine, bob and weave, stretch and grow until we are lost in the melody… lost in each other until the song ends.

Everything else fades away including my aunt.

Filled with joy, I smile and from the bough of the ship about a quarter of a mile away he smiles back, his amethyst eyes shimmering like rare jewels. He is impossibly handsome. Ridiculously mesmerizing and he knows this.

"You've gotten better," I compliment in a whisper knowing he can hear me even from this distance. "If that's possible since you were already amazing."

Just like Ando, he chuckles and blushes at the same time.

"That is quite a compliment coming from a Siren," Ares replies, his cheeks reddening several shades more.

ACAPELLA

Remembering that we are not alone, I make the mistake of glancing down at my aunt who silently treads water near the base of the stalagmite, debating what to do next. I drop my concentration briefly to hear her thoughts, but she too has erected a mental wall so difficult to breach that it actually gives me a headache. She looks up at me knowing that I am unable to spy on her.

The expression she wears is grave, and her customarily bright aquamarine eyes have transformed into an ominous shade of sapphire as her fire-red locks begin to slither of their accord like crimson snakes. The vision is the stuff of nightmares.

"What in Zeus' name have you done?" she shouts, the intensity assaults my eardrums.

Unnerved by the hideous sight, I form my reply and am about to speak when from my peripheral vision I see two fishermen tending their nets look up. Their eyes glazed over and docile. Immediately, they drop their equipment and dive head-first into the azure seawater.

"Chert!" My aunt growls in Siren as she disappears beneath the surface. I am not sure what that means, but I am positive it is not good.

Seconds later, she has returned the men to their boat and erased the damage that I have done. They shake their heads as if waking from a dream startled by their soggy clothing. The crafty Siren plants a memory of a partially blind wandering whale accidentally bumping into their vessel then convinces them to take the rest of the day off and return to shore.

Just as quickly as she left, she returns, but this time she is on the opposite side of the rock formation.

"You are always followed by chaos," my tia practically spits like a feral cat. "God of War indeed!"

Still on his yacht, Ares also makes the mistake of making eye contact with Aunt Ligeia who studies him, her facial expression now neutral, yet still terrifying.

"Ligeia," Ares acknowledges her presence with a respectful nod accompanied with a regal half bow.

My aunt nods back.

"Ares," she responds with a menacing scowl, her gaze locked onto his. "I did not expect the God of War had time to seduce baby Sirens."

Umm, baby?

Ares grins, amused for the moment at their strained, yet cordial banter.

"There are several wars going on as we speak. Why are you not there enjoying the carnage?" she blatantly mocks.

"What about you, my lady?" He jibes back, without fear.

Ligeia's eyes narrow and a crack of lightening whips across the sky, landing where, I do not know. In the wake of her growing fury, the air around us takes on a slight electrical charge and the water itself increases in density. From Ares' expression, he notices the bleakness in our surroundings too, but being *Ares*, he ignores the warning.

"I am certain there is a sick dolphin or a dying coral reef that needs tending to, but instead you are here… *vacationing*," he pokes back, disappointed when the ancient sea warrior's expression stays the same.

"Release her," Ligeia growls as she angles her body to better view the Olympian prince.

As the sky continues to darken, I can clearly see that he is moving toward the wheel of his vessel. Not surprisingly, he looks like a model in a boating magazine dressed in navy cargo shorts, a beige and navy striped, button-down shirt with tan boat-shoes. Naturally highlighted wisps of golden strands blown by the rapidly increasing summer breeze entangle in his long lashes, so long they appear artificial, and his beautiful smile is enhanced tenfold by his tanned skin.

Deftly, he steers the ship closer, unafraid of being near my more than formidable aunt. Personally, if it were me, I would be steering the yacht in the opposite direction. In fact, I would already be docked in Naples sipping a fruity beverage and nibbling on a sugary chocolate gelato cone.

Realizing this, I draw the conclusion that he is either extremely brave or mentally challenged, for my own peace of mind, I settle on brave.

"What are you doing?!" I snap at his reckless behavior. "You are taking your life into your own hands!"

He grins impishly, even though he stands on the verge of a duel with a more than formidable opponent; an opponent that I have seen subdue an eighteen-foot pregnant great white shark with one hand and a fully-grown male orca with the other (and that was on a bad day when she was not feeling well). Later, I determined it was from eating too many oysters the night before.

"I do not understand what you mean," the male god states coyly, using his overly abundant charm then suddenly realizing that his *charm* has no effect on this particular being.

I shake my head in disbelief.

"Provoking a Siren is not smart," I warn. "Not smart at all!"

"Listen to her, boy." Ligeia chimes in.

Ares only glares at her as he continues his task of ticking her off.

Oh boy!

"'*Boy?*' I am no boy," his voice deepens and another charge of electricity envelopes us. This time, I assume he is the cause. "*I am older than you, Siren!* I am one of the original twelve Olympian gods! *The son of Zeus and Hera!*"

Ligeia only stares; her face still unchanged. However, the expanse above tells another more sinister story. What was once a clear sky is now covered with clouds as black as coal which loom like a death-shroud over a breathless body, while the howling wind blows ice-cold and relentless. The feel of it against my skin is painfully sharp.

"You will show me some respect, half-breed!" he glowers, temporarily losing his cool.

Half-breed? My aunt he deems a half-breed? Then what exactly am I?

Within a minute, the *Anna-Sofia* stops a few yards away and drops anchor. Still unintimidated, Ligeia sends him a warning glare as the breeze strengthens to gale-force gusts that almost knock me off of my perch. Even Ares loses his balance once or twice. Elated with herself, my aunt grins when he grabs onto the railing to remain upright.

"Leave my niece alone, Ares," Ligeia calmly reasons as the wind increases again, causing the boat to rock violently.

"I will not," he answers, defiance radiating from his icy stare.

The Siren sighs and in that one sound is a plethora of pain and sorrow.

"You cannot have her," she warns as her talons appear. "She is just a child."

"In prior centuries, she would already be married with children," he reminds coolly.

Wait a doggon minute!

"*You! Cannot! Have! Her!*" The enraged Siren emphasizes each word as a dense fog rolls in blocking our spectacle from prying eyes, and then, without breaking a sweat, she creates a whirlpool below the *Anna-Sofia* making it spin.

Can gods die?

"*Stop!*" I shout, but she ignores me. "Aunt Ligeia! Please stop!"

As the vortex quickens and grows, the ship's hull creaks under the stress then begins to sink as it begins to be sucked into the sea with Ares clinging to it. Granted, I have imagined many scenarios where the god of war came face-to-face with one of the original Sirens, but a death-match had never occurred to me. I figured there was some unspoken supernatural code that could not be broken. Kind of like the signs in store windows stating:

No shirt... No shoes... No service!

Clear, concise, and understandable. I know now there is nothing like that. Perhaps this is why the ancient world had so much turmoil.

Dear Father!

"Cease your actions!" Ares orders gruffly from the pitching deck.

Stubborn to a fault, Ligeia spins the boat faster, so fast in fact that the wave caps are mostly foam.

"Do not make me hurt you, Ligeia!" the god bellows angrily, amethyst eyes glowing red.

"Release her!" my aunt shouts again and I think it is in Greek.

"I cannot!" he rages back. "I command you to cease your actions!"

When my aunt ignores his wishes, the air around him thickens and blurs, the salty spray burns with the nauseating funk of sulfur and ozone, then a blinding golden light engulfs him, and when it fades, Ares' true form is revealed. No longer appearing as a preppy college student, but a battle-god dressed in intricately embellished bronze armor, helmet and golden sandals on his feet. In his left hand a sturdy shield embossed with an octopus whose eyes are bejeweled with aquamarine gems, and in his right, an impressive spear obviously forged by *Hephaistos* the Greek God of the Forge. Even his four supernatural horses have specially designed armor around their athletic bodies.

As my eyes adjust, I realize he is no longer standing on the deck, but instead he floats several feet above it in a gold chariot pulled by four black, fire-breathing stallions. A sudden shiver travels down my spine as I study the entity before me. Every part of his physique exemplifies military prowess and courage, and I am drawn to him like a moth enticed by the flame.

"I will have her," he threatens, sending a warning bolt in her direction which she effortlessly dodges. "We will rule this world together!"

"Release her!" Ligeia repeats more emphatically. "Or I will kill you!"

"You will not!" Ares sneers with an upturned lip.

Ligeia, not one to make idle threats, raises both arms out of the water and calls upon the ocean's tallest and fiercest waves, and in the distance the sea swells as they develop and mature into high, angry walls of destruction.

"Aunt Ligeia, stop this!" I scream at the top of my lungs so I can be heard. "I've made my choice!"

As the first wave hits, I am pushed off of the rock into the water. Fortunately, my gills activate along with my scales and webbing. Unlike prior times, my body has learned to adapt to rapidly changing environments; however, nothing could have prepared it for this epic showdown between the *God of War* and one of the original *Sirens*.

While I am being battered by the surf, Ares, on the other hand, is still safe in his chariot as his ship disappears under the assaulting waves. Rage stretches across his features and the air around his chariot crackles and fumes like lava when it meets the sea.

"Ares!" I yell for him to notice me. "Be reasonable! Don't do this!"

"I was not the one who started this, Selena, but I will be the one to finish it!" he informs with a harsh growl, all signs of the gentleman I not so long ago met are gone.

"I doubt you will win anything," Ligeia teases, her features incensed as well.

As she speaks these words, a rapidly moving wave hits his chariot from behind causing it and the horses to crash into the Tyrrhenian Sea. Thankfully, he does not stay submerged for long and when he does reemerge, undeniable hatred mars his handsome features.

"If you want to live another day then you will leave!" he bellows at the top of his lungs as the wheels of his vehicle hover a foot above the waterline.

My aunt simply continues to stare, unaffected by his ultimatum.

"You do not frighten me!" she retorts, sending another battalion of waves his way. This time the strength of them throws Ares from his chariot into the turbulent sea.

Seeing her opportunity, the Siren races towards him, secures him in a chokehold and pulls him under.

"Please stop!" I scream as they vanish below the rolling whitecaps.

As I stand watching the swells increase, I see the brief glimmer of Ares' spear. With it he stabs at Ligeia, his weapon gashing her left side near the hip. Blood instantly appears, but that does not slow her down.

"Ligeia!" I screech like a barn owl.

Furiously, she slashes at him with her talons and lands several blows to his face and upper right arm. The water is now tinted red, and I worry about sharks coming to investigate. That would not be a good thing. Sharks are naturally hard to control, and when blood is added to the equation, there is no telling what might happen.

To make matters worse, another crop of blonde tresses emerge from the breakers.

Oh no!

"Aunt Leukosia!"

Frantically, she searches for her sister then recedes from view once again. Several seconds later, all goes quiet. Unnaturally quiet like the calm before an impending storm. As I helplessly tread water, a thunderous boom breaks the silence then all three reappear in a wail of screeches and shouts. Their bodies decorated with scratches, gashes, oozing open wounds, and dark bruises. At this rate, someone will definitely die. The idea of losing any of them makes me physically ill.

This has gone far enough!

Determined to get them to stop fighting, I grasp the volcanic glass charm and squeeze it in my left palm as I duck under the churning sea. Beneath, all I see are the three wrestling and battling to the death. My heart tightens and I get that swirling in my stomach that warns of what might come up.

Closing my eyes to concentrate while taking shallow breaths and tightly clenching the glass, I whisper:

"Flame."

Just like when I fought Amphitrite, the water temperature around me becomes hotter and hotter.

"Stop this!" I instruct loudly in Siren. "I will not ask again!"

Ignoring me, they continue which only makes me more determined, angrier.

"I command the earth to shake!" I continue chanting.

Again, the power fills every crevice of my body, radiating from my pores like pheromones. My head becomes dizzy, and the energy that I feel is more addictive than dark chocolate. Every cell in my body is buzzing!

From far away, I hear the Sirens calling me.

"Selena!" They shout in unison.

Ignoring them, I refocus my gaze on the task at hand, separating them. Like in a dream, I hear them gasp as their bodies are gently relocated several feet apart, out of harm's way.

Then I turn my effort to Ares' yacht.

Using the entire ocean's power to fuel my efforts, I concentrate.

"Gaia, Mother of the Earth," I begin, not really knowing what to say, but allowing my instincts to lead the way. "Mother of the mighty Titans! Let the strength of the Sirens flowing through my veins manifest and become corporeal!"

Suddenly, my skin begins to tingle where the glass touches until it practically burns. My flesh is on fire, but I cannot suppress what I have awakened, and beside me, something moves as if the ocean has taken a solid form.

"Veniforas!"

Every part of my body begins to burn, from the roots of my hair to my taloned feet and the unseen entity that I have created grows larger.

"Veniforas!" I state, louder, bolder.

Sweat particles appear above my upper lip.

"Veniforas!" My volume increases. *"I command you to do my will!"*

"Selena, wait! Do not do this for me!" Ares shouts, but I cannot stop. Consumed, I become more reticent than before. *How can I possess so much power?*

"Veniforas!" I shout and hear the sound of my own voice in the water surrounding me.

Surprisingly, I am the only Siren who can speak underwater. *Damn!* That still amazes me being able to do something that Mom and the aunts cannot.

'*Stubborn child!*' Ligeia bellows in my head. '*There are consequences for using all of this power!*'

Pretending not to hear her warning, I shout again.

"Veniforas! I command you… Come Forth!"

At my will, the sea begins to move in slow motion; it is weird and a bit disturbing. Leukosia and Ligeia are calling to me, but their words are too lethargic to recognize, even Ares is moving at a snail's pace. Only I seem to be moving normally.

"Come Forth… *Veniforas!"* I call out again. *"Encantato siempre, Veniforas! Acum! Acum!"*

At last, it happens.

As the particles of sand resettle onto the bottom, I see the *Anna-Sofia* resting upright on the seabed, its hull undamaged and without a scratch. It looks great except for being more than a little waterlogged. Below the ship, the sand begins to shift and whirl, creating a gigantic upside-down whirlpool that I use to secure the several ton sailing vessel. As I watch, the water pushes it up to the surface where it rights itself.

Proud of my success, I stand on the sandy sea bottom staring at the shadow above me where the *Anna-Sofia* now waits; all the while my aunts and the God of War stare at me.

CHAPTER SIXTEEN

Needless to say, Ares sped off on his yacht choosing to remove his presence from the Siren conference currently occurring. My aunts of course, are lecturing me about the hazards of falling in love with an unpredictable supernatural being like the God of War. Patiently, I sit on one of several secluded beaches near Capri not too far from the *Marina Piccolo.*

"Are you out of your Siren mind?" Leukosia huffs as she paces in front of me (I guess it is a family trait, on both sides).

Ligeia sits several feet away mumbling and grumbling about the perils that young maidens face when gods want them for their own. Her voice is clipped and harsh. If it is possible, she appears to be even more distressed.

Ligeia rambles, "I remember Zeus' shenanigans when he transformed himself into a shower of gold to seduce, Danaë, the daughter of Acrisius, King of Argos."

Leukosia agrees, nodding in remembrance.

"Perseus resulted from that affair," the second Siren reaffirms.

"What's wrong with that?" I make the mistake of asking, earning a look of disgust.

"The entire city of Argos was destroyed when Acrisius threw his daughter and her newborn son into the sea," Leukosia informs with a mighty huff. "Thank heavens the princess and Perseus were saved from certain death—"

"*By us!*" Ligeia bursts out. "Zeus summoned *us* to fix his *'problem'*!"

Then she rants in the original Siren tongue and whatever she is saying makes her sister almost blush, almost.

My eyes widen with shock when I recognize the word for *'poop'* and one other shocking expletive regarding procreation and mothers.

"It never ends well!" The redheaded Siren complains as she flails her arms over her head lost in her own rant.

"I'm not going to shack-up with Ares!" I blurt loudly. "I'm only sixteen!"

"What about calling on Gaia?" they both remind.

"You must be insane!" Leukosia continues alone, ignoring the ongoing ruckus coming from the direction of her sister.

"You never abuse the power of the Earth!" Ligeia growls. *"Never!"*

The sound of damp sand being thrown into the air and landing with a muffled thump makes me glance over at Aunt Ligeia who is now on her feet kicking furiously at the beach, her olive complexion now ruddy and overheated. Finally, she notices me staring and uses her powers to call a bolt of lightning that strikes a few feet away from where I am sitting. The electric current lingers in the air making my hair frizz under the static charge.

"I can handle it," I announce confidently. "I can—"

"There are *always* consequences to one's actions, Selena!" Ligeia interrupts. "Sirens are not immune to this!"

I pout, avoiding her disappointed look.

"Melody learned that the hard way!" Leukosia exclaims and is halted from saying any more by Ligeia's steely glare.

"What?" I ask, studying their pained expressions.

'Stupid child!' I hear Ligeia berate me internally.

She even has the audacity to clickity-clack the word, *Idiot!*

"I am not an idiot," I mumble under my breath loud enough for her to hear me.

"You certainly are an idiot!" she chortles. "You have Zeus' stubbornness and propensity for wanting what does not belong to you."

Then she makes the most ridiculous face at me. I cannot believe my brother taught her how to do that. It is strange to see a several thousand-year-old mythological sea nymph sticking out her tongue like a loopy lizard. I should start calling her Vern. Vern is the name Ando gives to every lizard he meets whether it is a boy or a girl. I guess being loopy is a family trait.

"You're being overdramatic," I insult, not making eye contact for fear of receiving her full wrath.

"Do not insult me, young lady," Ligeia cautions.

"What did I say?" I ask feeling no guilt.

"Vern?" she scoffs. "I am no Vern! Vern indeed."

"Stop invading my mind!" I bark viciously, tired of explaining myself. "That's an invasion of privacy! Or don't they teach you about that in Siren one-O-one?"

"You will do as you are told, young one!" Ligeia fires back. "You will stay away from Ares, or I will—"

"Or you'll what?" I shout at the top of my lungs. "Kill him?"

She glares at me, lips pursed tightly together.

"Obviously, you can't kill him," I mock. "You are evenly matched."

Angrily, she throws insults at me in ancient Greek.

"Ha!" I laugh. "I don't understand what you are saying, so double Ha!"

That did it!

Ligeia advances towards me, but I refuse to cower, not even to her.

"*Stop it!*" Leukosia snaps, jumping between us. "You two are behaving like infants, whining, and bickering! It is a wonder why I have not kicked both of you off of this beach! Why did you have to be just like Zeus?"

Suddenly, my aunt's words pierce my brain.

"Wait!" I exclaim, realizing that this is the second reference to my connection with Zeus in less than a minute. "Explain what you just said."

Leukosia covers her mouth with her hand, her face pales and Ligeia rolls her eyes.

"How could I have *Zeus'* traits?" My eyes narrow too.

They both stare at me like I have just sprouted another head.

"I thought Zeus was in love with Melody, I mean Melpomene, my great grandmother, *ugg!* You know what I mean."

They remain silent.

Then I understand. Truly understand why the Father of the Gods created a protected island for a Muse.

"Zeus breathed life into her form," I recall to no one in particular. "His *'life force'* animated her."

All is quiet as I speak aloud.

"Why would gods and goddesses fear *us*?" I continue, letting my mind remember what I have learned thus far.

We are intelligent.

Strong, and fierce.

Well-versed in every battle skill and strategy.

We are cunning seductresses.

Other beings fear and admire us.

Poseidon, Ruler of the Seas, also helped to create Melody. He physically molded her in his likeness. Something that comes as close to being unselfish as an arrogant god could do.

"We are just as powerful as the gods," I say aloud so my aunts can hear.

As all of these thoughts converge, merge, collide, and then reform, the stunning realization slams into me hard. Finally, the blinders that I have worn for my entire short-lived existence suddenly breakaway, and in their absence, I am exposed to my true nature, my true self, and for better or worse, the harsh reality of my lineage has been laid naked at my feet.

"Zeus didn't love her in a *passionate* way." I steady my voice. "He loved her because she was his daughter!"

They both nod, reluctantly, yes.

"Loosely translated," they answer together. "We contain his *'life force'*, yes."

"But that would mean that Ares and I—"

"He is your distant uncle," they pause. "In Human definitions, you are similar to a niece."

A few minutes pass before I whimper.

"You should have told me," I sneer. "All of it."

"We did not know how to tell you." They both confess. "How could we know you and Ares would be, *close*?"

"Do you think he knows that I am his distant relative?" I question feeling sick to my stomach, a heaviness growing on my soul. "I mean, *'lifeforce'* is almost the same as *'blood'*."

"We are sure he understands," they say, looking away.

Shocked, well, more than shocked, I stand peering at the outstretched blue expanse calling me home. The sun is high in the sky now; its rays should be warming my skin, but for some reason I feel cold and empty. Even the soft breeze no longer caresses my limbs.

"That's gross!" I shout, hearing the thunder in the distance, knowing I am the cause of it and not caring.

"It was not *'gross'* in the ancient world," the Sirens explain nonchalantly.

"I see," I mumble, wanting to disappear.

"Selena are you alright?" They question.

My stomach lurches and I stop for the moment needing to escape.

"May I go now?"

Their faces darken as I do not wait to be dismissed, but instead start walking toward the sea.

"Where are you going?" They both enquire. "Are you going home to your parents?"

I shake my head no.

"We forbid you to go back to Ares!" they shout.

"I'm not going to Ares," I admit with growing disgust.

Confused, they continue staring at me.

"How could you not tell me that I'm Zeus' *great-great-granddaughter*?" I shake my head in disbelief. "Now, I understand why Ares said that I am a descendant of gods, but not any gods, the most influential gods in the hierarchy of the gods."

The aunts appear bewildered.

"Marina did not want to overwhelm you with everything at once," Leukosia states meekly.

"This is too much," I reveal, turning to face the sea, needing to leave. "I don't want any of this. I just want to be left alone."

That is when I feel the first raindrop. It hits me in the middle of the forehead making me look up. Overhead, the sky is now dark with storm clouds blocking the sun. A few seconds more and an onslaught of rain beats down on us, followed by cracks of lightning and booming rolls of thunder.

I know that I am causing the storm, but I no longer care. Deep inside my mind, I locate the *'switch'* that allows me to choose: Siren, Human or a combination of both. I turn it on *'Siren'*. Not a little, but all the way. I actually feel when my humanity turns off. There are no more human emotions left in me. They have left. I think the Sisters feel it too.

High above where we stand, the remaining white clouds begin to compress and darken too. The wind picks up speed and the once placid waves transform into slithering squirming sea serpents undulating in time to the worsening weather. Both aunts glare at me knowing that I am the cause.

"Selena?" They question in unison as the first flash of blue lightning brightens the gloomy heavens. "What did you do?"

"I want to be alone," I announce to no one in particular as the hurricane-strength gusts thrash my curls to and fro, but I stand insolently against its will.

"Do not abandon your humanity," Ligeia instructs sternly.

"I don't need it," I reply just as sternly, reducing the speed of the winds around me, but increasing it around my aunts. With difficulty, Leukosia steps cautiously towards me; her blonde mane slashing against her face like a legion of wicked whips.

"Of course, you need your humanity!" she pleads. "Even Ligeia and I cherish it! *Need it!*"

Her words do not register, and I continue to ignore her as I resume my walk.

"Where will you go?" Leukosia probes, voice competing against the rising volume of the oncoming storm.

"I'm going to Paradiso." I shrug, looking toward the gloomy horizon.

Then they glance at each other, then back at me, puzzled expressions on their exquisitely gorgeous faces.

"I do not know if that is wise," Leukosia speaks first.

"Why is that a bad idea?" I whine as I roll my eyes.

"Being alone too long for a Siren is not good," Ligeia replies next.

"I'm tired of talking," I respond, longing to be back in the sea.

"We will come with you," they both answer sweetly, making me more irritated.

Then the idea comes to me.

"I forbid you to enter the Siren Grotto or to inhabit Paradiso," I inform much too passively, and at this proclamation their radiant aquamarine irises dilate and morph to a deeper more dangerous hue.

"You cannot forbid us from going home," Ligeia's voice hardens as she challenges me.

When she reaches out to touch my shoulder, I spin around and grab her by the wrist. It does not appear to hurt her, but she is unable to escape my determined grip. Startled, she tries to pull away, but cannot. Coming to her sister's defense, Leukosia grabs my wrist, but before she can secure her hold, I yank it away and secure hers instead.

"Paradiso is mine," I sneer like a rabid dog. "It is my birthright!"

Unable to strike me, I look up in time to see another streak of lightning light up the heavens and realize that that streak came from one of the aunts.

"Scatter," I speak the word and the clouds obediently disperse and return to their previous state.

The aunts watch me curiously, their expressions grave.

"Stay away from Paradiso," I express again, slowly releasing their hands. "Or suffer the consequences."

Without another word, I quickly dash to the water's edge. In the distance, the sun shines down on the sea, its rays creating tiny glittering particles of warm light that sparkle against the aquamarine waves, but not even this sight, this wonder, warms my heart anymore.

Looking straight ahead, I wade into the warm water and dive beneath the surface. Like they are supposed to, my gills activate followed by my webbing, but this time I choose not to bring my scales to the surface. After all, there is nothing in the ocean that can harm me now.

Nothing at all.

I am truly…

… unequivocally…

Free.

CHAPTER SEVENTEEN

The swim from the harbor to the Siren Grotto is uneventful. No family members persuading me to come home. No gods or goddesses wanting to annihilate me for being a 'half-breed'. Only quiet and the peace of being liberated from familial obligations and restrictions. Now, as I swim through the long tunnel that leads from the cave into the second chamber, my eyes slowly begin to adjust to the bright lighting. Somehow, I telepathically request that the light dim and surprisingly, it does!

Wow!

As before, I catch a glimpse of land up ahead, but this time it is all mine. Everything the light touches including whatever lies beneath. Mine.

At a leisurely pace, I make my way toward the landmass. Knowing better, I ascend at a timed pace in order to avoid pressure in my ears. The water is warm, but not stifling and I can feel the particles of volcanic ashes and other metals in the water as they brush against my skin. After a few minutes, I break through the surface near the shallow part of the lagoon close to the beach.

"My grandmother and aunts all grew up here," I say to myself and smile. "Mom, for a time, did too."

Unhurried, I allow the current to wash me up onto the black, powder-like shore. Against my feet the texture is like finely ground powder. Fascinated by it, I take a little between my palms and rub with all of my Siren strength, and almost immediately it disintegrates.

Amused beyond words, I brush my hands off, and then leisurely make my way up the beach, lumbering through the soft sand toward the thick tree line surrounding the narrow stretch of shore. As I get closer, the sugary sweet scent of ripening pineapples tickles my nose, jogging my memory of the scratchy plants nearby. This area reminds me so much of Coconut Palm Beach near our house on Isla Flora, excluding the pineapples and black sand, of course.

Recalling the delightfully perfect fruit, I stop to pick one of the many ripe ones when it unexpectedly gets dark, extremely dark. So dark that I cannot see my hands in front of my face, and

Acapella

I wish I had a flashlight or a lighter. Then I remember the trick Mom showed me.

Turning my attention to the limestone cliffs stretching for a great distance upward, I recollect that there are hundreds, possibly thousands of small gaps in the limestone that allow light to enter.

"The island of Paradiso is protected by this huge limestone stack," I say to myself. "Like *the Faraglioni* and whatever happens outside, affects inside."

Knowing what I must do, I close my eyes and picture the sky outside beyond the walls. The slight breeze filtering throughout the space increases exponentially. The strength of it almost knocks me off my feet, and when the wind dies down, the cavern surrounding Paradiso starts to fill with muted sunshine.

Much better!

With that task done, I turn my attention to finding food. Practically starving, I start a fire with a small stack of dried twigs and leaves by clicking two of my talons together. The spark ignites after the third or fourth hit, surprisingly. Next thing I know, I have a well-built campfire. Silently, I watch as the persimmon-colored flames begin to grow and expand until every piece of kindling is engulfed with it. Warmth spreads across my limbs making me grin at my success.

What should I eat?

The shallows are teaming with all sorts of fish, everything from barramundi to slipper lobsters, grouper, and tuna, as well as tons of oysters, clams, and mussels that cling to the lagoon rocks.

After much deliberation, I decide on clams and inspect the area where the water meets the shore, and there along the beach are clams galore waiting to be found. With a glimmer in my eyes, I dig up a dozen or so and take them back to my makeshift cooking area.

Using wet seaweed that has washed onto shore as a covering to steam them, I pile them over the flames. About five minutes later, the shells crack open gifting me with the most succulent tasty morsels of meat. Already salty from the sea, they need no other seasoning.

After lunch is devoured, I split open a coconut and consume every last drop of its goodness. By the time I am finished, my lips and hands are sticky, but who cares. It is just me and the beautiful island I now call home.

The only thing that saddens me is the thought of not seeing Andrew and the rest of the gang again.

"Enjoying yourself?" I hear my mother's voice behind me.

The sound almost makes me jump out of my skin.

"I was," I respond, bombarded with annoyance.

"Your meal smells delicious," my mother compliments as she notices the discarded shells resting on the dying embers.

"It was." I do not elaborate as I kick sand onto the pit in order to put the fire out completely.

"Are you ready to come home?" Mom questions with pleading eyes.

"The villa is not my home," I do not look at her when I reply.

Mom opens her mouth to speak, but I cut her off.

"I've told you before. I'm already home," I grumble, eyes toward the cavern ceiling.

"Selena," Mom sighs. "The reason you feel this way is because you haven't completed *The Joining*."

"So what?!" I abruptly snap.

Ignoring my caustic tone, she slowly sits on the fallen log that acts as seating. Her movements are deliberate and steady as if she is trying her best not to spook me.

Am I that unpredictable?

Hmm.

I guess I am.

"The process gives you stability," she educates in that parental tone she has without a doubt mastered throughout her tenure as a mother. "Without that balance, you are shifting toward your true nature, your Siren side."

Suddenly, I feel tense. Needing to keep calm, I focus on the island. All around us, everything from the tops of the palm fronds to the limestone walls that hide Paradiso from the outside world is bathed in soft sunshine. Not harsh, glaring light like on an ordinary sunny day, but gentle and comforting.

Mom clears her throat to remind me that she is still there.

"Please sit," she requests, and out of habit, I comply.

Another soft gust of wind rushes past us rearranging my hair into my face.

"We've been worried about you," she reveals, reaching to touch my riotous curls, but I stop her before she can complete her action.

"Really?" is all I can say.

Ignoring my attitude, she looks up at the ceiling too.

"This place never ceases to amaze me," she announces softly. "Spectacular, isn't it?"

"It is," I whisper, keeping a neutral face.

Without asking, she takes my left hand in hers and I do not pull away. Quietly, we sit watching the shadows of clouds as they float weightlessly past the openings in the limestone. As we rest, avoiding eye contact, I hear her thoughts. I do not know when my telepathy switched on, but apparently it does so at the right time, allowing me to spy on my mother.

"I haven't lost my way!" I bark, rising quickly to a standing position.

Mom remains seated.

"You have," she says, voice calm and even.

"You don't know what you're talking about, Marina," I snarl then wait for her wrath, but it never comes.

Mom nods.

"I do understand," she adds. "Do you think you're the only Siren who has ever felt this way?"

This time, I nod.

"Well, you're not," she glares, and I take a step back, just in case.

As you know, Sirens are unpredictable, especially when provoked.

"Do you remember what age I was when I returned to the sea?"

"Yes," I reply. "You were sixteen."

"Do you know why I did that?" she interrogates, her eyes narrowing.

I think for a moment.

"You left because your father, Marcus, died," I whisper, feeling sorry for her.

She frowns.

"That's right," Mom sighs, and the heaviness of the sound hurts my heart. "I never told you how he died, did I?"

I shake my head.

My mother has never spoken about those details and I, not wanting to pry, never prodded her to spill the beans. I figured she would tell me if she wanted to. Since she never has, I thought it must have been unremarkable.

"He died because of me," she blurts, and tears instantly begin to roll down her cheeks. "I killed him."

Stunned, I sit down; my legs too shaky to remain standing. All I can do is stare at her in horror.

"Y-you… *killed* your father?" I stammer, not knowing what else to do. "How?"

My mother's right foot begins to tap, then her left and then both.

"My own mother told me about *The Calling* and *The Joining*," she begins as she wipes away her tears with an angry swipe. "But I didn't want to do either of them."

Still shocked, I stare at her, glued to every single word.

"I was a cocky teenager," she grins, but it is rather scary. "I thought I knew everything."

Her statement makes me squirm, realizing what she is implying.

"Yaya Parthenope and the aunts told me I had to do both," she responds with a snarky tone. "I told them I could control myself; after all, I was only half Siren."

Uneasily, I clear my throat; wishing this stunning piece of Mom's history was never revealed.

"The four of us had a terrible argument," she continues, her mind replaying the event. "And I left here, furious at all of them."

"You went back home?" I gulp, my tummy lurching. "Back to the villa?"

"Yes," she answers, tears starting anew.

"What happened next?" I mumble, feeling my innards winding around like snakes.

"Somehow, my mother got to the villa before I did," she frowns. "She had already told my father what had happened and of course, he took her side."

There is a long pause, a very uncomfortable long pause.

Finally, she continues.

"They were both yelling at me," she remembers, shutting her eyes, reliving the pain. "I got so—"

"Angry," I interrupt, understanding.

"Furious," she clarifies, expression stern.

My palms begin to sweat.

"I yelled back!" her voice grows louder. "I cursed; I started throwing things—"

Suddenly, she stands and starts to pace.

"I damned them to Hades for creating me!" my mother growls to herself. "I wished every horrible thing upon them and then…"

"And then, what?" I whisper, my temples throbbing.

Mom stops pacing and stares at the lagoon.

"I struck her," she whimpers.

My eyes widen.

"Yaya Parthenope?" I gulp.

My mother nods.

"Holy crap!" I blurt then cover my mouth with both hands.

"My father jumped between us to stop me—"

"But?" I interrupt, mesmerized by every detail.

"But I shoved him out of the way," she sniffles, the color in her face draining.

Double crap!

"I shoved him, and he fell and hit his head on the edge of his desk," Mom continues, her voice barely audible.

"Oh my God!" flies from my lips before I can halt it.

"My mother tried to heal him," she states blankly. "She tried."

Oh no!

"But he wouldn't wake up," the grief ridden Siren informs, the sound indescribable, and then her gaze focuses on me.

"So, you see," she says, wiping away the wet rivulets decorating her face. "I understand completely."

I do not know how much time passes before I speak.

"You're trying to trick me," I accuse hearing her thoughts once again. "You only told me about this because you want me to do what *you* want."

Mom nods and tries to speak, but I do not give her the opportunity.

"It's time for you to leave," I announce, wanting to be by myself.

"Dad and Ando have been missing you," my mother says sweetly, squeezing my hand. "I miss you too."

"Please tell them that I'm okay," I comment, changing the subject.

"Wouldn't you like to tell them yourself?" she questions optimistically.

"No," I answer without emotion then turn and begin walking toward the jungle.

My mother tries to follow me, but before she can take a step, I drop to my knees, placing both hands palms down flat on the warm sand. I do not know why I decide to do this, but something tells me that there is unseen power hidden deep beneath.

I close my eyes and concentrate.

In a hushed tone, I command, *"Veniforas."*

Mom's mouth gawks when she realizes what I am doing.

"Selena!" she shouts as she tries to pull my hands away from the ground. *"This is forbidden!"*

Fueled by adrenaline, I stop briefly to push her away. Unaware of my newly developing strength, she flies through the air, landing several yards away near the shoreline.

"Leave… This… Place!" I scream, almost hurting my throat.

Mom begins to sob; her eyes turn dark sapphire.

"There are consequences to using this power, Selena!" she informs, trying to stand. "Serious consequences!"

"Stay there!" I order, allowing the Earth's energy to surge from me.

To my surprise, she stays sprawled upon the water's edge, unable to move, face wet with tears.

"What consequences?" I ask arrogantly with a large smirk. "What could the punishment be for using powers that were clearly meant for me?"

Mom shakes her head in defeat.

"There's a reason why your great grandmother can't return to Paradiso," she whimpers, wiping away teardrops. "Don't go down this path, Selena! I beg you!"

Her words intrigue me, so I inquire calmly.

"What could a Muse possibly do that was so horrible she would get kicked out of paradise?"

My mother only glares at me with a sad expression, her eyes lined red.

"On the far west side of the island, there is something you need to see," she tells, finally able to rise to her feet. "There you will find the answers you seek."

Finally, her posture straightens, sadness morphing into disappointment.

"You don't know what you're playing with," she reminds. "Come home with me before it's too late."

Annoyed by her comment, my heartbeat accelerates, and my palms begin to sweat. Waning patience transforms into fury as I watch her, watching me. Before I can stop myself, I feel the *'switch'* being thrown. Everything I feel for her, good or bad, evaporates like snowflakes on a warm spring day.

"Whatever happens is your fault!" I yell, placing my hands back on the volcanic sand. "You shouldn't have kept secrets! You and the aunts want to control me!"

"I was trying to protect you, the family!" Marina shouts at the top of her lungs and the wind strengthens more, shaking several coconuts from the surrounding trees.

"Liar!"

Again, I tap into the Earth, filtering and amplifying the particles of obsidian on Paradiso to draw more energy. Without much effort, I fling her body into the middle of the shallows. Off balance, she does not have enough time to react. Taking the opportunity, I send another burst of energy her way which plunges her body into the deep where I use the strong current to take hold of her.

Unable to break free of the mini whirlpool, she is pulled downward and into the tunnel. Reading her mind, I know that it takes her only a second to call her scales, webbing, and talons.

'*Selena!*' she shouts inside of my head. '*I order you to stop this! Right now!*'

Finding it humorous, I laugh as I wade into the shallows then dive under already in full Siren-suit. Quickly, I grab her legs and begin to pull her out of the narrow channel into the Siren Grotto until we reach the entrance to the sea.

Without avail, her talons scrape at my scales, but they are not strong enough to do any damage.

'*You weren't trying to protect the family,*' I respond casually. '*You wanted to hide what we are. You wanted to control us!*'

'*That's not true! That's* The Surge *talking! Not you!*' she tries to wiggle out of my grasp but cannot.

The Surge? What's that?

'*You don't want to end up like Melody!*' she pleads. '*Fight it! You have to fight it!*'

Pretending not to hear her warning, I say aloud this time, not surprised that I can speak underwater:

"*Veniforas!* I command you, come forth! *Powers of the Interregnum* I order thee!"

'Listen to me, Selena!' she begs, once again. 'Please, the powers you're tapping into will consume you if you don't stop using them!'

"What would you know about it?" I reply in Siren.

'Because that's why I fought with the aunts and your grandmother!'

'What?' I switch to telepathy.

'That's why they were so upset with me!' Mom confesses with guilt. 'I tapped into the power of Paradiso and used it for my own personal gain!'

Huh?

'The power you're feeling is called The Surge!' she continues, still squirming. 'It's too much power for one person!'

Determined not to fall for her tricks, I shake my head.

"I'm in control, for the first time in my whole life and you can't stand it," I hiss vehemently. Once more, I repeat, "Come Forth… Veniforas."

As I speak, the sea begins to move in slow motion; everything looks strange especially my mother who is still determined to break free, but just like before, only I seem to be moving at regular speed. I do not know how I am doing this, but it feels amazing!

Illuminated by the jewels embedded in the grotto's walls, my scales shimmer in varying shades of aquamarine, silver, gold, and emerald with a smattering of onyx. In no hurry, I admire how they sparkle. Each one seems to be lit from within.

When we arrive at the cave's entrance, I scan the ocean and quickly find who I am looking for: *The Aunts!* As usual, they are tending to the wounds of an injured sea creature.

Great! They are distracted and their guard is down! Before they can block my mind probe, I invade their memories and locate the information that I need.

Ahh! There it is!

Then with all of my determination, I throw my mother out and away, far enough from the entrance as I can.

"Alhajiz," I say the word with authority which means *'barrier up'* in Arabic.

This immediately invokes the barrier spell which should keep any unwanted supernatural entities out which includes my aunts, Mom and even Ando. Filled with rage, she swims towards me, but runs into the invisible wall that now separates and seals the entrance from the rest of the world. With all of her might, she punches and kicks at it, but it does not budge.

"You can't do this!" Mom informs loudly with high-pitched clicks and clacks. "Take this down immediately!"

Shaking my head, I smile.

"I don't follow your rules anymore, *Marina*," I grin, blocking her thoughts.

Slowly, I turn, heading back to Paradiso.

"What about your family?" she shouts in Siren.

"I don't need a family anymore," I reply, turning my back on her dismissively. "I'm married to the sea."

CHAPTER EIGHTEEN

With my mother gone and the invisible barrier barring the entrance to the Siren Grotto, I swim back to the island with a light heart and a carefree attitude. This time, I take the opportunity to truly explore the tunnel and lagoon, wandering like a bard experiencing all of the wonders of Paradiso, my new dwelling.

Life below the surface is fascinating. Strange and unique sea life swims and plays without fear of other predators, except for me, of course. The current is much stronger here which makes it dangerous if you are not a skilled swimmer, but for a Siren it is a piece of cake.

Back on land, the flora of the island is similar to Capri. It consists mainly of Mediterranean shrubs and trees like towering mastics, brightly flowering myrtles, as well as arbutus trees with their red, flaking bark and their edible, red berries. Clusters of heather plants dot the landscape as well, while tall, slender cypresses and the occasional oak bring character to the isolated land mass.

No longer a part of the human world, I head directly to the jungle. Weary of the dangerous thickets of pineapple bushes with their slender razor-edged leaves that cut flesh, I immediately call the scales on my legs. Unlike the first time Mom brought me here, my legs remain untouched.

Needing to drink fresh water, I find my way to the crystal-clear pool near the base of the tallest hill. The pool's surface continuously ripples as it is constantly being fed by several small waterfalls that break off from a much larger river, ending its journey in front of me. Thirsty, I kneel and cup my hands using them to scoop up the incredibly sweet liquid. When I am finished, I splash some on my face and instantly I feel refreshed and reinvigorated.

As I stand, admiring the lush scenery, movement in the bushes several yards away catches my attention.

"It's a deer!" I gasp, smiling at its graceful gait and slender physique.

The lovely animal stares at me from a gap in the underbrush. It is beautiful with its neutral markings of cream, beige, white, and specks of dark brown. Its large, soulful eyes glimmer playfully.

'Selena,' I hear from the direction where the deer stands.

'Follow me,' I hear in my head.

My entire body tenses as my heart skips a beat.

What the hell?!

"Who's there?!" I exclaim, wishing for my mother's bow and arrows.

Cautiously, I begin backing away.

"I've got a knife and I'm not afraid to use it!" I shout, pretending to reach into my pocket.

"There is something you must see," the deer speaks again, but this time I hear it all around me.

Dear Father! What is happening?

Have I somehow lost my mind? Did I eat a bad clam? Is this punishment for disowning my family and kicking my mother out of her childhood home? All of these thoughts run through my head as I stand motionless waiting for the *Stay-Puft Marshmallow Man* to attack me.

"Selena," the familiar voice calls to me again.

That is when I recognize it.

"Gaia?" I whisper. "Is that you?"

"Of course, it is," she laughs. "Who else would it be?"

Whew!

"Thank heaven!" I rejoice, thrilled to know that I do not have an aneurism.

"Why are you disguised as a woodland creature?" I stare at the lovely animal.

"I get bored in my original form," she giggles, easing my anxiety even more.

"Oh!" I giggle too.

There is a brief silence before she asks, "Who is the Stay-Puft Marshmallow Man and why would he attack you?"

Embarrassed, I chuckle to myself.

"The Stay-Puft Marshmallow Man is a character in a movie called Ghostbusters," I try explaining already knowing that the reference will go right over her head.

She pauses.

"What is a *'moo-vee'*?" Gaia stretches out the word making it sound like she is part cow.

Again, I scoff.

"A movie is a story depicted by actors on a screen," I explain to the most influential goddess in the echelon of mythological beings.

There is a short period of silence.

"I do not understand," she pouts, sounding irritated.

Stifling a snicker, I shake my head.

"Don't worry about it," I mutter with amusement. "It's silly human stuff."

"Ahh," she sighs. "I see."

Unsure of what to say next, I weigh my next question, not wanting to insult my only friend at the moment.

"Why are you contacting me this way?"

"I am a goddess," she reminds. "Sometimes I like being dramatic."

Her candor makes me smile again, and then from out of the blue, she kicks back into Mother Nature mode.

"I know what has been happening with you," she reveals, making my face heat.

"Oh," I mumble slightly miffed. "What exactly do you know?"

"Everything."

Hating to be put on the spot, I swallow the lump that is forming in my throat but refuse to admit guilt. Instead, I wrap a strand of hair around my pointer finger and begin to twirl it until it transforms into an even tighter, bouncier curl, successfully avoiding the uncomfortable subject altogether, or so I hope.

Unfortunately, before I can answer, the Earth responds for me. Not in words, mind you, but in the only way it can. The sky darkens and tiny raindrops begin to fall, light at first then stronger and harder until there are puddles at my feet. What was once gentle wisps of wind are now short choppy bursts that threaten to blow me off of my feet. The boughs of ancient trees, that only a few moments previously were stoic and proud, have begun to sag and droop, while healthy wildflowers wither for no reason at all; their soft petals falling to the burnt grass they stand on.

All the while, Gaia stands motionless, her body untouched by what is going on around her. She stays this way for a short time, but for me it is an eternity as I wait for what will happen next. Too afraid to run away, I stand before the mother of the entire world and await my judgement.

Slowly, Paradiso returns to normal. The rain ceases, the winds recede, the trees stand tall again, even the flowers and grassy carpet are fervent and alive. When the goddess finally opens her eyes, she frowns, and I know there is more to be said.

"What have you done?" her question is straight forward and right to the point.

Instantly, I freeze. The hairs on my arms and legs stand straight up. Even the ones on the back of my neck are on high alert.

"Wha-what do you ma-mean?' I stammer, knowing exactly what I have done.

Quietly, she studies me.

"The Earth weakens every time you pull from it," Gaia reminds flatly, her irises shifting from amber to chocolate brown and then back again.

"But how—"

"I know all," Gaia interrupts with that same flatness.

As I stand speechless, I feel that all too familiar tightening in my chest. It is that *'human'* sensation that reminds me of who I was, what kind of *'person'* I was, but I am not a *'person'*, am I? No, I am not. So instead of listening to that feeling, I push it down deep where no one, not even me, can hear it.

"There is a darkness encompassing you," Gaia continues at last with a deep frown.

"What do you mean?" I feel my pulse accelerate and my palms beginning to sweat. "'A darkness?'"

"Selena, you, like your family, straddle two worlds," she explains. "You are the bridge that connects the supernatural realm to the human one."

Terrified to move, I stand listening intently as she gathers her thoughts.

"You walk a complicated tightrope," she continues, amber irises darkening to the same intense shade of my obsidian charm. "A slight push to the right or to the left will send you into turmoil."

Everything she says sounds like a riddle, an incomprehensible, Sphinx-like enigma.

"I don't understand what—"

The goddess raises her right hand, effectively halting what was meant to be a rant.

"We need to go to the opposite side of the island," Gaia states flatly, pointing in that direction with one of her front hooves, her smile gone.

I recall my mother wanted me to do the same thing but did not explain why. Truthfully, I did not give her the opportunity to tell me why it is so important. Suddenly, I feel guilty.

"What's on the opposite side of the island?" I gulp as nervous chills travel down my spine.

The Goddess of the Earth pauses briefly.

"Your past."

It takes almost twenty minutes to reach the west side of the island. It is nothing like the east side, which is decorated with palm trees and picturesque vistas of wildflower-covered rolling green hills. Gone are the flowing streams and rivers that sound like music as they wind through the ground and the songbirds of many different types singing their praises to the world.

No.

Unlike the east, the west is harshly different, unfortunately, not in a good way.

Immediately, I know I have reached the other side of the island because of the sudden darkening of the sky. I look up and realize why. The limestone here does not have as many holes in its walls, so only limited light from the outside can enter. Plus, the tall hills block the light from the opposite side almost completely, only their tops glow dimly.

"How much farther?" I question, knowing that the Earth Goddess can hear me. The idea actually comforts me more than I would like to admit.

"It is straight ahead," she apprises patiently from all around me.

"I can't see anything," I complain, shuffling my feet and reaching out with my arms like a blind person.

"Adjust your eyes, young one," Gaia entreaties, so I do. Switching to Siren-vision, everything is now visible even the bats hanging upside down in the trees looming above.

"Eeek!" I squeal, surprised that there are bats on Paradiso.

Gaia chuckles.

"You are not afraid of sharks, but you are squeamish about harmless bats," she teases.

"Bats freak me out," I admit embarrassedly with a blush.

"Why?" She questions sounding innocent.

"When I was seven or eight years old, I snuck out of bed to watch a vampire movie, and Dracula, the main character, could transform into a bat and bite people," I explain in a rushed jumble.

Quite scholarly, she explains: "There are bats that survive only on blood, but they primarily feed on chickens, cows, and other animals. They are only as big a person's thumb and are quite good-natured, unlike your friend, Dracula."

As we turn the corner, I see a squat shape in the distance.

"What is that?" I probe, pointing in that direction.

Gaia goes silent.

"Is that a house?" I ask, making out the shape.

Still silence.

"Gaia?"

More disturbing silence.

"Could you please show yourself?"

Grr!

"This talking animal thing is starting to give me the heebie-jeebies," I blab before the goddess can respond.

She laughs then and the sound resembles twinkling bells.

"As you wish," she bleats.

Just as before, the earth starts to gently shake. The soil at my feet begins to stack on top of itself like *Legos* creating that human-shaped mound. Underfoot, emerald-colored grass grows out of the mound then transforms into a long emerald gown. Where the top of her head will be, dark brown tresses appear adorned with a majestic wreath of yellow broom flowers studded with sprigs of fragrant jasmine.

"Is this better?" the goddess questions with an alluring smile.

Her lovely mocha complexion combined with sparkling amber eyes overshadows everything around her until all you see is *Her*.

"Much better," I grin, enjoying the company.

"Thank you," she unexpectedly blushes.

"Who lives there?" I ask, getting back to the matter at hand.

"That, my dear, is the first home that housed your great grandmother and her children."

"Really?" My mouth gapes as Gaia nods.

Fascinated, I take a closer look at the structure.

"I've seen these types of houses before in an article I read about Celtic tribes," I inform, still studying the ramshackle edifice.

Cautiously, I approach stopping right in front of the main door which hangs precariously on its hinges. It creeks every time the wind blows like a haunted house in a horror movie. It is unnerving, to say the least.

"The Celts lived in round houses with thatched roofs made of straw or sometimes heather, just like this one," I continue, eager to share my knowledge. "Did they build this themselves?"

"Yes, they did," the goddess advises with admiration.

Admiring their ingenuity, I enter the low-lying structure. The walls of the house are made from woven wood and a mixture of straw and mud since there is an ample supply of wood from the surrounding forest. The building has no windows, and from what I can see of the underlying ceiling, the roof is made from straw with mud placed on top of a simple bamboo grid to keep the warmth in, while large stones held together with clay keep it in place. In the middle of the home is a smooth, stone hearth where a fire can be lit for cooking and heating. Above, there is a hole in the ceiling so smoke can escape, but I do not see what keeps the area protected from rain.

"This is awesome!" I whisper like I am in a house of worship and service is about to start.

Gaia grins and nods.

"They did a fantastic job with the materials they had available," the deity agrees with a graceful nod.

Wanting to see the entire area, I exit through the back door as the goddess follows. Her footsteps are silent against the leaf-littered stone floor, unlike my feet that thud like an ogre.

Around back is an overgrown plot of land that was once used to grow wheat and barley which I conclude based on the distant aroma of hot bread currently wafting around us. Several yards away, a smaller version of the house overrun with climbing vines of dark purple grapes surrounded by a low wooden fence teeming with bee balm blossoms that was probably where the family reared sheep, goats and maybe pigs. The idea of the aunts as toddlers running after animals makes me smile.

Then, without warning, that unnerving sense of déjà vu rears its ugly head as rapid movement to my left catches my attention and quickly, I turn to see what it is. To my shock, an intensely colored hummingbird feasts upon the nectar of the biggest bee balm blossom growing nearby. This time I know that he sees me, but I deduce that he just does not care about my nearness. Everything about his appearance is enthralling, especially his rapidly fluttering wings of lime green, pumpkin, plum, lapis and gold; elegantly sleek and aerodynamic, moving faster than my eyes can focus.

"Just one minute!" I blurt, emphatically. "I know this bird! He was in Melody's garden on Capri!"

Gaia's eyebrows hitch, but she does not reply.

"What are you doing here, bird?" I grill, not expecting a response, but instead this hummingbird stops eating, darts over to me and hovers a few inches away from my face, studying me.

Weird!

"Hello, little bird," I greet more gently, afraid to make any sudden movement for fear of startling him. "I'm Selena. What's your name?"

Quizzically, the hummingbird flutters in place, cocking his head from left to right then back again, I presume trying to size me up.

"How did you get to Paradiso?" I continue to interrogate in a soothing tone. "Did Melody invite you to come here?"

Acapella

As expected, there is no answer, just the delicate buzzing that his quicksilver wings create as they flutter.

From behind me, Gaia clears her throat to get my attention and when I turn back, the mysterious bird is gone.

So incredibly weird!

"Here is where they kept the garden," my companion states whimsically, bringing me back to reality.

"My mother started a garden back home on Isla Flora," I mention casually.

"I know," she grins girlishly.

"Sorry, I forgot," I blush. "You know everything that happens which deals with the earth."

In typical fashion, she nods, showing her impeccable smile.

"Mom planted the same herbs that they grew here: basil, marjoram, oregano," I grin, remembering our lovely garden back home. "Here's curly parsley and wild thyme."

Enjoying the memory, I bend, plucking a tiny lavender flower from the thyme bush. My mother loves cooking with the fragrant herb. Back home, we have a healthy supply of it. There is even a window box with it on the kitchen ledge where it sits and soaks up the Caribbean sunshine.

"See, they did not have such strange upbringings," the goddess proclaims.

"Is this why you brought me here?" I probe with one arched *Mr. Spock* brow.

"This is only part of what I wanted you to see," she admits, sternly.

I gulp noticing the lump in my throat.

"What's the other part?" I press, wanting to get it over with.

Like the *Ghost of Christmas Future* from Charles Dickens', *A Christmas Carol*, she points across the field toward the final set of grassy knolls. Dark shadows loom and no animal sounds are present, and the only thing I hear is my own heartbeat as it accelerates.

"Will you come with me?" I beg with a trembling voice.

Gaia shakes her head.

"I will join you after," she promises sincerely leaving no room for negotiations.

"Great!" I blurt, the solitary word dripping with sarcasm.

"I will be right here," my newfound friend promises, making me more comfortable. "Call for me if you need me."

"Okay," I take a deep breath. "Wish me luck finding *'whatever'* it is I'm supposed to find."

"You will know it, when you see it," the Goddess of Nature encourages with a wink.

"Wish me luck," I exhale loudly. "Here I go."

CHAPTER NINETEEN

Slowly, timidly, I leave the goddess and trudge toward the dark shape looming ahead. As I get closer, my vision begins to filter more light allowing me to see the object more clearly. It resembles something you would see on *The Discovery Channel* on an archeological dig site.

"What is this place?" I gasp looking at the ancient structure, dumbfounded that it is still standing.

Unlike the remains of the round house that my family lived in, this building looks more dilapidated and slightly wobbly. I stop in my tracks to debate if I should go inside, fearful that the entire thing will come crashing down on top of me. I have no doubt, no doubt whatsoever, that one misplaced bump, the giant boulders will crush my skull and flatten me like a pancake.

"Selena," I hear a voice on the wind, but it is not Gaia's.

Immediately, I stand still.

"Who's there?" I ask, breathing heavily. "Is that you, Ares?"

"May I show myself?" the male voice deepens.

All the hair on my body instantly stands at attention.

"Who is this?" I half growl, clenching my hands into tight fists and calling my talons.

"*Proskaléste me,*" the voice whispers seductively.

"What?" I bark, not understanding the uttered phrase.

Again, he states, "*Proskaléste me.*"

Irritated and confused, I roll my eyes with a huff.

"Sure, yeah, whatever," uneasily, I reply.

As I wait, an intense golden light fills the temple almost blinding me. When they readjust, I identify my mystery visitor. I should have recognized the voice.

"Ares," I sigh, relief filling me.

"Is it safe to be here?" He tries to joke but ends up sounding more apprehensive than anything else.

"What are you doing here?" I rebuff, even though I am glad for the company. "If Gaia finds you here, she'll—"

"*Shh!* Lower your voice," the Olympian orders as he places a finger over my lips ceasing my intended rant.

"What are you doing on Paradiso?" I repeat, slapping his hand away. "No one is allowed here without an invitation."

Ignoring my comment, he smiles that lovely smile of his.

"You just invited me, silly Siren," he jokes.

"No, I didn't!" I hiss.

"Yes, you did," he smiles smugly. "I said, *'Invite me in'*, albeit in Greek, and you agreed."

Tricky bastard!

"That's all it takes, huh?" I interrogate, not believing it could be so easy.

"Yes," he says casually. "That is all it takes. Not even Gaia can evict me without provocation and so far, I have not broken any rules."

I pause to consider his response and it makes sense.

"Alright, you can stay," I concede. "Just don't touch anything."

Glancing around, he whistles.

"I would not dare," he acknowledges with a disgusted expression. "This thing might topple over with just a nudge."

Without my permission, he takes my left hand in his.

"What are you doing?" I chastise, looking down where we are joined.

Mischievously, he chuckles.

"You commanded me not to touch anything," his bright eyes glimmer playfully. "Holding hands ensure that I cannot."

Son of a biscuit!

"Do you know what this place is?" I interrogate the God of War.

"I have heard rumors of it," he reveals with a straight face. "But I have never seen it. I did not think it really existed."

"You still haven't told me what *it* is," I remind.

"Sorry," he genuinely apologizes. "*Knisja tas-Sirena Ġganti.*"

I repeat the mysterious words before asking, "What does that mean?"

"Translated from Maltese it means, '*Church of the Giant Siren*'," he tells it like he is saying a prayer to the gods.

"Whoa!" I exclaim.

"There are supposed to be three of these churches interconnected by underground tunnels," he informs like a history professor; all he would need is an ascot and a pipe. "Sadly, no one knows where the other two are located, or if they even exist. Something like that. Like I said, it is all speculation."

"I saw huge pieces of debris in two other places when I was walking across the field to the knoll. That's probably where the other two buildings were." I educate, pointing behind me.

"Perhaps," Ares nods in agreement as he scans the area.

"They must have been relocated somehow, but this one managed to remain here," I add hypothetically.

"That sounds logical to me," he beams.

"They look archaic," I mumble, daring to run my hand over the rough squared, limestone pillars etched with unfamiliar glyphs and carvings of extinct sea creatures.

"According to legend, they are over six-thousand years old," Ares mutters this information like he is revealing a well-kept secret.

"I believe it," I respond, still examining the design and style.

"The site was supposedly constructed by a noble race of giants, hence the word *'ggant'* which means 'giant'," Ares informs with confidence. "Regardless of its age, the monument has survived in a substantially decent state of preservation."

"It's most likely due to the boundary wall that encloses the temple which is built using coralline limestone blocks," eager to show my ability to figure things out, I mention. "Some of the megaliths exceed five meters long and probably weigh more than fifty tons."

Speechlessly, he stares at me, mouth gaping.

I giggle, patting myself mentally on the back.

"My stepfather, David, is a scientist," I clear my throat. "He likes to share his knowledge with my brother and me hoping one day we'll follow in his footsteps."

Ares smiles.

"He sounds like a great man," the god states honestly.

I smile too.

"He is."

A sudden wave of sadness slams into me as I think about David.

Needing to change the subject, I add, "See that surface over there?"

Ares nods.

"That type of limestone is called Globigerina limestone. It's much softer and is usually used for inner furnishings like doorways, decorative slabs, and altars."

Next, I point.

"Like that one over there," I amaze even myself with all the facts I have learned over the years.

Pleased with myself, we continue our tour in silence; Ares still holding my hand in his. The way he moves is so graceful, unlike me who has tripped at least twice since entering the temple. Thankfully, I manage not to go sprawling onto the dusty ground.

As we venture further inside, I realize that the church consists of several large semicircular recesses along with a domed roof toward the eastern end where the altar stands. Clay pots and vases still containing dried flowers and herbs decorate the inner sanctum. The internal walls still show evidence of once being plastered with deep red ochre. I happily tell him this as we continue our adventure.

Ares laughs.

"You know what ocre is?" He prods, obviously impressed.

"*Ocre* is an earthy pigment found in clay that contains ferric oxide," I expound. "It varies from a subtle, light yellow to a rich brown or in this case, red."

"How do you know this morsel of goodness?"

Again, one of David's planned family vacations we took three years ago bubbles up from my memory.

"I saw something similar at the *Gozo Museum of Archaeology*," I clarify, excited to share, but my sadness grows as we continue walking.

I push it away not wanting to ruin our *'date'*.

No!

Not *'date'*!

Friendly outing. *Yeah!*

ACAPELLA

Only an outing!

As we enter another area, the skeletal remains of an animal suggest some sort of ritual sacrifice. Also, the use of fire is evident by the presence of three stone hearths behind the altar. A few holes in the floor might have been used for pouring liquid offerings. Most likely, one or all of my fellow Sirens were conducting strange ceremonies, for what, I have absolutely no idea.

"Why is it so important to Gaia that you see this church?" the God of War grills.

"I'm not exactly sure," I admit glumly.

Realizing he still holds my hand, I pull away.

"What is wrong?" he stands, watching me with a sad puppy-dog expression.

"This can't continue," I announce sternly.

"Why not?" the deity huffs.

"Because you *may* be the half-brother of my great-grandmother, that's why!" I bark, suddenly feeling trapped.

"Who told you that?" His eyes widen.

I remain quiet.

"Why would it matter if I was?" he quizzes, seeming confused.

"Because it's freaky and gross!" I exclaim, my temper growing.

"Selena," Ares begins. "Do you really think if we were related that I would pursue you?"

I shrug.

"I don't know," I whine. "From what I've read, ancient deities are quite scandalous."

He reaches out to touch my cheek and I dodge it.

"Would you please let me explain—"

Suddenly, my stomach starts to violently churn, and I worry that I will lose my last meal.

"I have a boyfriend! His name is Andrew!" I blurt, suddenly feeling relieved. "I love him!"

Ares' brow furrows.

"Then why did you lead me on?" he compels, expression grave.

"I didn't lead you on!" I turn to leave, but he steps in front of me.

"What about our first meeting?" he reminds, making me feel worse.

"I was using my *Sireny-whatnot* on you," I confess, glancing away. "I wasn't in my right mind."

Stunned, he continues to stare.

"I was going to drown you!" I bark, hoping to snap him back to reality.

Still, he stares, saying nothing.

"This is too much," I announce heading back to the entrance.

As soon as we exit the building, I take several cleansing breaths. It seems to help, unlike the god standing beside me with a blank look on his face.

"Are you ill?" Ares asks, placing his palm on my forehead to check for a temperature.

"It was too stuffy in there," I lie, shaking my head. "I just needed some fresh air."

"Are you sure?"

"I'm positive," I answer with a faux grin.

Ignoring my previous rant, he leans to kiss me, but I stop him.

"You should leave," I say sadly.

"Do you really want me to go?" he queries as one eyebrow arcs towards his hairline.

I nod.

Be strong!

"Gaia is waiting for me," I announce, making him scan the darkness for any sign of the Earth Goddess.

Avoiding another confrontation, he bows low, and kisses my hand.

"Thank you for inviting me, Selena," he coos. "I truly have missed you."

Knowing that we may be distantly related, I answer.

"It was nice seeing you again, Ares, but this will be the last time."

Without one of his witty responses, he fades away surrounded by a sparkling shower of gold, leaving nothing behind except more confusion and doubt.

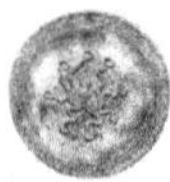

Gaia is waiting in the same exact spot where I left her. Her amber eyes light up when she sees me, and there is a soft glow that seems to surround her entire form. I, on the other hand, cannot get my knees to stop knocking or my palms to stop sweating. I invited him, inadvertently of course, but still, I am responsible. My mind is racing at a hundred miles per hour, and unfortunately, I have never been an adrenaline junkie.

Nope! Not at all. I like calm, cool, and collected.

"Selena?" the intuitive deity coos. "Is something the matter?"

Oh no!

Does she know that Ares was on the island?

Did she somehow sense his presence?

Not knowing what else to do, I do the only thing that I can. I make up a story.

"Nope," I blush, while clearing my throat. "Nothing's the matter… why would something be the matter? *Geez!* Everything is hunky-dory! Right as rain… *peaches and cream…* sunshine and—"

A loud roll of thunder shakes the island, and a spear-like streak of lightning brightens the sky beyond the stalagmite stacks.

"Why, may I ask, are you rambling?" Gaia's eyes narrow as if she can see right through my deception, so I decide to do a little probing of my own.

"Why is that temple so important?" I forcefully probe, needing to take the higher ground, but she only stares at me.

On instinct, I begin to pace, biting my already short nails in the process. I can feel my stomach turning into a ball of knots and my heartbeat is so loud, I am certain the wily goddess can hear it too.

"Why do *you* think it is important?" She answers my question with another question, which I abhor.

Massive clouds move in and cover Paradiso in darkness which instructs the foliage on the island to turn on their natural lighting. All around us, the soft soothing glow acts like a nightlight, adding the perfect amount of brightness. The birds assume that it is nighttime and settle in their nests, tucking their heads under their wings and temporarily bidding goodnight to the world. Hundreds of night-blooming jasmine wake with their full white blooms, delicately scenting Paradiso with their alluring perfume. Even the giant wetas are informed that the curtains have been lifted, the stage lights are on, and it is time to start their rather loud serenade of mating love songs.

Regrettably, I find no comfort in this. All I can think of is getting to the bottom of all of this. Actually, what I want to do is go back to being a Siren in solitude. All I really want is to be alone.

"Don't speak in riddles," I request, my blood pressure elevated from seeing Ares and realizing that animal sacrifices were being made in a house of worship. "Did you know about the animal sacrifices? *Did you?* Did The Sisters do it?"

Gaia's face saddens.

Acapella

"I'll take that as a *'yes'*," I blather, wanting to run away and hide in the woods or maybe find a nursery of raccoons and hope that they will adopt me as an honorary woodland creature. Anything not to be a part of my crazy messed up family.

I feel my chest tighten again, but angrily push it away.

"It is time," the Goddess of the Earth announces.

Immediately, I cease my pacing.

"Time for what?" I snap, not caring about my clipped tone.

"It is time to talk to the Muse." She frowns, and gently takes my hand.

CHAPTER TWENTY

The following night, just before midnight, I leave the Siren Grotto and make my journey back to Capri carrying my waterproof duffle bag to keep my change of clothes dry. The sea is serene, which makes for an easier trip, and with a weak undertow, I am able to make it to the island of Capri fifteen minutes quicker than usual.

On a small hidden beach, bathed in pale moonlight, I quickly change into a pair of black shorts and a dark grey T-shirt. Wasting no time, I hide the bag behind a large rock before calling the webbing and talons on my feet as well as my hands. Like the *Amazing Spiderman*, I scale the steep face of the cliff to the plateau several hundred feet above. It takes me ten minutes just to get to the top. Getting down the cliff is so much easier than getting up; for me it takes just one leap.

Once I catch my breath, I jog to the spot where Melody's cottage normally manifests. This is the first time I have been here alone. Normally, Ando is with me and for some reason I feel the need to glance behind me with the hope of seeing him there; gathering stones or twigs and putting them in his pockets to use at a later time for some strange experiment he has thought of on the fly.

Right now, a slow-moving processional of clouds has covered the moon, leaving me in almost complete darkness. When I was much younger, this would have entirely freaked me out, but now it is not so bad. Still, I have never been a fan of dark spaces; however, because I will be visiting Melody, I am willing to deal with it.

I am not nervous, just anxious.

Wanting to take my newly enhanced powers out for a spin, I grasp my obsidian charm and concentrate. My mother once told me that I cannot control what I, myself, did not muster, so with great curiosity I attempt the impossible, and without much effort, I command the wind to increase in speed and the remaining clouds to:

"Scatter."

Obeying my wishes, the clouds continue to travel, and it suddenly becomes brighter due to a now cloudless sky covered in twinkling stars and a brightly glowing moon.

"Couldn't be done, huh?" I say to myself as I pompously stare upward, admiring what I can do. "Not bad for a *newbie* Siren. Not bad at all."

As I stand admiring my work, a screeching tawny owl startles me. Its rounded, stocky form and short tail makes it easy to recognize. David once told me and Ando that there are only a few pairs of these birds of prey left on the island of Capri. That makes me wonder if Belen has a mate.

Nope! I quickly conclude that that is doubtful since *that* particular great horned owl is stubborn, moody, and a pain in the neck.

"Melody!" I call into the woods. "It's me, Selena! Please show yourself!"

Then I make the mistake of taking a step forward and notice the ground is uneven here, and covered with pebbles, dried branches, slippery moss-covered rocks, and a butt-load of wild mushrooms clinging to various mediums. Not wanting to slip and fall, I carefully step over these seemingly innocuous barriers, realizing that I am still a wee bit clumsy. Not as bad as I was before, but still danger prone.

Soon, I reach an area where the bushes are almost waist high that seems vaguely familiar, and as I venture into the heavily wooded area, I notice another patch of weeds including one spot of dried dandelion seeds. Instantly, my mind ventures back to the first time I came to the cottage and witnessed a wicked wind scattering the fluffy objects into the night leaving only one stem holding onto six seeds.

As my footsteps gently shake the leaf-lined ground, all the fluffy dandelion seeds tremor, but instead of taking to the air as they would normally, they drop off of their shriveled dried stems. The oddity of the action captivates me as I stare at the delicate strands lying as if in sleep; hoping that one of its brethren will take root in the fertile soil and live again another day. To my surprise, one lone seed remains on its stem, defiant until the end.

A sudden shudder runs over me, but I quickly chase the disturbing thought from my brain.

Where is my great grandmother's cottage?

"Melody!" I shout again at the top of my lungs not caring about anyone passing by at this time of night.

Then I feel the first bite and add: "Mosquitos are biting!"

After the third bite, I hear Melody's lyrical voice. It is that wonderfully familiar sound of effervescent Champagne bubbles being poured into a crystal flute right before midnight of a new year. It is music unto itself.

"I have been waiting for you," the Muse gives her usual pleasant greeting.

I grin; pleased to hear her melodious voice once again.

"How did you know I was coming for a visit?" I glance around the woods.

As I keep an eye on the clearing, the charming cottage emerges from the darkness with a crackle accompanied by pops of lights and electricity. Against the darkness of the woods, it resembles that of Fourth of July fireworks, but on a smaller scale with bursts of cobalt, silver, crimson, and neon green. It is still impressive and absolutely spectacular to witness.

Quickly switching off Siren-vision, I see the Muse; her short, robust silhouette draped by her favorite hooded jacket. Slowly, she removes the cloak revealing her round face and sparkling emerald eyes with a swirl of gold. Those eyes are able to change as her mood does, and as always, she looks lovely. Fortunately, she is in a relaxed state and a cheerful mood, but then again, when is she not?

"Come inside, my dear child," Melody welcomes as she blesses me with a hug. Immediately, I feel inspired to sing. Sing like I have never sung before; however, I suppress the urge knowing now that her natural ability to give inspiration is the cause of my distraction. No matter how it bends me to its will, I must remain focused.

"I've missed you," I inform, inhaling her incredible floral scent combined with warm baked goods. It is a fragrance that I never get enough of.

"Come inside, dearest." Warmly, she smiles.

Then politely, she steps aside, gesturing to me to enter, and then motions for me to go to the living area. Making myself at home, I settle on the floral sofa and lean back to admire the space. Soon after, she returns carrying a tray of finger sandwiches and two glasses of cold apple juice.

"I hope you are hungry," she says trying to entice me.

I chuckle.

"I'm always hungry," I confess with a deep blush.

She chuckles too.

Before I can chicken out, I ask, "Would you answer a few questions for me?"

"You may ask me anything," Melody encourages, placing the tray of goodies on the coffee table.

As the tray lands on the solid surface, I help myself to the closest sandwich. It is delicious! Crisp cucumbers paired with extra-sharp white cheddar on simple, yet mouthwatering white bread with a light smear of homemade mayonnaise.

"I hope you like these as much as your aunts did when they were your age," the Muse smirks.

My eyebrows hitch.

"They ate *cucumber* and *cheddar finger sandwiches*?" I snort in disbelief.

This comment makes her grin too.

"One summer, we traveled to Naples for a festival. It was on that trip that the girls fell in love with bread and cheese," she educates, her mind drifting back to the event as her smile widens.

Before I bite into the first rectangular-shaped sandwich, I query.

"What do you know about the *Knisja tas-Sirena Ġganti*?"

Being a Siren, I know that my pronunciation is dead-on accurate.

Her eyes close with recollection.

"Ahh, yes," Melody sighs. "Although, I have not been back to Paradiso for many millennia, I will never forget the Church of the Giant Siren."

Eager to hear more, I sit straighter, hungry for more information about the strange building, or rather *buildings*.

"The Church of the Giant Siren," I repeat the words, but do not like the sound of them.

Melody nods as she refills her glass then sits once more with hands clasped tightly then decides to reach for her cup. Outwardly, her demeanor is calm, but her irises are in a constant state of flux; first gray then amber, next, a stormy violet. Finally, they settle on grayish green.

"What are they for?" I press her more forcefully.

The Muse remains silent, all the while sipping her beverage.

"Who built it?" I ask, taking a bite of the impeccable sandwich as I wait for her response.

She starts to reply but pauses before the words can be released.

"Great grandmother," I complain, almost to the brink of wanting to shake the answer out of her. "Did you build it?"

"How do you know about the temple?" the renowned mythological being responds at last, sidestepping the question.

"I found one of them," I confess, narrowing my eyes.

Again, she remains mute.

"What are they used for?" I continue to pry, determined to get to the truth once and for all.

"Why is this matter so important to you, child?" Melody heavy-heartedly exhales.

"Because the Goddess of the Earth was determined to show it to me," I confess with a shrug. "I'm not sure why though."

Melody nervously clears her throat.

"Why would she do that?" the beautiful Muse questions with narrowing eyes, but I am not sure if she is asking me or herself.

"She didn't explain," I add, reaching for another appetizer. "All she kept saying is that it was time to talk to the Muse. The only Muse I know is you."

Bowing her head, she breaks eye contact and now, instead of waves of inspiration ebbing from her, I feel another emotion instead. This new sensation is weighty and dark; it slithers over me like evil fingers and my body shivers with horror. Menacing images flash through my mind of the tour guide in Anacapri and how her life left her as I squeezed. Also, of Ares when I called him to a watery near-death. Every single malicious thing I have ever thought—ever done—punches me dead in the face.

"We live in complex times," my great grandmother sighs woefully, as she contemplates her answer.

I nod my understanding, but my gaze never leaves hers.

Acapella

Since the first time I met Melody, I have trusted her, loved her. She is the kindest, most understanding individual I have ever encountered. Whenever I feel unsure, I think of her, and my mood immediately shifts, and I am whole again. This time though, my heart is pounding, my palms are sweating, and my throat is dry.

Picking up on her mood, I brace for what is to come, knowing that it cannot be anything good.

"Great grandma?" I whisper. "Are you alright?"

Finally, she nods and continues.

"The world has changed so much, Selena," the Muse frowns. "In my day, things were not as complicated. It was black or white, never gray."

"Yes, we live in a world where people you love lie and deceive you," I agree with a nod. "Without blinking an eye, they ruin your entire future, who you are, who you were going to be all the while proclaiming that they only did it to protect you.

"*Pfff!* What a crock!"

"Are you are referring to your mother?" she simply states.

Angrily, I nod.

Wanting to comfort me, Melody takes my hands in hers. The Muse's warmth and strength are undeniable. She exudes goodness, but now there is something shifting underneath her placid exterior.

"Forgive her," she states firmly.

"Why?" I pout, feeling the hate bubble to the surface.

"It is best for the soul," she expands, taking her first sandwich in contrast to my seventh.

"I don't understand," I respond, truly mystified by her remark.

"There is a darkness that surrounds you, my dear," she meekly replies which catches me off-guard. "A strangling cloud that I felt as soon as I opened the door for you tonight."

Goosebumps appear on my arms and legs as her words soak in.

"That's not possible!" I brusquely retort, needing to defend myself. "I feel exactly as I've always felt."

My great-grandmother gently reaches up and smooths my riotous curls. In her patient gray eyes is pity combined with regret and repentance. It breaks my heart to see her so upset.

"This is my fault," Melody mumbles, suddenly removing her hands from mine altogether, and instantly, I miss their warmth.

Intrigued, I rest the remaining piece of my sandwich back on the tray replacing it with the cool juice. The condensation around the smooth glass calms me, and unhurried, I take a small sip of the tangy, yet sweet, liquid.

"Why do you think this is your fault?" I study the worry lines currently marring her normally flawless complexion.

She takes a breath before speaking.

"You know of my origin?"

I nod.

"According to my mother," I begin. "Poseidon sculpted you and had Zeus breathe life into your vessel, but recently I have heard conflicting accounts of what occurred after that."

I pause, debating whether or not to burden her with what may or may not be the truth.

"I have recently heard a different recollection," I continue, examining her expression.

Melody braces herself and I can tell that she is both intrigued and concerned about my statement.

"What is the *other* version?" She practically dares me to spill the beans, so I do.

"I was told that you are the *daughter* of Zeus," I nervously retell.

Embarrassed, she blushes.

"Which version is accurate?!" I exclaim, wanting clarification.

"Both versions intertwined are the correct one," the Muse mumbles with a mysterious half smile.

"This is so confusing," I groan, flinging my body back onto the sofa cushions dramatically. "Please clarify before my head explodes."

This makes her chuckle. I guess she does have a little darkness inside of her after all. Knowing this makes me feel better.

"Yes and no," she mutters offhandedly.

I feel a headache coming on.

"Huh?"

"When the great Olympian Zeus breathed into me, it was his essence, his life force that animated me," she explains.

"I still don't understand," I huff, my aggravation doubling.

"When a man and woman create a baby, the child will have half of the mother's essence and half of the father's."

I nod my comprehension, albeit feeling a bit uneasy as my great grandmother gives me *'the-birds-and-the-bees'* talk.

"When you were conceived, your mother created you with only *her* essence; you do not have a father, correct?"

"Correct," the word sticks in my throat.

"We are the same," Melody grins. "I have no maternal or paternal parents, umm…"

She ponders how to continue her example, but I inject my idea before she can continue.

"Your DNA has that of your father, Zeus," I add with a grin. "But it's not like *actual* DNA."

"Yes," she agrees. "Zeus is *not* my biological father, but it was his life force that animated me, my cells. However, my genetic material is that of the earth, of Gaia. My essence is that of the sea and also of the land. It contains volcanic ashes along with every particle of every sea creature that has ever swum in *any* body of water, as well as those of dry land, because they are all interconnected.

"That is why my offspring became the embodiment of the seas and oceans, but they also have a small dominion over some land creatures. Like me, like your aunts and grandmother, our chemical makeup is strictly our own; no one else's."

"Also of the Earth," I repeat, and she nods in agreement, but does not expand on this particular fact. "That makes us related to Gaia as well."

She nods.

"We are related to her most of all," she replies with misty eyes, and I wonder why that makes her sad.

Quickly, I decide to change the subject.

"Could we have inherited some of Zeus' abilities because of this?" I inquire abruptly.

She thinks for a moment.

"It is a great possibility," she beams.

"What about Mom and Ando?" I continue, mulling over the possibilities.

"They are a combination of Siren genes and Human ones," she instructs. "They are unique unto themselves."

At last, she exhales, and her eyes change to a mellow chocolate-brown, accented with subtle specks of amber.

Unable to wait any longer, I ask the question that has been burning on my tongue.

"Am I related to Ares?"

Horrified, she glowers at me with wide eyes and an even wider mouth.

"Dear heavens!" she almost spits her disgust. *"Absolutely not!"*

Relieved of her proclamation, I release a held breath.

"Are you sure?" I grill one more time.

"Of this I am positive," Melody finally answers after several tense seconds.

"What a relief!" I grin, my apprehension fading. "Zeus is *not* my biological great-great-grandfather."

Melody adamantly shakes her head.

"That would be like calling the bee who delivers the pollen to the flower its father," she chuckles, painting such a concise picture.

When Melody regains her composure, she adds: "However, you *are* aligned with Ares."

"What do you mean?" I huff, cocking my head to one side, as is my custom when hearing disturbing news.

"The darkness that surrounds you, the one I spoke of earlier—"

"Yes, I remember," I frown, not liking the direction this conversation is now heading.

"Unfortunately, I believe that you and he are somehow *linked*."

Outside, right above the roof of the cozy cottage, a brash roll of thunder announces itself.

Unable to answer, I can only stare at her.

"No way!" I shout at last, losing my temper and not caring.

More thunder roars and Melody realizes who is causing it and subtly softens her tone.

"You have given a part of you to him and him to you," she speaks in riddles.

Through the glass windows of the living room, furious lightning flashes in warning almost in rhythm with my pounding heart.

"Great grandmother!" I sneer at her inappropriate remark. "I promise you, I have *not* given myself, to *him*! *To anyone!*"

Her cheeks become heated, and she looks away.

"I realize that silly girl!" she snaps back. "Magical beings can sometimes *'join'* their essences, usually by mistake. Your great grandfather joined our essences when we were married."

The lightning and thunder lessen to a distant groan.

"You actually physically got married?" I blurt, stunned by that fact.

Melody smiles, showing her perfect teeth.

"We certainly did," she brags with a wide grin. "Gaia performed the ceremony on the highest knoll on Paradiso."

Instantly, my brain pictures the exact place where the ceremony took place. I know it well. There is a spot almost exactly in the middle of Paradiso where the grassy slopes of wild lavender and giant sunflowers merge to overlook the clearest river on the island. At that place, a myriad of assorted multihued butterflies' flit and flutter from every open flower, stopping briefly at each to sample their delicious wares. Directly above the knoll, lyrical songbirds perch atop the tallest branches to perform, their chorus accompanied by the soft buzzing of an orchestra of insects all in complete harmony. It is the perfect location to be joined.

As soon as that vision leaves me, one of Ares replaces it. Angrily, I chase it out of my mind, but it claws its way back almost as soon as it leaves.

Ugg!

"Can this link with Ares be broken?" I demand with hope in my heart then gulp down the remaining freshly pressed apple juice.

"Yes," Melody reassures, sensing my growing frustration. "It can."

"How?" the word rushes past my lips.

"Sadly, it will take an act of violence between you two," she explains in all honesty and then her tone hardens. "An extremely vicious act, that should break the bond that has connected you."

An act of violence? Against the God of War?

Great!

I decide that now is the right time to ask the most important question of all.

"Great grandma?"

"Yes, young one?" She grins, returning to her snack.

Here goes nothing.

"Why haven't you been back to Paradiso?" I blurt before chickening out.

"I was expelled," the Muse admits without hesitation, her words dripping with shame.

Of their own accord, my eyes widen.

"Who banned you?" I ask then answer my own question. "It was Gaia, wasn't it?"

The soft thumping of raindrops begins to smack the glass panes. In the distance, the increasing wind howls like a wounded wolf and the trees surrounding the cottage blow and bend to my will. Unable to rein my emotions back, I simply sigh and listen to the song that it creates.

Melody nods, tears welling in her now watery-blue eyes. Quickly, she reaches into her apron pocket and retrieves a delicate handkerchief that she uses to dab the moist corners.

"Why would she do that?" I interrogate, filled with rage over my great grandmother's harsh treatment by the Earth goddess.

No answer follows.

"You *must* tell me," I push harder.

"Why is my punishment so important for you to know?" her brow furrows and her lips tighten.

"Because the Goddess of the Earth says that it is... that's why," I say in a jumble of words not sure if I even make sense.

A few minutes go by before Melody finally responds.

"Ares killed Akheloios," she bawls. "He killed your great grandfather!"

Shocked into silence, I sit on the whimsical floral print couch just staring at my great grandmother who rocks back and forth trying to console herself, her hand still in mine. Unsure of what to say next or how to comfort her, I glance nervously around the nicely decorated room while wondering if finishing my sandwich would be considered rude or uncouth. I have never been in a situation like this before, and I wish I could blink myself back to Paradiso like Barbara Eden in *I Dream of Jeannie*.

"I am sorry, my dear." Melody finally gasps after a few moments of sniffling.

"It's alright," I ease. "Are you feeling better?"

Please say you're feeling better.

"Not really," she confesses, discarding her handkerchief and this time reaching for a tissue.

When Grandpa Theo passed away, I was sad of course, but I did not comprehend what it truly meant. My mother, on the other hand, was numb, then angry, and then finally, accepting. It took her a long time though to go through all the stages of grief. I remember it well. One morning, she woke up and was able to look at his picture and smile.

"Are you sure that it was Ares?" I practically choke on the question.

Melody nods.

"I can't believe he would do that," I grumble, shaking my head.

"He is the God of War for a reason!" the hysterical Muse barks and sits bolt upright; her expression hard like granite as another wave of tumultuous emotions radiates from her. It is then that I truly feel her fury; a fevered torrent from a wall that I imagine will never be breached, never be broken, and I now understand why she has erected it.

I do not know what I would do if I lost someone that I loved more than life itself. It is strange feeling everything that she does, but I remain steadfast against it as best as I can.

When her rage subsides at last, the Muse wipes her nose, and continues.

"I do not know what caused the final altercation, but Akheloios and Ares were feuding long before I came along." Melody pauses, staring blankly at the fire; her admission and expression grave. "After your great grandfather was murdered, I did something so horrible... so forbidden... that I was banished from my home, forever."

Shaken to our core, we sit silently for a long while. I am not sure how much time has passed before I speak again.

"What did you do that was so awful?" I gently push for a more complete explanation, placing my second sandwich back on the plate, fully intending to return to it.

Tears begin to stream down her face again, salty, and wet.

"Melody," I take her hand in mine once more. "Tell me."

"I wanted revenge," she discloses with trembling lips.

My eyes narrow as I mull over what she has said.

"What did you do?" I plead in a whisper.

The rain increases to the strength of a tropical depression, and I know that I am not the one causing it. At least, I do not think that I am. I doubt a Muse can control the weather. *Right?*

Taking a deep breath, she replies rather shakily.

"I used the temple on Paradiso to channel the power of the Earth through my children and then used it for my own personal gain," she confesses as if her tongue has a mind of its own.

From where we sit, the woods around the cottage can be seen. Their branches are being whipped around as if they are made from leather instead of sturdy timber that have stood against many a powerful storm, but this storm is not like the rest. This storm is fueled by the rage of one ticked-off Muse that could possibly have the combined strength of Gaia, Poseidon, and Zeus.

"Do you truly believe that Ares murdered your husband?" I probe, continuing to process the information.

Squeezing my hand, Melody swears.

"Yes, I truly do."

CHAPTER TWENTY-ONE

Paradiso is brimming with activity this morning. The birds are singing. The fish in the inlet are jumping as they catch water bugs flying too close to the surface. Bright sunlight filters through the holes in the limestone crags protecting the island making everything seem more enchanting, but none of these things comforts my heavy heart.

Unable to sleep since returning to the island, I have decided to get a start on fixing up my new home. Yes, I have made up my mind to repair the small, round house built by Melody and her young Sirens. With my hands perched on my hips, I stand for several minutes, hair up in a messy bun, wearing light-gray sweatpants, a white tank top and my once white sneakers, trying to decide the best way to approach this looming project. Over and over in my mind, I try to formulate a plan.

As I review everything that needs to be addressed, a brave bunny hops out of the woods and stops at my feet.

"Good morning," I greet in my warmest tone. "You're up early too."

The tan-colored creature blinks at me as he twitches his tiny pink nose.

"If you have any suggestions on how to attack this massive project, please feel free to give your input," I smirk, wondering if the cute bunny will respond.

Taking a closer look at the edifice, I begin talking to myself.

"I've never had to do this sort of thing before," I remind myself. "Not even when my family and I moved from Ohio to Isla Flora."

The rabbit looks at me then at the house then back to me. Suddenly, it sneezes and hops away, and just as quickly as it arrived, it vanishes into the low-lying brush.

I giggle.

"Thanks for the help!" I call after him.

Channeling my inner-handyman, I run my hand over the main door which hangs insecurely on the doorframe. The worn wood creeks as soon as it is touched. It is dangerous, to say the least.

"Ouch!" I shout as a splinter jabs my right index finger causing it to bleed, but almost instantaneously it heals.

Another minute passes before I announce to no one in particular:

"I guess I'll start with the door."

Knowing now that it needs to be sanded, I remember seeing sea cucumbers that were arranged in a neat pile on the beach. David said that loofahs are made from dried sea cucumbers.

"I can use a couple of those to smoothen the wood," I smile as I continue conversing with myself.

Then on winged feet, I race as fast as I can back to the beach to gather as many of the sea cucumbers as I can carry. It takes me a few hours to get the wood as smooth as silk, but it is worth it, and using several strands of palm fronds, braided together, I create a makeshift rope that I use to reattach the front door.

Proud of my work, I smile broadly.

"Not bad," I compliment myself. "Not bad at all."

Wait!

I forgot about the leaks in the roof due to gaps caused by strong winds and heavy rains. That task should be easy. First, I build an improvised ladder with bamboo poles secured with the thick vines that had once covered the penned area. Now all I have to do is locate more palm fronds to fill in the bare areas. These I find at the coconut grove near the lagoon and use them to patch the roof.

Being careful not to fall, I deftly layer the vegetation over the holes in order to keep water away from the sub-roof. Since the majority of the shrubbery stays dry because of being so densely packed, it traps air and functions as natural insulation. When I am finished, I stand down below approving my newly found thatcher skills.

"Now, inside will stay nice and dry." I beam from ear to ear.

Next, I make a mental note that the central hearth used for cooking needs cleaning. Actually, the entire house needs to be cleaned from top to bottom, but the rumbling in my stomach reminds me that I have not eaten all day.

"Time to find some food," I announce, looking around. Oddly, my mind drifts back to the adorable rabbit from earlier and then to the ones in Melody's garden that were boldly pilfering carrots, but those creatures are fast and I know that my skills with my mother's bow are not at that level yet. Plus, after meeting the other bunny earlier, I feel kind of guilty for even thinking about eating one of his brethren.

Trying to find a happy compromise, I make my way back to the beach, strip down to my birthday suit, and dive into the refreshing lagoon teeming with schools of different species of fish. Before long, a medium-sized striped mullet swims lackadaisically by practically daring me to eat him, so… *I do!* Raw and wriggly.

I think of it as fast-food sushi and convince myself that no one will miss it.

Nearly full (for the moment), I stop by the grove to get a ripe coconut. With expert precision, I use my talons to puncture holes at the top in order to get to the sweet liquid inside. When I have consumed every last drop, I split it open and devour the soft succulent jelly that still clings to the inner shell.

"Mmm!" I hum, patting my belly. "That's some good eats."

Back to work!

However, before I can leave the area, I notice the surrounding field. I do not recognize exactly what I am looking at, but somehow, I know that it does not belong here on Paradiso. Moving quickly, I sprint toward the object. When I get close enough to get a better look, I realize what it is: a plastic bag.

Instantly rage flares, thunder rolls, lightning flashes, and the winds pick up, but is quickly suppressed. Immediately, I begin gathering the unwanted debris. Farther up the field, what I find infuriates me even more: plastic soda rings, bottles, fishing line, used hooks, tattered netting, and an assortment of trash that has somehow accumulated here. My OCD rears its ugly head and I angrily begin my clean-up efforts until the entire field is rubbish free.

"There!" I beam, reviewing my work as I dust off my hands. "That's much better!"

It is then that I notice the beehive high in the upper branches of a nearby tree. I do not know how long the hive has been here, but by the enormous size of it, it must be decades of Sundays. The massive swarm of buzzing inhabitants flying around it confirms my conclusion.

Again, my stomach growls and the idea of something sweet pops into my brain.

Honey! What could be healthier than a food naturally sweet and delicious?

Nothing I can think of at the moment.

"How do I do this without getting stung?" I question myself, still staring at the extremely active beehive.

Scales of course!

Grinning like a fool, I call for my scales, including the ones on my face. Carefully, using my talons as natural pickaxes, I attempt the steep climb up the trunk of the extremely tall tree. Immediately, the bees are alerted to my presence and in response their buzzing becomes louder, angrier, and more alarming. Needless to say, the fear of their wrath does not deter me from pursuing my sweet prize. In fact, it only makes me more determined to retrieve the amber-colored nectar, whether or not it is a good idea does not even occur to me.

Halfway up the tree trunk, the first soldier bee lands on my head and stings me on my scales, but in this attempt to protect his home, he loses his stinger and I know that he will eventually die. Being a protector of the Earth, I realize that I would basically be killing hundreds, if not thousands, of innocent drones if I continue upwards.

My heart clenches in protest, and slowly, I climb back down, but the desire for honey still plagues me.

Standing in the same place as I stood before my first climb, I review my choices.

Climb the tree, agitate the bees, they sting me and die, and I feel like crap.

Nope! I do not like that scenario.

Is there an option number two?

Determined to find another way, I contemplate other means to reach my end goal.

At last, it comes to me.

Clearing my mind, I focus on the bees. More accurately, I focus on their '*song*.' It is unique unto their genus, their species and embedded in their song is their ancient language. Closing my eyes, I listen intently as I separate it from the breeze that lightly blows across the lavender-covered field. Then I remove the percussion of the pounding waves against the outer limestone cliffs. Finally, I listen with my soul and within a few minutes, I hear *it*. I hear and I understand.

With newly found awareness, I close my eyes and sing.

I sing with every particle of my being.

I sing with all of the compassion that binds me to the Earth.

I use my connection to the very foundation of Paradiso.

I thank them for their talents at pollinating the flowers which replenish all of the trees, plants, bushes, wildflowers, every form of greenery that lives and flourishes on this carefully hidden island. This perfect island was created by Zeus to protect a Muse and her newborn Siren daughters. I do not even realize that I am crying until I feel the cool rivulets running down my cheeks.

When I open my eyes, I see what my song has done.

To my amazement, all of the bees, including the queen who is much larger in size than the rest of the hive, are hovering a few feet away from their nest. Their buzzing has softened to a temperate hum as they watch me intently.

Wasting no time, I climb up and slice off just a two-inch piece of the honeycomb's insides using one talon to make the precise cut, taking care not to harm any other part of their home. Just as fast, I scamper down the trunk and kindly thank them with a small nod. Before I can blink, they return to their residence to resume their labors.

"Wow!" I whimper to myself, awestruck and tickled pink. "Just... *Wow!*"

Still standing in the same spot, gazing up at the hive, I consume the sticky substance, relishing that I have never tasted anything so incredible as this perfect food. The bees, back to their routine, ignore me as I ogle their busy motions as they care for their abode.

Not sure why I am hungry again, my mind wanders back to my choices for another meal. Unable to decide, I head in the direction of the wooded area. As I walk, I mull over what I am in the mood for, decisions, decisions. By the time I reach the tree line, I figure out what I am craving: pheasant!

"I need Mercury!" I squeal, and as fast as my feet can carry me, I dash toward the hilly area not too far ahead where my mother revealed the secret hiding spot of her beloved hunting bow. I sprint excitedly, willing my feet to move faster, and to my genuine surprise my muscles kick into overdrive, my lungs expand to take in more oxygen and then it happens. My speed increases exponentially! My entire body transforms into a well-oiled machine allowing me to run more rapidly than I ever could before.

Oh! My! Gravy!

"What the Hell!" I exclaim at the top of my lungs, enjoying the power that I have tapped into.

Within seconds, I arrive at the base of the towering mango grove. Recognizing the area, I suddenly come to an abrupt stop, drop to my hands and knees, and commence to dig near the roots of the tallest tree.

"I know it's here," I grumble to myself. "C'mon! Where are you?"

Ah ha!

"Found it!" I exuberantly squeak, holding up the weathered burlap protecting Mom's prized possession. With steady hands, I unwrap the exquisitely crafted wooden bow along with the quiver of six razor-sharp, pink shell-tipped arrows.

"Hello, gorgeous!" I gasp, overjoyed, grinning from ear to ear.

It truly is gorgeous, in my opinion.

"Nice to see you again, Mercury," I giggle over the fact that my mom loves to name her favorite items.

I recall why she named *'him'* Mercury.

"Mom said that you are as fast as lightning and you never miss your mark," I talk to the bow with all seriousness. "Just like the messenger of the gods, Mercury."

"Let's go, my friend!"

Beaming, I secure the items over my shoulder and begin my journey to locate a generously sized pheasant.

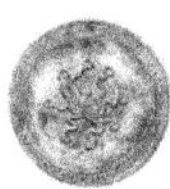

It took almost forty-five minutes to find my prey.

Never in my wildest dreams could I have ever imagined that I, Selena Marquez, would be crouching in the woods stalking my meal. On high alert, I study my surroundings, keeping an attentive eye out for the elusive bird. Inside of my chest, my heart is beating an excited tune, a tune of anticipation along with a small helping of nervousness.

"Be calm," I remind myself.

Having more control over my body, I will my pulse to decrease, shocked that it obeys. Just like Mom, I listen to the sounds around me: birds chirping, leaves rustling, insects buzzing…

Up ahead, movement catches my attention.

"Let me see you," I whisper, filled with curiosity. "Come out of the brush."

As if hearing my request, a small creature steps into view.

Please, let it be a pheasant.

'Just a little bit more,' I encourage telepathically so not to startle whatever it is.

Then patiently, I wait.

When the shadow does not comply, but instead heads in the direction of a small clearing up ahead where another set of bamboo stalks are growing in bunches near a shallow, stony stream, I follow. These stalks, unlike the massive ones nearby, are younger and much less developed; however, they still appear verdant and healthy due to the clean water that they are partially growing in.

Now, out in the open, I recognize what it is.

Good day, Mr. Muskrat? I greet in my head. *Are Muskrat's good to eat?*

ACAPELLA

Sadly, I have no idea, and the notion of eating the rather homely creature does not appeal to me at all. My stomach, however, growls in disagreement.

Muskrat it is! I guess.

Deliberately, I crouch low using the brush to conceal my location.

Focus on the head, I think to myself, wrapping my mind around what must be done.

I do not want him to suffer. Make it a quick death. It will be humane; I try consoling myself. It is either him or I, and right now, my stomach convinces me that it has to be him.

Father, give me strength!

Seemingly unaware of my close position, the plump muskrat sniffs at the base of the clump of bamboo, his short, thick orange-brown coloring making him stand out against the surrounding moss-colored stalks. His fur is partially wet, and his eyes are black like onyx crystals. Leisurely, he forages for what, I have no idea.

Aww! He's kinda cute! I smile, ignoring my complaining stomach.

I've got to do it now, or I never will, I shake the notion out of my brain.

"You're a *Siren*," I whisper and blow a strand of hair out of my eye. "I can do this."

Just as I saw my mother do, I bring the bow up to my face, adjust my hold on the weapon, and take aim, all the while holding my breath. Next, I purse my lips as I had seen her do and slowly release my held breath as if I am a deflating balloon. With much hesitation, I release the arrow and as the fletching skims my cheek it leaves a thin scratch, but of course it heals as quickly as it is formed.

With the release of the bolt, the unsuspecting muskrat looks up *at me*. Silently, we both watch as the handmade shaft whizzes through the air towards it. All it would take is that one arrow directly to the muskrat's brain to instantly kill it, ending the hunt. Instead, the projectile pierces the trunk of the thinnest bamboo, several inches above the animal's head. Obviously surprised, he stares at me, and I stare at him; both of us were relieved that my arrow did not do what it was supposed to do.

No words are spoken as I recover the weapon. With steady hands, I pull it out of the bamboo with a strong tug. I do not even need to clean the shell-tipped point or the top of the shaft. Saying not a word, I take a seat on the ground and am pleasantly surprised when the curious semiaquatic rodent wanders over and sniffs my hand. Not wanting to frighten him, I remain still.

He is sort of cute, if I do say so, with kind eyes.

"Are you hungry, boy?" I ask with a small smile.

He answers with a funny sound and a twitch of his nose which makes me laugh.

"I'll take that as a *'yes'*," I chuckle, rising to a standing position.

The wetland creature starts to follow me.

"What do you eat?" I question, sounding like a curious child. "I'm guessing fish."

On silent paws, Mr. Muskrat follows me to the beach.

Hold on! You came from the pond, so you probably eat freshwater fish… maybe?

Mr. Muskrat simply stares at me and twitches his wet nose.

"Ok then," I add confidently. "Let's see what freshwater fish are in the stream."

My new companion stays silent.

"You're no help," I giggle, bending to gently stroke his fur, delighted that he lets me.

The remainder of our trip to the stream is done in silence. Fortunately, the stream does have a few deeper sections where I find a variety of fish such as rainbow trout and grayling, and believe it or not, crayfish. Thrilled at the find, I use my talons as hooks and skewer three good-sized trout, six or seven crayfish, and I rustle up some small potatoes, wild mushrooms, onions, and a handful of multicolored carrots from the woods nearby.

"This will make a fantastic dinner," I announce to my friend.

Slowly, he turns to head back to the stream where I first saw him. As if on a mission, he walks quickly. Well, as quickly as his short, stumpy legs can carry his pudgy body. He does not even look back.

"Wait, Mr. Muskrat!" I shout to get his attention. "What about dinner?"

More than a little disappointed, I pause, staring after him, but before I can walk away, he returns. This time he has another muskrat, about the same size as him along with three smaller ones.

"Is this your family?" I grin, happy that I was not deserted.

Again, he twitches his nose, and makes a cute chattering sound.

"I'm assuming that's another 'yes'," I clarify for my own peace of mind.

Slowly, I kneel, allowing Mr. Muskrat's family to sniff my hands and feet.

"You have a lovely little clan," I compliment with all sincerity.

Their twitching noses tickle my skin.

"I think we're going to need a few more fish!"

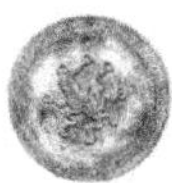

Several minutes later, we settled beside the stream.

Quickly, I call the talons on my right hand and strike with one determined swipe against a smooth rock that I have used to construct my fire pit. All of the stones have come from the stream and unlike the cooking area on the beach it is much smaller, but more easily managed.

Now starving, I use my talons to light the fire and place the smallest fish over it on several elevated spits that I have built to roast it. The crayfish I put directly on the coals around the fire's edge, being careful to turn them often so they will not burn. My veggies are sautéing on a medium rock that I preheated in the pit.

With a pleased grin, I present my dinner guests with the rest of the fish.

"Bon appetite!"

They all twitch their noses at me and begin to eat their meal.

My heart leaps with joy.

Mr. Muskrat and his family almost make me miss my own (almost), but instead of caring about it, I return to tending to my dinner. We eat in comfortable silence, then after our meal, I say goodbye to the muskrat bunch and decide to go back to the beach.

The night is quiet with a lovely cool breeze to fall asleep in.

Hastily, I arrange a pile of palm fronds on the soft sand, and then lie on my back staring up at the cavernous ceiling. Closing my eyes, I grasp my obsidian charm and concentrate on the task of calling the clouds outside the stacks to cover the moon. That makes the illumination on Paradiso turn on and as my vision adjusts to the subtle glow, I realize just how amazing everything on the island is.

I never want to leave.

Ever.

CHAPTER TWENTY-TWO

For three days, I live blissfully alone. I suppose not really alone. Most of the days are spent assisting Mr. Muskrat and his wonderful wife and children. Mrs. Muskrat is an amazing huntress and knows where the biggest and best tasting crayfish hide. Their offspring: Rolly, their only son, named because of his round tummy that tends to get in his way as he moves. Ginger, the eldest of the three whose fur has a lovely ginger tint to it, and lastly, Pinky named for the small dot of pink on her nose.

These three are incredibly bright and are able to work as a team to find food and gather cattails that grow around the edges of the stream. They are also still small enough to squeeze into holes and crevices to find food for the family. Mostly, they play and keep out of the way of their parents who are always working to maintain the family's nest that is burrowed into the bank.

Cleverly, the entrance to their home is located underwater and hidden from predators.

My nights are spent lounging, singing songs to the animals on Paradiso, and hunting for food. I have actually gotten quite skillful with Mercury and am able to successfully hunt animals from several hundred feet away. However, I tend to lean toward seafood, since I love the taste of anything that comes out of the ocean.

Today, I have decided to return to my task of fixing up Melody's old cottage. I have been putting it off and now after some downtime, I have made up my mind to get it done. It will be nice to have a warm place to rest when the temperature drops.

After a quick swim in the lagoon, I use a woven mat I find to dry off, and then I redress and head back to the homestead ready to continue my chores. As I walk up the narrow path, I hear a familiar voice behind me.

"Beautiful day, is it not?"

Ares!

Turning around quickly, I bark, "What are you doing here?!"

Ares' chuckles as he rakes me with his eyes from head to toe then back again.

"I just wanted to drop by for a visit," he leers.

"I didn't invite you this time," I complain, turning back around.

"Once invited, always invited," he informs, a little arrogantly.

"How do I disinvite you?" I ask, wanting to get myself riled up in order to break the stupid bond between us.

"I do not know." The god winks then snickers. "But if I did, do you honestly think I would tell you?"

"Seriously, I don't want you here!" I shout, causing him to stop in his tracks.

"What did I do to make you so irate with me?"

"I know what you've done," I growl, showing my teeth. "Don't pretend to be innocent!"

He holds his hands up like he is being arrested.

"I honestly do not know why you are so upset with me."

With lightning speed, I turn on my heels, and punch him hard in his nonexistent gut.

"Well, according to a reliable source, you killed my great-grandfather," I snarl. "Among other things."

Before he can right himself, I call my talons, but before I can use them, he grabs my wrists and holds me securely in place, eyes flashing deep indigo.

My right foot automatically begins to tap a staccato.

"Let me go, Ares!" I bark at the much too powerful Olympian.

"I did not—"

"Liar!"

Somehow, I manage to pull away and this time I strike him right on the nose with all of my force. To my surprise, he stumbles back, but instead of retaliating, he captures my hands instead. This time, no matter how hard I try, I cannot break free.

"Damn it, Selena!" Ares chastises harshly. *"Stop!"*

For a brief moment, I do as he requests. I do not know why, but I do.

"I admit to several duels between Akheloios and me, but I did not kill him," he confesses indignantly.

"Then why does my great-grandmother think that you did?" I narrow my eyes sharply.

"Poseidon," he interjects, slowly releasing my hands. "It has to be Poseidon."

"The God of the Sea?"

He nods.

"Why would he do that?" I probe, wondering if all gods are jerks.

"He has always been in love with the women of your family," Ares chortles, stepping back and away from my reach.

Ahh!

"I've heard about his amorous feelings toward my great grandmother and my grandmother," I acknowledge. "Did he care for the other women too?"

"No," Ares reemphasizes with a shake of his head. "Gods cannot truly love."

"Huh?" I state, not understanding.

Ares looks away at something across the field. I am not certain what it is, but it has caught his attention and holds it. Nosey to a fault, I turn to stare in that direction, but see nothing noteworthy.

After a while, he speaks.

"Gods and goddesses are inherently pompous and self-serving beings," he admits without heat. "Great power makes it so."

"I see," I mumble, realizing the finality of this statement.

"They view Humans as prized possessions, like interesting baubles," he continues. "However, rumor has it that Poseidon has turned his eyes on you."

Everything in my digestive system threatens to erupt.

"Ugg!" I groan, sick to my stomach. "Please, don't even joke about that."

He convulses with laughter, earning him another hard punch to the abdomen which causes him to double over in pain.

"Ha! Ha!" I mock. "That's not funny!"

"It is!" the God of War replies still folded in half. "It is hilarious!"

When I cannot stay mad any longer, I giggle at his playfulness. In his presence, with this carefree aura, it is impossible to view him negatively no matter how hard one might try.

"You are a beast!" I snort, earning a hitched eyebrow.

As we enter the clearing, he whistles low when his gaze makes contact with my ancestral dwelling. Wide eyes lock onto the semi-completed D.I.Y. project with horror, and all he can do is shake his head.

"This is where you *live*?" He stares in shock, making me self-conscious.

"Not yet," I apprise, determined to keep my composure. "Soon though, I hope."

Without an invitation, he pushes by into the living area. Obviously disgusted by what he sees, he crinkles his nose like he has smelled something revolting, and just as he is examining my soon to be living quarters, a two-foot black snake slithers across the ground startling me. Without missing a beat, I scream.

Ares laughs as he picks up the quickly moving reptile.

"It is just a Whip Snake," he chuckles at my expense.

"Is it poisonous?" I blurt, not caring if I appear squeamish.

"No," he grins, revealing his dimples. "But it will still bite if provoked."

"Good to know," I exhale.

"Would you like it as a pet?" Ares snickers.

"Thanks, but no thanks," I stick my tongue out at him.

Gallantly, he takes the snake outside near the forest and releases it into the wild. The animal rapidly hurries away, hopefully, never to return.

"Why are you afraid of a silly snake?" he probes.

"I don't know," I huff wanting to change the uncomfortable and embarrassing subject.

"You are an all-powerful Siren," he jokes as I blush.

"Keep it up," I warn. "Don't make me banish you from my island."

Holding up his hands in surrender, he laughs.

"Anything but that," he scoffs, playfully.

Impishly, I shove him. Not judging my own strength, he is slammed into the closest wall. As he stands, recovering from the unexpected motion, he studies the structure. Gently, he touches the edifice, seemingly afraid it will collapse below the weight of his palm.

"Are you certain this place is safe?" he asks, voice laced with concern.

"It has lasted for eons," I state confidently. "Why shouldn't it last a few eons more?"

He makes a strange face like he has bitten into a piece of bitter melon.

"It is filthy," the overly indulged deity states snidely, brushing off his hands like he has touched garbage.

"I haven't gotten to cleaning yet!" My temper rises, insulted by his callous, although true, observation. "Right now, I am focusing on repairs."

"You cannot be serious," Ares scolds with a closed mind.

Offended, I scowl.

"This is my ancestral home, and I can't wait to live here."

Tired of his elitist attitude, I exit the low-lying structure to check the outer walls of the house.

Acapella

"The walls are woven wood with a mixture of straw and mud to hold it together," I say aloud, speaking to myself. "I can easily get that from the surrounding forest."

A minute later, Ares joins me outside, a more nonjudgmental look plastered on his face.

"This building has no windows," observantly, he mentions. "I can add a few for you to help let in more light."

Knowing he is trying to make up for his impudence, I blush.

"I would appreciate it," I graciously accept his offer.

After all, the *'man'* has been around for a ridiculous amount of time and should remember when houses looked like this.

"Also, the roof still needs some straw and mud placed on top—"

"Why?" I interrupt, feeling a bit insulted that my work is not quite up to his standards.

Softly, as if he is comforting a wounded animal, he answers.

"To keep the warmth in."

"Oh!" I agree, blushing; slightly embarrassed. "Alright."

Confidently, he continues.

"If it is pleasing to you," he placates as he examines the roof. "I can rig something across the hole over the hearth so smoke can escape, but the rain does not get inside."

This time I hug him, making us both blush, but instead of releasing me, his grip on my hips tightens. Against my will, a rush of inappropriate ideas materializes in my mind. Realizing that we are alone, and anything could happen, I swiftly pull away.

"That's incredibly thoughtful," I commend, taking a much-needed step back. "I'd appreciate it."

Needing to put even more space between us, I exit through the back door as the God of War tries to follow again. Before he can try anything else, I place my hand on his broad chest and make my request.

"You work on the house, and I'll take care of the smaller building."

Disappointed, he nods and trudges toward the forest. Unlike me, his footsteps are silent against the leaf-littered ground. He is definitely impressive. Hoping to get Ares out of my mind, I go to the backyard to deal with the overgrown plot of land that was once where Melody and her daughters grew wheat and barley.

Several yards away, where the smaller version of the house stands overrun with climbing grapevines and surrounded by a low wooden fence badly in need of repair, is where I begin. Not wanting to get scraped by rotten debris, bitten by bugs, or scraped by splintering wood, I call my scales, but only the ones on my arms, hands and legs.

Time to get started!

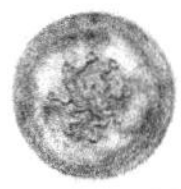

Several hours later, Ares appears from inside the main house, shirt off, wearing nothing but jeans and a smile. When he catches me staring, he chortles. Not knowing how to cover up my obvious attraction to him, I turn back around and continue what I was doing.

"I am finished," he boasts, brushing dirt from his hands. "Come see."

Taking a break from my duties, I inspect his work. To my delight, the god has created three simple windows by cutting squares in the walls. To keep the rain out, he has woven additional mats and secured them to the opening to function as shades. He has also attached pieces of dried braided vines to adjust the length of the coverings.

"These are wonderful," I whisper, touching them like they are made of gold or some other valuable material.

He grins, pleased with himself and his work.

"Look," he shows me how to adjust the blinds. "When you need them to stay open, all you have to do is tie them like this."

"I didn't think you were so clever," I jest, nudging his elbow with mine.

"Sometimes I even surprise myself," he says making us both laugh.

"What about the roof?"

"That was easy," he grins. "I constructed a conical shaped piece of mat with a kind of mushroom cap on top. When you are cooking, all you have to do is pull this cord, which flips the cap to the side and, *Voila!* Instant ventilation!"

"Instead of being in the business of war, you should change your field to construction or architecture," I respond, smiling.

"How are your tasks going?" Ares snickers, ignoring my comment.

"I've finished cleaning out the *'shed'* now I'm working on the garden."

Wanting to get a better view, he steps in front of me, accidentally shoulder-checking me, but does not apologize.

"The garden is still here?" he questions, looking around.

I point in the direction of the tallest weeds.

"Over there is where they kept it," I explain, envisioning the final product. "Right now, it's so overgrown with weeds, you can't really see it, but when it's cleared, it will return to its former glory."

Ares sits on an upside-down wooden cask like the ones that store aged liquors, his legs long enough to straddle it without any effort. Strange that he can seem so normal when he is clearly not normal at all. Even his action of brushing dirt off his hands is intriguing and provocative.

"What will you plant?" His question startles me out of my musings.

"I found tomatoes, some sort of pumpkin, I think onions, garlic, sweet potatoes—"

Laughing, he manages to reply, "I understand, all different kinds of vegetables."

I nod, shyly.

"I am only teasing," he apologizes. "You are doing a great job restoring this farm."

"I know," I giggle as I wipe the sweat from my brow with the back of my hand.

Recognizing a particularly bright yellow flower, he educates as he stands.

"Do not harm these," he points then bends to touch several dandelions. "These are edible... These are not some common weed. Modern man considers them to be pests, but in actuality, they are quite nutritious. Sadly though, many villainize them to sell their herbicides.

"Pathetic *Humans*," he finishes with a snide scowl at the thought.

"I didn't know that." I reply, more than a tad bit impressed. "I mean about the importance of dandelions. I appreciate the tip."

He bows teasingly.

"I've already started pruning the basil, parsley, rosemary, and thyme which have held up pretty well, all things considered," I add, breaking off a piece of mint and a sprig of rosemary.

My stomach growls when I smell the fragrant herbs.

"Does this mean we can take a break for dinner?" Ares smirks.

"I think so," I blush. "As long as you catch it."

"Whatever your heart desires."

Filled with mirth, he grins.

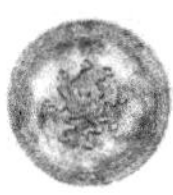

"Son of a grouper!" I exclaim passionately as I examine the wild boar flung over the God of War's muscular shoulder.

"Do you like ribs?" Ares grins proudly, looking at his catch.

Overwhelmed, I scratch my head as I wonder how to cook the hefty beast.

"I do, but—"

"But what?" he asks, skeptically.

"That can't fit inside bamboo stalks," I grumble, staring at the large animal.

"What was that?" Ares' brows hitch at my comment.

"Nothing," I fib, covering it up.

"I can find something else," he frowns, staring at me.

"No need to do that," I state with a frown of my own while Ares continues to stare.

"I don't know how to cook something so gigantic," I use my arms to emphasize the animal's tremendous girth.

My suave dinner companion breathes a sigh of relief.

"Do not worry," he pacifies, resting the carcass on the grass. "Tonight, I will cook."

My brows immediately hitch at his proclamation.

"You can cook?" I joke, earning a stern glare.

"I can," he smirks, good-naturedly. "Genghis Khan taught me."

Wow!

"Fine," I snicker, folding my arms across my chest. "Show me your culinary skills."

Up for the challenge, the agile god goes to work digging a shallow pit in the clearing several feet away from the main house with his bare hands. Wide-eyed, I sit cross-legged on the grass covered ground, watching in amazement. Skillfully, he digs a three-foot hole which is deep enough to hold the one-hundred-pound boar.

Then without a word, he disappears, *literally*, only to reappear holding an eight-foot banana tree. I continue staring at him as he resumes the task at hand. I truly am impressed.

"Why do you need a banana tree?" I question curiously as he tears off the broad green leaves.

He formulates his answer before replying.

"The trunk has a large amount of water inside. When you cook a pig in the ground, a lot of steam is required, and a banana tree's trunk is the perfect way to create this as well as imparting flavor."

"I didn't know that," I grin. "That's good trivia."

He adds: "Did you know that when you cut down a banana tree, it will regrow within just a few months?"

I shake my head no but make a mental note just in case I need that bit of information if I ever appear on the television show *Jeopardy.*

As he finishes constructing the structure that will hold the massive pig above the hot rocks and smoking wood, he turns to me and asks, "Could you do me a huge favor?"

"Sure."

"Soak these in freshwater," he requests, handing me the leaves.

"Anything else?" I grumble, pretending to be irritated by his command.

"While you are soaking the banana leaves, could you look for some lava rocks for the pit?" he answers without looking up.

I clear my throat which makes him turn in my direction.

"You've got it," I salute, jokingly. "Is that all, General Ares?"

He thinks for a minute.

"Do you have seasonings?" he grins at my actions.

"I've got garlic, onions, ginger, black sea salt, thyme, all sorts of things," I beam. "What do you need?"

He smiles.

"Everything."

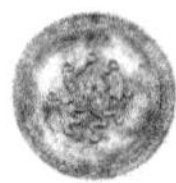

With my mind racing, I run to the pool and soak the leaves while gathering the lava rocks from around the area making sure to choose the ones that are around four to eight inches wide like Ares requested. Thirty minutes later, I return to find the cooking area constructed and the wild boar cleaned and seasoned. The aroma of fresh herbs and spices fill the area making my stomach growl even louder than before.

"Just in time," he grins, standing to greet me.

"I got everything that you asked for," I brag.

"Great!" he exclaims, pointing to the cooking pit. "Place the rocks around the bottom. Be careful not to fall in."

"I will do my best," I respond sticking out my tongue when he turns his back.

In awe, I watch as he lights the fire then returns to the awaiting boar and wraps the entire animal in the wet banana leaves. Carefully, he lowers the marinated meat onto the platform, covers it with more layers of leaves, then fills back the hole with dirt. I cannot wait to eat.

"How long will it take for the boar to cook?" I query, mouth already salivating.

"About eight to nine hours," he says off-handedly.

My mouth gapes.

"We have to wait for eight or nine hours?" I repeat, shaking my head with disappointment.

"We do," he chuckles at my expression of disbelief.

"I'm hungry now!" I whine, listening to my stomach complain.

"We will eat this tomorrow," he responds.

Instantly, my eyes narrow.

"You're inviting yourself for dinner tomorrow?" I add with an arched brow.

He smiles, dimples showing.

"It is for an early lunch," he chuckles, adding one final leaf over the pit.

"This is extremely presumptuous of you," I scold as though he is a cat who just sprayed the couch.

My comment makes him laugh; a full belly laugh that almost makes me laugh too.

Almost.

"Yes, I realize that," he beams using that boyish charm that he has had centuries to master.

"Alright, smart aleck," I insult, losing my patience. "What will we eat right now?"

He considers our choices then states, "I will be right back."

With that said, he disappears in a cloud of sparkling gold dust.

Only a few minutes pass before he returns carrying a flat cardboard pizza box and cup holder with two beverages. I stare at him and then at the items in his hands. My expression must be one of bewilderment.

"What is that?" finally I interrogate.

"It is dinner," he snickers.

"Where did you get it?" I ask, hands on hips, right foot tapping my annoyance.

"I figured you would enjoy something that you did not have to kill and cook, so I popped over to Naples and got us some comfort food," he grins, obviously pleased with himself.

"I have to admit, I've missed pizza," I reply with glee.

Thrilled to eat, I settle on the soft ground and wait until he is sitting on the grass beside me. Knowing that I am starving, he places the box between us.

"Bon appetite!" Ares announces while opening the lid to reveal the steaming, Neapolitan masterpiece. My entire body heats as the scent of melty cheese and freshly baked dough overloads my senses. Inhaling deeply, I allow the fragrance to permeate the air around me. It is the scent of heaven.

"Is that—"

"Pizza Margherita?" he teases, quickly closing the lid. "It definitely is."

I feel a dollop of drool form as I inhale the tangy aroma again.

"Would you like a slice?" he playfully tempts like the biblical serpent, but with handspun pizza instead of an apple.

Unable to speak, I nod.

"Will you allow me back on the island for lunch tomorrow?" He uses my hunger against me.

"Is this another bribe?" I joke, reaching for my first slice, but he pulls it out of reach.

"Yes," he grins impishly while handing me a paper napkin he also procured from the restaurant. "I will not deny it."

I pause, letting him suffer.

Slowly, provocatively, he turns the reopened box toward me and uses his hand to fan the steam coming off of it in my direction. He is torturing me on purpose.

Butthead!

In an attempt to further antagonize me, he artfully describes, "Can you see how lovingly this is made using only simple, fresh ingredients: a basic dough recipe that dates back to the late eighteen-hundreds, vine-ripened tomatoes, fresh mozzarella cheese, sweet organic basil, and pure Italian olive oil—no fancy toppings?"

"You are incorrigible," I groan, wanting a piece.

"Come on," he torments. "You know you want it."

I sit motionless, debating.

"Look at all of this delicious goodness," he continues.

Still, I remain quiet.

"Do not be stubborn," he sighs, impatiently.

Defiantly, I fold my arms across my chest.

When I remain silent, he huffs: "Here, you difficult Siren! Eat!"

Giving up, he hands me a slice then takes one for himself. Immediately, I take a big bite. *Oh! My! Gravy!* This is what I have been craving, mouthwatering pizza still bubbling and oozing with goodness.

"Thank you," I moan after a few more bites, and he blushes.

"You are welcome, my dearest Selena."

Sitting quietly, we finish the entire thing. Afterwards, Ares pats his stomach and chuckles, causing me to chuckle too. I could not have wished for a better evening.

CHAPTER TWENTY-THREE

The following morning, I wake feeling odd, for lack of a better word. Everything bothers me: the sound of the birds chirping, the brightness of the sunlight as it filters through the crevices in the limestone, the balmy temperature so early in the day, even the taste of a perfectly ripened coconut has lost its appeal.

"Yuck!" I mumble to myself, tossing aside the one-seeded drupe.

Hoping to improve my mood, I quickly strip-down to skin so I can take a relaxing swim. Filled with anticipation, I race toward the water, smiling as I get closer. Without hesitation, I dive below the calm surface, but when the saltwater touches my skin, it burns. Immediately, I call my scales and webbing, hoping to counteract whatever is in the water that is causing me irritation.

Unfortunately, it does not help much.

ACAPELLA

As I drift along the current, I close my eyes and begin to breathe deeply, letting the oxygen flood my system. Slowly, I feel better. My scales are doing their job, and the sea no longer burns.

Ahh! Much better!

In fact, I am so comfortable that I drift into a light slumber; however, my peacefulness lasts only ten or so minutes before I feel something bite onto my right ankle, but it does not go all the way through my scales. Jolted out of sleep, my eyes instantly open.

"Ouch!" I scream underwater, and the sound echoes throughout the water-filled space.

Glancing down, I see the light-gray, three foot long, torpedo-like shape still attached to where it initially bit. It is a pup. Shaking my head, I try without success to pry him off.

"Stupid Spinner shark!" I click and clack, examining his markings. "I am not a meal! Let go!"

Belligerently, and true to his species, he ignores my command.

"You're pissing me off!" I click then whistle at the top of my lungs, emphasizing my exasperation.

Still, he, wait, *she* ignores me.

"Do you want to be made into soup?" I threaten at the end of my rope, but still there is no response.

The young shark even has the nerve to shake back and forth as she attempts to saw through my defenses.   Trying another tactic, I poke at her eyes hoping she will let go, but instead she just rolls them back.

"This is your last chance," I warn. "Release me or suffer the consequences."

The bold beast actually grins at me.

"I've tried reasoning with you," I sternly chastise. "But you refuse to listen!"

Stubbornly, she bites down harder.

More annoyed than hurt, I shake my leg attempting one last time to get her attention, but defiantly she readjusts her grip to get a better hold. This time she manages to get my entire foot into her mouth.

Left with no other choice, I call my talons, skewer her mouth and pry apart her jaws. Needing to send a message to any onlookers with delusions of grandeur, I rip her body apart and eat everything except the tail and fins. With a satisfied burp, I pick the excess flesh from my teeth as I leisurely swim back towards the shore.

"Anyone else want a piece of me?" Arrogantly, I yell into the surrounding depths and to my delight, all of the sea life in the small inlet suddenly disappears.

"Don't you forget it!"

I close my eyes again, but my moment of solace is gone. Sadly, I begin to swim to shore. This is not how I envisioned my day starting. Usually, being in the sea comforts me, but today, not even that helps. When I arrive back to shore, Ares is waiting for me with a huge smile on his face.

"What are you doing here?" I rudely comment.

"I have missed you—" he responds, taken aback.

"We just saw each other last night," I interject brazenly. "Wasn't that enough?"

"I wanted to check on the wild boar. It should be cooked by now," The god counters, ignoring my poor attitude.

Pretending he is not there; I retract my webbing and scales exposing my human form. His expression immediately changes as he closes his eyes. With a wicked chortle, I grab my shorts and t-shirt and begin dressing, uncaring that he is standing only a few feet away. In a most gentlemanly fashion, he turns his back to give me some privacy. For some reason, I do not care whether he sees me naked or not.

"Ahem!" he nervously clears his throat.

"What?!" I snap.

"That was unexpected," he chastises.

"Did I embarrass you?" I provoke not caring that I have made him uncomfortable. "You are thousands of years old. I'm sure you've seen more than your share of naked bodies."

"I am only thinking of your virtue," he responds, but keeps his back to me.

"My virtue?" I repeat, outwardly mocking him. "Like you could make me do anything that I didn't want to do."

"I will meet you at the imu," Ares informs, choosing to avoid confrontation.

"What is an 'imu'?" I imitate his voice effortlessly as I pull on my top and stand, hands on hips, glaring at him.

He tries to look me in the eyes but cannot.

"It is the Hawaiian word that means an underground cooking pit."

"Oh! Good to know." I grumble, turning my back to him.

"Have I done something wrong?" He turns suddenly, his voice is shaky, and nothing resembling his normal confident self.

"I don't know," I say with a haughty tone. "Have you?"

This time, he does not answer, just turns toward the path that leads to the small house. With growing irritation, I stand watching him walk away, a scowl of epic proportion on my face. Suddenly, the vein at my temple throbs its annoyance as my mind races uncontrollably.

Dammit! What's wrong with me?

Needing to figure out why I am so angry, I take my time fixing my hair. Contemplatively, I replay everything that had happened last night to this morning and realize that there is absolutely nothing that can account for my nasty temperament. All I know is that I feel out of control and itching for a fight.

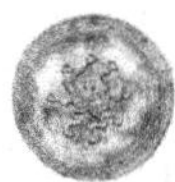

Several minutes later, I find Ares uncovering the pit in order to check the doneness of the meat. As he removes the last layer of banana leaves the intense aroma of seasoned wild boar tickles my nostrils. It smells disgusting!

"*Ugg!*" I groan and wheeze, feeling my stomach churn. "That smells horrible!"

Ares' face drops.

"Are you serious?" he whines in complete disbelief. "It smells amazing."

Carefully, he tears off a piece of the caramelized skin and takes a bite. Happy with the outcome, he moans in delight.

"You have to taste this," he grins like a little boy with his first ice cream cone. "It is better than amazing."

"I don't want any," I reply, holding my breath.

"Please," he pleads. "One bite— "

"No thank you," I protest, shooting him a nasty look.

Ignoring my wishes, he breaks off a tiny piece and begins to walk in my direction. As he reaches a foot in front of me, I grab him around the neck and pull him down to my lips. At first, he resists, but as I continue to assault his lips, he surrenders. His grip on my hips tightens as our kiss deepens.

Suddenly, he pulls away.

"Stop!" he orders, wiping his mouth with the back of his hand, his gaze icy.

"Why?" I pretend to be ignorant of his manly reaction.

Firmly, he holds me at arm's length. His breathing is labored like he has just run a marathon. His amethyst eyes have darkened to violet, and I can even hear his heart thumping wildly inside of his heaving chest.

"What's wrong?" I purr as I try to get closer, but he holds me easily in place.

"I do not know what game you are playing, but you need to stop," he orders.

"I don't want to stop." I pout.

"You must," Ares releases me, his eyes returning to normal.

As he continues to stand in front of me looking pathetic, something snaps inside of me. Rage fueled by contempt spreads like wildfire through my limbs filling me with something dark… something scary. Before I can stop, I kneel touching my hands to the ground. The earth begins to shake violently as I channel all the energy contained on Paradiso through my core. It feels like white lightning as it strikes, unforgiving, and unapologetic.

Like a bomb, the energy detonates from my arm as my fist meets his chest. The force sends him flying through the air depositing his limp body on the grassy area near the forest. He lays there for a minute or two, prostrate and motionless, both hands gripping his left side.

At last, he moves, groaning loudly.

"I think you broke my ribs."

"You're lucky that's all I broke," I hiss. "I was hoping to do more damage."

"You are not acting like yourself," he claims on a groan.

"You're wrong," I disagree. "I finally feel like a god. Isn't that what you offered when you took me to Mount Etna?"

"Yes, but— "

I hold up my hand, stopping his explanation.

"You offered me the world as my kingdom, didn't you?"

"My offer was for us to rule together," he clarifies with a puzzled expression.

Before I can give my retort, he groans again.

"There are rules governing supernatural beings," he educates, still clutching his wounded area. "You have just broken one of the most sacred rules."

"What rule is that?" I sneer.

Suddenly, his eyes narrow, the warning clear.

"Never use the power of the Earth without permission," he relays without humor.

Another surge of power builds inside of my core, radiating outwards until it is released through my fingertips. This time the God of War rolls out of the way before it can strike. Shakily, he stands. The wrath building until he morphs out of his civilian garb into his godly battle gear including his spear.

"I do not wish to fight you, Selena!" Ares snarls.

"You wish to die then?" I beam evilly as I extend my hands in the direction of the earth, but this time I do not need to touch it in order to tap into its power.

As easy as breathing, I focus on the sky hidden outside of the limestone walls that hide the island from the outside world. Immediately, it darkens and just like before, the foliage becomes lit from within, shedding their soft glow around us. Ares grips his weapon tighter as a crack of blue lightning breaks through the protective barrier, shattering part of the limestone as it comes for him. The bolt strikes the ground a few inches away from his sandaled feet, throwing him backwards toward the sharp thicket surrounding the woods. Luckily for him, he somehow manages to plunge his spearhead into the dry soil and uses it as a brake, skillfully somersaulting up and onto his feet.

"Impressive," I smirk.

Standing tall, he glowers at me, still weary of my actions.

"What has come over you?"

"You're a god for Pete's sake, you're meant to be invincible," I smirk, rolling my eyes. "Show what a badass you can be, God of War."

This time I call to the root systems hidden beneath the topsoil of Paradiso. He does not realize what is happening until the long, thick, tentacle-like roots have ensnared his legs and arms. Angrily, he struggles to get free, but they only tighten.

"Release me!" he roars causing the entire island to shake violently.

"Release yourself!" I shout back as I send another bolt at him; however, he uses the spear he clutches to soak up the energy, redirecting it at me. The supernatural object hits my abdomen knocking me onto my gluteus maximus, temporarily disorienting me.

From my seat sprawled on the hard packed dirt, I whimper, "Come Forth… *Veniforas!*"

"No more, Siren!" the God of War bellows.

Ignoring his rising temper, I raise my voice, "*Veniforas…* I invoke the sea and all of its fury!"

Suddenly, Ares breaks free of his bonds.

"What you are doing is forbidden!" he shouts over the din of crashing waves and booming thunder.

I only stare at his miserable face.

Taking a deep breath, I continue.

"*Veniforas!* I call to thee! Come forth!"

The next thing I hear is a loud whizzing sound coming from the beach as a hail of jagged volcanic rocks shoot out from the foaming sea; each deadly projectile aimed at the handsome god in front of me. They rain on him like bullets exiting the world's most powerful gun. With such force, they pierce his armor and even knock his helmet off his head, leaving him unprotected.

Well-seasoned as a fighter, he uses his spear like a shield, blocking most of the flying debris, but he is not fast enough to block them all. Several strike his dented chest plate while one four-inch fragment smashes into his left temple, sending him down to his knees then onto his back.

By this time, I am standing over him, watching as he sputters blood from his mouth. His once flawless face is now marred by blackish-blue bruises of varying sizes and shapes. Even his knuckles appear to be swollen and cracked, but I am not sure why, and his once manicured fingernails which now have volcanic grit lodged beneath them appear chipped and torn.

"Not so mighty, are you, son of Zeus?" I tease with a devilish grin, not caring that I have bested an ancient being, one of the twelve original Olympian gods.

Slowly, agonizingly, he sits upright, wearing the most pained expression. His entire body shaking like a leaf blowing in the wind, and for one brief moment, I almost feel guilty.

"You are behaving like a bi—" he mumbles when he is able to speak.

My hackles rise as does my blood pressure.

"Go ahead!" I growl. "I dare you to say it!"

Instead of answering, he fades away in a golden shimmer.

"God of War, my ass!" I practically spit as I turn and walk away.

I get only a few feet before I hear a deep baritone behind me, the sound so familiar yet almost forgotten within such a short span of time.

"You are so grounded!" the man states with authority.

Stupefied, I blink several times as I swallow the lump in my throat. It cannot be. He cannot be here.

Slowly, I turn around to face him.

My brain instantly freezes as I stand face to face with my stepfather.

CHAPTER TWENTY-FOUR

He looks just as I remember, but then again it has only been a few weeks. His hair is wet and slicked away from his face with its exotic Spanish good looks, but the tiny bit of gray at his temples have doubled, almost tripled. I guess it is from the stress I have caused during my self-inflicted solitary confinement. On his athletic form, he wears a wetsuit while he carries his Scuba gear in his hands.

"Dad?" I gasp, horrified. "How are you here?"

I look around for the others, but I do not see them.

"Wu-what are you d-doing here?" I stammer, unable to make sense of what I am seeing.

He does not answer, only watches me intently.

"I thought Mom said that you could not be here because the sediment in the water would make you deathly ill," I recall.

Still, he says nothing, yet his eyes dart to different parts of the clearing. First, they land on the grassy knoll behind me then further to the jagged mountain on the opposite side of the island. The blowing palm fronds cause him to look up, when he notices the illumination coming from the foliage and ground, he smiles.

At last, he speaks.

"Wow!" He whistles in amazement, eyes glistening even in the dark. "It's like Dr. Who's TARDIS in here. *Wow!*"

His expression is that of a schoolboy hungry for knowledge.

"I never imagined it would be as gorgeous as this."

His comment makes me giggle, but immediately I harden my outer shell.

Clearing my throat, I interrogate.

"You still haven't answered my question."

He turns back to me.

"Do you remember the samples you brought back for me to study?"

I nod.

"You wanted to do research," I answer blandly, hiding my excitement to have him here with me, the person who has encouraged and loved me unconditionally.

"I've learned a lot about the makeup of the chemicals that surround the island," he smiles warmly.

"That's good, I guess," I reply uneasily waiting for the next shoe to fall.

"The cells of your body are programed to be Siren," he educates. "So without *The Joining* your body is in a constant state of flux, never leveling out, unable to evolve—"

"I don't understand why any of this would matter to me," I interrupt, not caring that I am being rude.

"Enough of this." David sighs.

"Enough of what?" I ask, cocking my head to the side.

"It's time," he states calmly, but winces briefly as if in pain.

"Time for what?" I act like I do not know what he is referring to. "Wait!"

Slowly, he turns away, his attention back on the glowing palm tree in front of us. Gently, like his touch will harm the sturdy tree, he runs his hands along the trunk, enjoying the slight imperfections that he feels under his palm.

"Dad?"

"Yes?" he answers, but his tone is heavily burdened.

My mind is racing once more.

"How did you get through the barrier at the entrance of the Siren Grotto?"

He shrugs.

"Apparently, the chant you used can only work on Sirens, so I being human, was able to pass right through," he winks cheekily.

"Good to know," I growl. "I'll know better next time."

He chuckles, but this time I not only hear my father's deep tone, but I hear Ando's playful giggle shadowing it like two radio stations accidentally merging, but you can still decipher music from both, just compressed together. It is difficult to understand either of them, but you know that something is not right.

Not right in the least.

"Why do I hear an echo?" I look around the area for my little brother. "Is Ando here too?"

David nods, turning to face me once more.

I look around, but we are the only ones here.

"Where is he?" I cross-examine my parent.

Lightly, he touches his chest confusing me even more.

"What the heck does that mean?!" my voice raises an octave.

"Ando is inside of me," he mentions casually. "Along with the others."

I blink without any comprehension.

"I have no idea what you are meaning," I admit, feeling like an idiot.

David smiles eerily, not at all like himself, more like Ligeia.

"They are all inside of me," he announces again as he leans against the tree trunk appearing to keep himself upright.

"Who are all inside of you?" I question his incoherent admission.

"Your mother, the aunts, Ando, of course," he grins with more effort than it should take. "Oh! I forgot about Melody. Melody is in there too."

I glare at him as though he has lost his ever-loving mind.

"Are you drunk?" I blurt still not understanding the cryptic crap he is speaking of.

Slowly, he shakes his head and all of the hairs on my arms stand like soldiers at attention.

"David?" I huff getting annoyed. "How can all of those people be inside of you?"

As I continue to glare at his disjointed movements, I realize that during the few minutes that he has been on Paradiso, it seems he has aged twenty years. Stiffly, he kneels and grabs a handful of black sand, smiling the entire time. The twinkle in his lovely hazel eyes is the only thing that resembles his former self.

"Your great grandmother did a spell to link us all together."

He waves it off like this sort of thing happens every day.

Inquisitively, I study his labored movement as he tries to stand, bracing himself when he walks as if struggling to do the simple task. Noticeably, there is also a thin layer of sweat above his upper lip and his forehead is covered too. Even his rapidly pounding heart can be heard without placing my head to his chest to listen.

"Why would they do that?" I continue to stare at him.

"You know why," he scoffs, voice now sounding like Aunt Ligeia. "We should have done *The Joining* months ago. This would not be happening if we did."

My eyes widen to the size of saucers.

"Ligeia!" I shout. "Is that you?"

"Do not sound so surprised," Melody answers next, the sudden changes between the female entities apparently inside of my stepfather is making my head spin and not in a good way.

Dear Father!

"Stop talking all of you!" I screech grabbing my ears, wishing they would all just, *"Shut up!"*

"You are being extremely rude, young lady," Aunt Leukosia speaks next, her lovely soothing voice incapable of seeming harsh even when chastising.

It hits me.

"Why am I hearing you inside of my head as well as out here?!"

Instinctively, I close my eyes in order to concentrate on blocking them, but I cannot.

"What have you done to me?!" I yell, still gripping my ears in agony.

At last, I hear my mother.

"Ares helped us," she informs sternly, tone harsh and unapologetic.

"How did he help?" I glare at my stepdad who sounds like my mom.

"Last night, after your meal together, he appeared to us at the villa," she answers without malice which surprises me.

"What did he say?" I frown.

"He told us that you were acting strangely, and he realized, so was he."

My eyebrows hitch to my hairline.

"What do you mean?" I ask with all sincerity.

"Somehow *you* connected the two of you," Mom informs without heat.

"You're lying!"

"No, I'm not," she remains calm. "You took on his aggressive warmongering personality while he became gentler… more sensitive… susceptible to Human feelings."

Rapidly, I shake my head, not wanting to believe that I could make that happen.

"That's not true!" I shout; the sound reverberating against the limestone. "I just mastered calling my webbing and scales. How could I now be able to join myself to Ares?"

"Ares had never felt love before, never," my mother continues, "Until he met you. That's how he realized what you had unknowingly done."

"I don't believe you!" I snarl, shaking my head.

Then I hear Melody.

"I realized what you were doing when you visited me at the cottage," the soothing voice of the Muse accuses.

"Do?" I yell at David who is housing her essence. "I did nothing!"

"While you were there, I was being bombarded by menacing thoughts," she admits. "But they were not my thoughts… they were *yours*."

Violently, I shake my head while fighting against my urge to strike out.

"That is why I stopped holding your hand," she sadly informs, her face lined with worry, worry for me.

Stubbornly, I shake off her words.

"That still doesn't explain how you all were able to get back into my brain," I whimper as a migraine begins to grow.

"Melody knew that in order for her spell to work your defenses would need to be weakened, weakened enough for you to lower your guard."

"Ares volunteered to be your punching bag," David chimes in. "Turns out, he really does care about you, spell or not."

Damn him! That little scoundrel! I begin to comprehend.

Ares got me to use my energy on him in order to help make me more vulnerable, so my family could get through the barrier without me stopping them. He then made me burn off some of my strength fighting him, I summarize as best as I can in my current state of mind.

David nods weakly, eyes shadowed with dark circles, something he never has.

Suddenly, the ground beneath our feet begins to tremble then grows into a small earthquake almost causing my stepfather and me to lose our balance. Just as before, the dirt shifts and reshapes into a statuesque female adorned with a crown of shamrocks, her voluptuous figure regal and perfect. The first thing I notice is that her amber eyes are redlined and puffy, I can only assume from crying. With unadulterated disappointment, her gaze cuts through me like a laser beam cuts through metal. Usually, she is filled with joy and compassion, but at this moment, she has the look of death.

"Gaia?" I mumble. "Why are you here?"

Her eyes narrow.

"I tried to warn you," the Goddess of the Earth sniffles, but remains unyielding.

"Warn me about what?" I fake innocence.

"Using the power of the Earth for your own personal gain is prohibited, even for me," she reveals.

"But I can control it," I reply arrogantly, standing my ground.

The beautiful Earth Mother shakes her head.

"Dear child, this great power will corrupt you if you allow it," she whispers as her irises glow like cat's eyes.

"I can control it," I argue. "I really can."

"*You cannot!*" Her voice booms startling every creature currently on Paradiso, causing them to flee from the area. "One taste, one drop of strength that you stole from the ocean, from the sea, from everybody of water that flows into it…

"*You* have stolen from *Me!*"

"I didn't mean to," I try to apologize, but she only holds up her hand to stop me.

"It's time, Lena," Ando's sad voice gets my attention.

"*No!*" I scream so loud that my throat hurts. "I don't want to go back to the human world! *I won't let you do this!*"

Enraged, I lunge at David, who stands motionless, but the same roots that I used to bind Ares are now being used against me. With Gaia's command, they wrap around my legs and arms keeping me in place, and with all of my might, I struggle, but eventually tire myself out.

David bows low to Gaia, before announcing, "Let '*The Joining*' begin!"

"Wait!" I yell. "We can't do the ceremony without the full moon!"

At last, Gaia smiles.

"Look up, dearest Selena," she requests with tenderness.

Without argument, I follow her instructions looking up at the topmost part of the limestone crag cracks. Gracefully, she raises her hands which opens an invisible seam in the stone that reminds me of a skylight, allowing us to see the sky. Above Paradiso is an enormously full moon shining down on the constantly moving sea.

"I didn't realize so much time had passed," I murmur self-consciously.

Before I can say anything more, David begins to chant in a language I do not understand. It sounds like a mixture of Siren, Latin, and possibly Swahili? Whatever language it is, it sounds guttural and terrifying.

"Dad!" I finally release my stubborn exterior. "I'm not ready!"

Not sure that he heard me over the roar of the sea, I try again. *"Daddy, please stop!"*

Still, he ignores my complaints. Then all goes quiet right before he bellows:

> *"Alagreo! Encanto wannee et su porto!*
> *Alagreo! Encanto wannee et su magga!*
> *Alagreo Ignis! Alagreo Glacies!"*

Then finally he utters something that I know, but instead of hearing my stepfather's voice, I hear my mother, Ando, Aunt Ligeia, Aunt Leukosia and Melody all in unison.

Then it switches to Siren.

"We call to the sea and every creature in it," they click, clack, whistle, and squeak. "We call to the moon and its quiet strength... we call on great Gaia to invoke *The Three*!

"*Alagreo!*"

Gaia speaks next.

"*Ajlonga exst suddo masala!*"

As I watch, storm clouds form overhead. Next, I hear the low roll of thunder as it ushers in the deafening wind. Behind the wall of bleakness, nasty black clouds conceal the streaks of horrifying lightning cracking and hissing behind. Then it forms that bizarre blue lighting that pierces the ominous darkness.

"*Alagreo Ignis!*" They chant with more fervor, more intent.

In a flash of electric blue, the first bolt strikes me in the chest, followed by several more in succession.

"*Alagreo Glacies!*" they add and with that last command a blinding bolt of steel-blue lightning breaks through the thickest cloud and strikes me with the force of an atom bomb.

"*Stop it!*" I screech, unbelieving that my family would do this to *me*.

Remarkably, it does not burn *at first*; instead, it feels ice-cold, so cold that it recharges me. However, that sensation does not last long. As the electricity intensifies it starts to burn, but not with heat. This must be the 'ice'. The 'lightning' is both the fire and the ice, but not these elements in the traditional sense. This, I imagine, is much worse than either of the two on their own.

As both components combine within my body, within my core like quicksilver, my limbs soak them in, letting it travel down my spine then along bone and sinew, stretching out to veins and corpuscles, until finally reaching flesh and skin. My entire body tingles, then surges like it has been plugged into an electrical socket. Suddenly, with this material coursing through my extremities, I begin to feel different. Tranquil. So different than I did before.

Then without warning, my breathing accelerates, and my heart feels like it will explode from out of my chest.

"I can't feel my legs!" I shriek in horror. *"You're killing me!"*

"Shh," the Sirens comfort. "Try not to panic. This is *The Christening*. Just let it happen."

Dear Father! Something else?

Trying to obey their instructions as best as I can, I take several deep breaths, but the burning sensation is inside of my lungs as well.

"I can't breathe!" I bellow and feel my tears escape down my cheeks, the salty liquid just as hot; just as molten.

"Be strong, Lena!" My brother comforts and I let his voice soothe my fears, finally understanding that my family would never, *ever* let any harm come to me.

I must be strong!

"I am Siren!" I whisper reassuringly to myself. "I am a descendant of Zeus! I am a descendant of Poseidon! I am born of Gaia!"

Damn right I am!

'Say the words out loud!' my mother requests firmly through telepathy. *'Say it and The Christening will be complete!'*

"I can't!" I scream against the pandemonium happening around me. "I can't do it!"

Then I hear *him*.

My stepfather.

My David!

Calmly, which is his way, he speaks just to me, his little girl.

"*Calmate, mija,*" he comforts in Spanish as our gaze's lock. "You are powerful."

"I don't wanna be, Dad!" I wail, overcome with emotions… *Human* emotions.

Ahh! There's the rub.

This is what they wanted.

Me to inadvertently turn back on my humanity.

"Daddy!" I plead with all honesty. "I can't be a Siren!"

David just smiles.

"Repeat after me," he continues in that same soft-spoken nature that Mom and I fell in love with all those years ago.

"My name is Selena Antonius Thermopolis Marquez," he says then waits for me to repeat.

Stubbornly, I remain silent.

"Come on, my love," he urges with determination. *"Por favor!* Please, repeat it."

Taking another painful breath, I mumble:

"My name is Se-Selena Antonius Thermopolis Marquez."

"I am the sea," he continues with urgency.

I close my eyes, finding strength.

"I am the Sea."

"I am the Earth," my stepfather adds.

Another barrage of white-hot, intense pain makes me almost double over.

"Selena!" Dad's voice snaps me back to the task at hand.

"I-I am the Earth," I follow his command.

"I am Fire, and I am Ice."

The pain mocks me, but something else begins to take over.

Something ancient…

Something more powerful than myself…

"I am Fire, and I am Ice," I declare with more confidence, more understanding.

The rest I know now, and on my own, I continue.

"I am the bridge; I am the portal that links the planes together and the glue that keeps the world in place. I am Heaven. I am Hell. I am the embodiment of all that is good in nature."

Unexpectedly, the winds begin to intensify, intensify to the point that I feel my body being lifted from the ground, but I do not fly off since the roots hold me in place.

"What's happening?!" I scream at the top of my lungs, praying that the restraints will not uproot and send me crashing into the stalagmite cliffs.

Just as before with Mom, from every direction, squalls of wind accost me, wanting to rip me apart. Unable to call for my scales, I am bombarded with a frigid northern stream along with a suffocating fiery stream from the south followed by a more moderate stream from the east and lastly, an unrelenting stinging one from the west.

Not again!

'Close your eyes,' Mom instructs telepathically, and I obey.

With my eyelids tightly shut, I start to feel the various winds intermingling, twirling, rushing faster and faster, whipping against my body, almost painfully they slash at my exposed human skin, but I can do nothing.

Then all of the streams converge becoming one, one massive airborne current that has a life of its own. First, it whips me clockwise then counterclockwise until I feel the need to hurl, but somehow, I manage to keep it contained. I scream, but the rush is so loud that I can hardly hear it.

What I do hear, is that ancient voice that calls from somewhere else, somewhere not of this place. I hear it and I answer with the only thing that makes sense to say:

"I… Am… Siren!" I yell those words with such force that my eardrums pop and a trickle of blood runs down either side of my face.

Slowly, my breathing returns to normal as the pain fades back into the ether and the winds release me to return to their rightful corners of the globe. My entire body is in pain and covered with scratches, but it does not matter because *The Joining* is complete.

ACAPELLA

"I am Siren," I whisper for only me to hear as my equilibrium returns to normal and my stomach settles in place once more.

In the background, with my eyes still closed, I hear the roar of the wind subside. I hear the sea calm to a gentle roll. I even hear as the angry clouds transform to soft puffy pillows.

Slowly, and with complete exhaustion, I open my eyes.

Where's my family? Ah!

There they are, still watching over me with shining aquamarine eyes within David's hazel ones.

"Hi, baby girl," Mom grins with relief.

"Are you feeling better, Lena?" my brother questions hopefully.

The only strength that remains inside of me allows me to nod and wink.

"See?" both aunts say as one. "Nothing to worry over."

Wanting to laugh, but unable to, I simply roll my eyes.

Where did David go?

"Please bring David back," I request with longing. "Please."

His eyes close and when they reopen hazel orbs greet me.

"I'm here," I hear as he weakly whimpers.

Excited, I grin from ear to ear.

"Hi, Dad!"

The last thing I see is him smile lovingly at me, as he mouths:

"I love you, my daughter," then in front of me, he clutches his chest right before his fatigued body crumples to the ground.

"Daddy!" is my only word as I fall into darkness…

CHAPTER TWENTY-FIVE

"Good afternoon, ladies and gentlemen. The weather on Isla Flora is a temperate eighty-one degrees with light winds coming from the east. Please remember to gather all of your belongings, take small children by the hand, and from the entire Caribe Airlines crew we thank you for flying with us..."

"Selena," Mom taps me on the shoulder, bringing me back to the here and now. "Help me with this duffle bag, please."

Her eyes are puffy and red, and I know she has been crying.

Beside me, staring out the airplane window at nothing in particular, is my brother. He has not spoken to me since the *'event'*. I understand why he has not. If he had done what I did, well, I would not talk to me either. Still, I hope that he will change his mind and forgive me in the future.

"Okay, Mom," I smile, but I know it does not reach my eyes.

As the other passengers file one-by-one past us disembarking the crowded commercial airline, Ando continues to sit in silence, looking out at the black pitch of the runway.

"Ando," I gently take his hand, but he pulls away. "It's time to go."

He nods, but still refuses to speak.

"Hold this," Mom hands him his teddy bear, Alfredo, who looks just as jetlagged as we all do, his left ear practically folded over with exhaustion.

Mutely, he takes the stuffed animal and clutches it to his chest, a lone teardrop rolls down his cheek and he angrily wipes it away.

"Hurry you guys!" Mom orders as she leads the way up the narrow aisle that heads off of the plane.

"Have a great night," the pretty Asian air hostess, with the flower in her dark hair, smiles brightly as we exit the state-of-the-art jetliner.

We all nod and smile politely as we make our way to baggage claim. In silence, we follow the crowd of passengers into the main building which is brightly decorated with original art prints by local artists. The furnishings are tasteful pieces in rattan and glass that makes it warm and inviting. On a mission, all of us filter into the baggage claim area at the far corner of the spacious warehouse-like building. We resemble a school of salmon swimming upstream to spawn.

Usually, I would smile at that image, but today it actually physically hurts to smile.

It hurts to breathe.

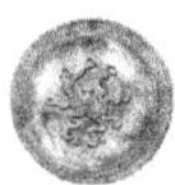

After a ten-minute wait, a small dome light begins to flash in unison with a steady alarm, then quiet, until the low drone of the motor switches on and the luggage carousel begins to move. Soon after, a slew of multicolored and styled luggage appears, all moving in a serpentine motion along its path. I notice that practically everyone smiles in relief when they spot their own suitcases. A few utter a litany of swears before stomping toward the Caribe Airlines counter. Thank goodness, I see our items almost immediately.

"There they are!" I point in that general direction.

"C'mon!" Mom snaps. "We don't want Nicole's mom to wait any longer than needed."

Ando and I nod.

We quickly grab our things and race to the arrival pick up area. Just as expected, Mrs. Wong and Nicole are already waiting. Both of them look miserable too.

Great!

This is the part I hate. The moment people look at you with pity in their eyes, not knowing what to say or what to do.

I wish I could say to them: *'No sympathy please!'* That is what I want to say, but instead refrain.

"I'm so sorry, Marina," Mrs. Wong hugs Mom tightly and she lets her. "How did it happen?"

Mom begins to tear up but stops herself.

"It was just an accident," she sniffles, removing a tissue from her purse.

"I'm so sorry," Mrs. Wong says again, giving her another tight squeeze. "If there is anything that you need, please let me know."

"Thank you," our mother manages a small, awkward smile.

My best friend, Nicole, finally speaks.

"Come here, little guy," Nicole gives my brother a warm hug and a sisterly kiss to the forehead.

To my surprise, Ando actually hugs her back. I suppose that is progress. He has not wanted or let anyone touch him, not even the aunts.

"How are you holding up?"

Ando only shrugs.

Then Nicole turns to me, eyes overflowing with tears.

"How are you doing?" she asks in a hollow sounding tone.

"Fine, all things considering," I lie and respond.

I hear Nicole's mother in the background saying again: "If there's anything, anything at all, just let me know, alright?"

Mom smiles again, but this time her demeanor stiffens.

"Right now, we just need to be home," my mother reminds.

"Of course," Mrs. Wong takes one of Mom's carryon bags and a medium-sized suitcase.

"Thank you so much for picking us up," Mom states as she helps load our things into the spacious minivan.

"No worries," the lovely Trinidadian woman waves off the compliment. "I made you a casserole for dinner, so you won't need to cook. I hope you all like chicken and broccoli with wild rice."

My stomach lurches in disgust.

"Sounds great," my mother fibs. "Thank you."

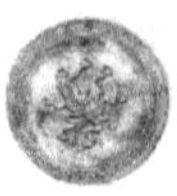

The ride to the country is done in complete silence. I spend the time reflecting on the summer's events leading up to *'my rebellion'*. That is how I refer to it. 'My rebellion.' It sounds better than: *'That period of time when I went bat-crap crazy.'* Plus, somehow it eases my guilty consciousness, but not by much.

Actually, not at all.

Our last week on Capri was spent packing, meeting with the groundskeeper, doing general cleaning, and other mundane and innocuous rituals. Ando spent that time in his room. Doing what, I have no idea. My brother only came out to eat and use the washroom. Many nights, I would hear him cry himself to sleep. Others, he spent in front of his window overlooking the *Marina Piccola*. I know this because I could see him from my window.

Our mother put on a brave face, most of the time. She accomplished this by making herself as busy as possible. However, when there were no more errands to run or suitcases to pack, she would lock herself in her room and weep.

Me? I visited Melody, often. Usually in the middle of the night when I could not sleep, which was basically every night. I felt safe with the Muse and her inspiration allowed me to relax and find solace. Many times, I would fall asleep on her floral print sofa, my head in her lap while she sung me to sleep. Her voice comforted me, and she was not one to judge since she knew what it felt like to let everyone in her family down.

Unfortunately, Belen remained in his usual Selena-disgusted-mode. He would screech at me from a distance while bobbing his head wildly as he flapped his wings. Once, he swooped down at me and almost knocked me on my butt.

Crazy bird!

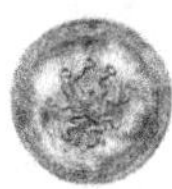

Twenty minutes later, we are opening our front door. The air inside is stale and musty from being closed up all summer. Mom and Ando immediately start opening the windows to let some fresh air in. I just walk around the room in a daze, my stomach still threatening to empty its contents.

"I'm going to take these upstairs," I announce grabbing as many bags as I can carry.

Ando ignores me while Mom nods and turns back to the task of airing out the house.

"Call me if you need me," I mumble.

She actually smiles this time.

"I will."

Gently, she touches my shoulder, but pulls it away like I have physically shocked her.

"I'll heat up the casserole," Mom informs with a trembling voice, and I know she only wants to be in the kitchen so she can cry without being seen.

Without a word, I trudged upstairs and into my room. Everything is just the same as when we left for our vacation. Except now, there is a thin layer of dust over my belongings, and I need to put fresh sheets on the bed. In a zombie-like state, I open the curtains to let in the light followed by the window. Fresh salty air billows inside welcoming me home. Unfortunately, home will never be the same again.

In my grief, I turn to my bedside table, and grab the frame that contains my favorite picture of David and my five-year-old self during our first trip to the aquarium in Ohio together.

He had been sick with the flu the previous week and had even missed work, yet he still kept his promise to visit the new sea lion exhibit that had just opened to the public. Later, we went to my favorite seafood restaurant and ended our outing at the family-owned ice cream parlor a few blocks from our house. We shared a hot fudge sundae and a chocolate-chip cookie the size of my head. It was terrific! A day I would treasure forever.

ACAPELLA

When we returned home hours later, David's fever was back: one-hundred-two-degrees, but instead of being grumpy about going out and not staying at the house to recuperate, he said that it was the best father-daughter-outing ever.

Touching his face lightly through the glass barrier, I whisper: "I'll miss you, Daddy."

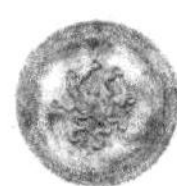

The next day, I tumble out of bed with tired eyes and a heavy heart. Immediately, I head to the far wall where the view of the Caribbean waits for me. From my bedroom window, ashen wisps of stratus clouds are arriving from the north, rapidly racing across the otherwise clear, azure Caribbean sky. The horizon is a few shades lighter, but for some reason there are no seabirds anywhere. By this time of morning, they are already diving for breakfast a few yards offshore in hungry flocks, strangely not today.

On the nightstand sits my alarm clock. The digital readout shows that it is almost seven a.m. on Saturday morning; the first Saturday we have been back on Isla Flora, without my father. In the distance, I hear only the light churning of the sea. No longer does it beckon me. No. Instead, it haunts my entire being and I wish with every ounce of my strength that I never fell in love with it, that I ever saw it.

The aunts no longer sing their Siren Song for me either. They decided to stay on Paradiso.

Why? I have no idea and they refused to explain.

Needless to say, our parting was not on good terms. As a matter of fact, they have banned me from the island until I mature; their words, not mine.

"Selena!" Mom calls from downstairs.

"Yes, Mom?"

"Your brother needs supervision on his swim," she reminds of my promise from the previous night.

All of a sudden, Ando appeared in my doorway. He still has not spoken to me since we have been back on Isla Flora. I want to drop to my knees and beg his forgiveness, but I understand why he will not. I would not forgive me either.

"Selena, take your brother for a swim!" Mom shouts louder.

Still exhausted, I turn to Ando.

"I'll be down in a few minutes," I reply in response to his angry grimace.

Without a word, he turns and heads back to the kitchen where our mother is washing dishes. My stomach growls loudly reminding me that I have not eaten yet. However, no amount of Crackleberry Crisp cereal can console me. Truthfully, I have barely had an appetite since *'the event'* that took Dad away from us... away from me.

Unhurried, I change into my bathing suit, grab a beach towel from out of the linen closet and walk with leaden feet to meet my brother, but when I get to the kitchen, he is not there.

"Mom?" I question meekly. "Have you seen, Ando?"

With heavy feet, she turns, soap still on her wet hands. This morning, my mother's eyes which are normally a vivid aquamarine are now a dark shade of gray. To my knowledge, she has not slept or eaten in several days.

"You're supposed to be looking after your brother," her voice is trembling and as she proclaims this, I hear the first crack of lightning over the house followed by the low roll of thunder. Seconds later, the heavens darken, and the soft pitter-patter of raindrops begin.

"Where is he?" I gulp down my misery, my guilt at the knowledge that it is my fault for what happened on Paradiso, and it is also my fault that my mother's anguish is calling the storm.

Glancing out of the kitchen window, she exhales, and the rain increases.

"He's already gone down to the shoreline," my mother responds in a robot-like trance.

"Great!" I mumble under my breath. "Don't worry. I'll catch up to him."

My mother gives a pained smile as she nods her thanks.

Not wanting to linger in case Mom's mood takes a turn for the worst, and the weather with it, I jog out of the house and down the rocky steps that cut through the cliffside to the platform below. As I take the last step, I see Ando sitting with his feet dangling in the sea; his cheeks streaked with salty tears.

"Are you ready to go swimming?" I ask, mussing his hair, but he slaps my hand away.

Without a sideways glance, he stands and jumps into the water and immediately disappears beneath the waves. Giving him some space, I wait a few seconds before following. It hurts my heart that he, my sibling and best friend, cannot or will not forgive me.

Gingerly, I step into the choppy sea entering my domain. The water is warm and inviting and fills me with the need to lose my troubles in it. Beneath the surface, the water which is usually serene is murky, and to my dismay, I can hardly see my hand in front of my face even though they are only inches away.

Acapella

Why won't my Siren-vision turn on?

Unfortunately, I cannot see where Ando went either.

Wait a minute!

I examine the spaces between my fingers as I tread water, not wanting to end up on the seafloor.

Where are the tiny purple dots between my fingers?

Still holding my breath, I call for my webbing.

Nothing!

As if my hands are covered in spider webs, I shake them both while calling for the errant, but needed webbing. In a near panic, I also call for my gills, surprised that they still have not automatically switched on, but nothing happens.

Concentrate!

Desperately, I try again, but still there is nothing.

Getting nervous, I click for my brother, but only more of the same occurs, but this time I swallow salty seawater.

Dear Father! I can't hold my breath much longer!

With every ounce of my willpower, I kick my feet *hard,* until I break through the choppy surface. Above, the sea resembles a washing machine on the 'bulky' cycle. The strength and fury of it whips me back and forth like a dried leaf in a cyclone, and with every deep breath I take, my mouth collects nasty-tasting seawater.

"Ando!" I shout, panic-filled and terrified.

The only sound that answers is the high-pitched howling of the typhoon-strength wind.

"Ando! Mom! Somebody!" I scream, hoping they respond telepathically.

More water gets into my mouth making me sputter and cough uncontrollably.

Then *it* happens!

With invisible hands, the undertow starts to pull me out towards the sapphire depths. Dread engulfs me as my body slips farther down until I land on the sandy bottom below. Wanting to live, I kick my feet and paddle my arms as I fight my way back to the surface, but still I feel like I am strapped with heavy weights. The watery embrace devours me as my lungs fill with salty liquid.

I'm a damn Siren!

I can't die by drowning!

It's too ironic for even my self-hatred mode.

Rapidly, this liquid world begins to fade as I drift into the abyss, and in the distance, swimming toward me is more of nothing.

Suddenly, a thought hits me.

There are no beautiful Sirens with aquamarine eyes coming to save me…

THE END
(I think not!)

ABOUT THE AUTHOR

 Alisa K. Michaels, an American author and schoolteacher, lives with her husband in the South-Eastern United States. Michaels is a Rollins College Alumna having degrees both in English and Secondary Education.

She brings to her authorship her experiences growing up on a beautiful, tropical island paradise in the U.S. Virgin Islands before coming to the mainland in her youth. She draws from those experiences to create her fantastical vision.

Alisa K. Michaels is a proud mother of three grown daughters, and a closet monster named Bucky.

ALSO AVAILABLE BY

Alisa K. Michaels

Available everywhere!

www.belenbookspublishing.com

COMING SOON

by Alisa K. Michaels!

SOLO

Book Four of The Siren Series